UNSUNG
Lullaby

UNSUNG

Lullaby

A Novel by

JOSI S. KILPACK

DESERET
BOOK

SALT LAKE CITY, UTAH

To my husband, Lee, and my children—for
the purpose they give me, the hugs they share,
and the love they bring into my life

This book is a work of fiction. The characters, places, and incidents in it are the product of the author's imagination or are represented fictitiously.

Library of Congress Cataloging-in-Publication Data

Kilpack, Josi S.
  Unsung lullaby / Josi S. Kilpack.
    p. cm.
  ISBN-10 1-59038-611-6 (pbk.)
  ISBN-13 978-1-59038-611-8 (pbk.)
  1. Mormons—Fiction. 2. Adultery—Fiction. 3. Domestic fiction. I. Title.
  PS3611.I412U57 2006
  813'.6—dc22   2006009061

Printed in the United States of America
Malloy Lithographing Incorporated, Ann Arbor, MI

10   9   8   7   6   5   4   3   2   1

ACKNOWLEDGMENTS

I love this part of the book, the place where I get to acknowledge publicly all those people who made this book happen. First off, thank you to my dear husband, Lee, for being my best friend, my biggest fan, and the kind of person a girl like me marvels to spend her life with. Thanks to my kids for their patience with my writing, their excitement for my accomplishments, and the sweet purpose they bring to my life. I'm lucky to come from a family that lifts and supports me as well as to have a family of my own that carries on that legacy. I only hope I give back as much as I receive.

Thanks to LDStorymakers for the unfailing support you have given to me over the years. I have grown so much because of each of you. Special thanks to my friend Carole Thayne and my sister Cindy Ellsworth for reading and commenting on the manuscript; Becca Birkin for her help on the legal issues; Olivia Ben for assistance with the Navajo elements; Dr. Darrin Housel, OB-GYN, of South Ogden for his help with both the professional and personal aspects of infertility; BJ Rowley, who did a great job with the editing before I submitted the manuscript to the publisher; Rachel Ann Nunes for encouraging me to submit to Deseret Book; and Julie Wright for being a tireless cheerleader and friend. Thank you also to the many fans who continually ask when the next book is coming—you have no idea how much that helps me.

I so appreciate Deseret Book for loving this story and breathing life into its pages, specifically Jana Erickson, for seeing the book through the production process, and Emily Watts and Lisa Mangum, for their excellent editing. Working with Deseret Book has been an absolute joy and pleasure for me.

And, most of all, thanks to my Father in Heaven for so much more than I can possibly say.

CHAPTER 1

*M*addie took a sip of lemonade while looking at the circle of women surrounding her. They talked and laughed, enjoying the chance to get out of their homes, away from their families, and to bask in the company of women for the evening—even if it was just a baby shower.

Maddie was not one of them.

Upon her arrival, she'd chatted with her aunts and cousins—the customary small talk. But conversations had evolved to—what else?—pregnancy and babies. Within moments she had become all but invisible, disappearing into the background while words like *Lamaze, epidural,* and *pitocin* echoed around her. She tried to ignore the pageantry—who had sacrificed the most to bring her child into the world—but found it impossible to disconnect completely. Maddie returned the lemonade cup to her lap, gripping tightly, as if letting go would somehow release all the feelings she was holding back.

If only Kim had been able to make it tonight. Her best friend turned sister-in-law would have made this bearable. They had been friends before Maddie had married Kim's brother Matt. A few months later, Kim had married Maddie's brother Allen. Marrying one another's brothers had only strengthened their friendship, and with their lives so interconnected, they were like true sisters. If Kim had been here, she would have known something was wrong and pressed until Maddie told her. Then she would have taken Maddie outside and let Maddie cry. But Kim wasn't here. Maddie had to face her aloneness all by herself.

Maddie had been tired and a little sick to her stomach for a few weeks, since before New Year's, but hadn't dared hope she could be pregnant. When her period hadn't come on time, she'd started to get excited—but not excited enough to buy a pregnancy test or tell Matt. Not again. Through almost four years of trying, and two in-vitro fertilizations, they had never once seen that plus sign show up on the little white stick. Why would this time be any different?

But she *had* told Matt a few days ago, and his enthusiasm was contagious. They had sacrificed so much, prayed so often, and wanted a baby for so long—maybe it had finally paid off. She was by then two weeks late, and their desperation clouded their objectivity. Saturday night they bought a pregnancy test and lost their minds when the test showed a positive result. They were ecstatic. Their prayers had been answered.

Maddie had called her doctor first thing Monday morning and made an appointment to confirm the home test by ultrasound on Friday. But this morning she'd had to borrow a pad from a woman at work. The dream had been shattered . . . again.

Since the brutal yank back to reality, Maddie had been numb. She hadn't even told Matt yet. How would she find the words? She'd told herself not to go to her cousin Tracy's baby shower tonight, but didn't want to explain to her mother why she had canceled at the last minute. She and Matt had held off telling anyone they were expecting.

"Maddie!" A voice called, pulling her away from her thoughts. *Thirteen minutes,* she thought as the woman she couldn't quite place sat down next to her. *In thirteen minutes I will have been here for forty-five minutes, and Mom will be satisfied.*

"I haven't seen you in ages," the woman said, and Maddie tried to weave the threads of remembrance together in order to come up with an actual identity for this person. Relative . . . cousin . . . Aunt Debbie's youngest . . . oh, yes: Laura. Maddie was older, and Laura had grown up in California, while Maddie was born and bred in Salt Lake City, Utah.

"Laura," she said just as her pause was becoming awkward. "How are you?"

"I'm good," Laura said with a laugh. "And how are you and your husband—what's his name again?"

"Matt," Maddie said, glancing at the clock again.

"That's right, Matt and Maddie. That's so cute."

Maddie forced her smile to get a little bit bigger and asked after Laura's family. Laura began prattling on and on about their move to Salt Lake a few months earlier, her husband's new job, and the apartment they were renting. She talked as if she and Maddie were old friends. Maddie smiled and made polite comments but had a hard time focusing. Her eyes were continually drawn to the front door, where she hoped to soon make her escape. At least Laura wasn't talking about childbirth.

"It's pathetic that I haven't found the time to connect with my own family," Laura said when she finished her update. She smoothed her pink broomstick skirt over her thick thighs and continued, "I can't believe how busy I am. I had my third kid six months ago, you know, and I just can't seem to catch up."

"Your third?" Maddie said with a little too much surprise. This twenty-five-year-old girl had three kids! The loss and anger Maddie had been holding back began to boil up. *Not yet,* she commanded herself. *You have to hold on a little longer. Six more minutes.*

"Can you believe it? And they're all boys," Laura said, oblivious to Maddie's discomfort. "Let me tell you, if I'd known Jeffery was going to be a boy, I may have reconsidered, or maybe sent him back. They're exhausting!" She laughed.

Maddie forced another smile, but the wall was crumbling.

"But how about you?" Laura said, touching Maddie's arm. "When are you going to trade the boardroom for a bassinette?"

Laura's concern over Maddie's career-committed lifestyle broke the bubble of cordiality. "Why?" Maddie asked with as much evenness as possible. "There's little sense in giving up everything for something I'll spend the rest of my life complaining about."

Laura was the one with the awkward pause this time. It lasted four interminable seconds. "Oh," she finally said. Her eyes darted around, as if she were trying to find an escape.

Maddie knew she should apologize, but she couldn't. Whatever loyalty had made her come tonight had worn too thin. The buzz in the room had quieted, and she wondered how many people had overheard her comment. She didn't really care. Let them feel uncomfortable for a few seconds. It was no match for the continual discomfort she lived in every day—in part because of them. So many women—these included—took their fertility for granted, daring to complain about the blessings she ached for so much. Right now she hated every one of them, her envy pulsing through her veins like liquid fire.

"Will you excuse me?" Maddie said, standing and setting her lemonade on the coffee table. She picked up her purse and hurried away, not meeting any of the eyes that followed her, not waiting to see the mom-to-be open the gift she'd brought, and hoping she could move fast enough that her mother wouldn't catch up.

Stepping into the gray winter evening, she shivered but didn't slow down, reaching her car in mere seconds. Every priesthood blessing she'd ever received for this issue had told her that someday she would understand. Well, she was tired of waiting, tired of playing nice. Having faith in the "plan" that seemed determined to keep her arms empty, and acting as if other people's insensitive comments didn't bother her, was getting harder and harder all the time.

With her hand on the car door, she felt pressure on her arm. She didn't have to look to see who it was.

"I'm okay, Mom," she said, fighting the tears and anger that were battling for first place on her emotional roster. "I need to go home. Matt's waiting for me." It was a lie. Matt was at a basketball game, but her mom didn't know that.

"I'm so sorry," her mother whispered in a way that took Maddie back to all the times her mom had tried to make things better. Off-key solos in church, bad boyfriends, unfortunate job interviews. Her sympathy did nothing this time.

"I just want to go home."

"Maddie," her mother said, a silent "don't be like that" echoing in her words.

"Please don't make me come to these things anymore." Maddie got in the car and pulled the door shut without another word. It was rude, and she would apologize later, but she needed to get away before she lost control of her tightly reined emotions. Being rude and insensitive was one thing, but becoming emotional and seeing the pity reflected in her mother's eyes was more than she could stand right now.

She drove through the Salt Lake suburbs, heading toward the canyons that cut through the eastern mountain range. As it was mid-January, some homes still had Christmas decorations up, creating glittery reflections of multicolored light on the wet roads. The dancing lights and dusky evening seemed to denote a certain coziness

5

within the homes, making her feel alone, encapsulated in her car and her own defeated feelings. For fifteen minutes she wound through neighborhood after neighborhood, the homes getting larger the farther east she drove. Soon she was curving up the side of the mountain, until she turned onto the dead-end street that ended in an empty cul-de-sac. The curb and gutter had been put in years earlier, but homes had yet to block the view. She often haunted this place when she needed solace. Lately, she had come here a lot.

Maddie got out of the car and looked over the sparkling valley below, lights blinking through tree branches and peeking around corners. Wrapping her arms around herself to fend off the January chill, she scanned the scene before her, trying to talk herself out of her bitterness but not doing a very good job. Her breath clouded with every exhale, and her cheeks tingled.

The city below her looked so perfect. She figured most things looked that way from a distance. She couldn't count the times people had told her how lucky she was to have such a good job, such a great marriage—their perspective based on their distance from her life. Since she and Matt both had college degrees and careers that matched, people always assumed they didn't have children yet by choice. She usually nodded and pretended to agree with them. It was awkward to bring up the truth. Most people didn't know what to say when she admitted the real reason, and when they did say something, it often reeked with pity—something she'd come to despise.

"I've done everything you asked," she whispered to the only one she knew still listened to her—well, maybe He listened. A cyst had cost Maddie one ovary at the age of fifteen, and the doctors had warned that it might be difficult for her to get pregnant when the time came. Knowing that would be a trial she would face, she'd felt prepared. She and Matt had never employed any birth-control measures, not wanting to lessen their odds of success even though Matt was still finishing up his degree those first two years of their marriage.

They were both sure that it would happen soon enough. During the third year, her faith began to wane. Matt had graduated with his master's in business from BYU and landed a good job as an investment broker for Zions Bank. She wondered why God hadn't opened those windows of heaven now that everything was perfect. Yet even with infertility counseling and tests, each month passed as another disappointment.

The fourth year of facing infertility had been the most miserable so far. She only wanted what everyone else took for granted. Was that so wrong? But after all the doctors, all the money, and all the prayers, the only thing she had to show for it was a bitter soul, an empty bank account, a crumbling marriage, and a heart full of unsung lullabies.

The last few days had been better for her and Matt, but that was because they thought they were having a baby. And they weren't. Which meant Matt would lose himself in his work while she kept her heartache to herself. They would tolerate one another, not because of love and endearment, but because they were committed to having a family and hanging onto the tenacious hope that a child would heal what was wrong between them.

The wind caught her long mahogany curls, sending them in a frenzy around her face. "You've abandoned me," she whispered. The wind carried the words away, but they echoed in her head. It *almost* hurt to say those things.

Almost. But not quite.

The cold stuck to the tear streaks on her face, and she turned back to the car. She needed to tell Matt.

CHAPTER 2

*M*att pulled the phone from his pocket and frowned. *Why would Maddie call in the middle of a game?*

"Hello," he said a split second later. He had to plug his other ear and lean down to hear her over the crowd.

"Hi," Maddie said, as if she didn't have anything important to say.

"Hi," Matt repeated, looking up so he could follow the ball as it traveled from player to player down the court to the home basket. "What's the matter?"

She paused. "Does something have to be the matter for me to call?"

"Usually," he said with distraction. The Jazz pass was intercepted, and he grumbled under his breath. This game should have been an easy win. *What is up with the team tonight?* It was the third quarter and the L. A. Clippers were ahead by three. "So what's up?" he asked after realizing she hadn't spoken for several seconds.

"Nothing," she said. "I guess I just . . . wanted to talk."

"About what? You know I'm at the game, right?" He could barely hear her over the crowd.

"Yeah," she said, and now he noticed the irritation in her voice.

No big surprise. She was often irritated about something, and he hardly bothered to notice anymore. Since finding out she was pregnant, it had been better, but it didn't surprise him that she'd reverted to her old habits.

"Never mind, I'll see ya later," she said.

"Yeah, see ya." He clicked off the phone and dropped it back into his pocket in time to jump to his feet and roar at the three-point shot Harpring had just made. The game was tied. *Sweet!*

"Who was that?" his friend James asked when they sat back down. James had been Matt's best friend since elementary school, and they attended a few games together each season. He'd been married for seven years and had three kids. Luckily for Matt, James's wife let him go out once in a while. Matt envied all the reasons James had to stay home—a loving wife and three cute kids—but he never said so.

"Maddie," Matt said with a shrug, raising his voice in order to be heard.

"Everything okay?" James yelled back as the Jazz got the ball.

"She didn't say it wasn't, and she always makes sure to tell me when things aren't okay."

The Clippers intercepted a pass and took a twenty-second time-out. The noise of the crowd died down enough that they didn't have to yell to be heard by one another. James chuckled. "That bad, huh?"

Matt shrugged again. "It's okay. Just the way she is, I guess. Did I tell you we think she's pregnant?"

"Really," James said with a smile. "Congratulations—all that practice paid off."

Matt grinned at the joke. "Well, we're not sure. The test came out positive, but with all the hormones and stuff she's been on, we need an ultrasound to confirm it. But we're pretty excited."

"That's great," James said. When the game started again, the Jazz made a basket, taking the lead. Matt jumped to his feet again. "Go, baby, go!" he shouted while James cheered next to him. Maddie's interruption was forgotten.

★   ★   ★

When Matt got home, the apartment was dark and quiet. He scanned the main area that encompassed the foyer, living room, dining area, and kitchen. The stove light illuminated the kitchen counter that separated the tiny square of linoleum from the boring brown apartment carpet. Three barstools were tucked beneath the overhang on the living room side, and a paper on the counter caught his eye. He pulled it close enough to read.

False alarm

He sat on a barstool and rested his elbows on the counter, dropping his head into his hands. A long, strangled breath seeped through his lips as he accepted yet another loss. That was why she'd called tonight—and he had blown her off. *I'm such a jerk,* he told himself.

With a frustrated groan, he crumpled the note and headed down the short hallway. Maddie was probably pretending to sleep but waiting for an apology. His saying he was sorry wouldn't satisfy her, though, and things would get worse before they got better. Eventually her anger would give way to depression, which would hang around until it wore itself out. Then they would try IVF for the third time, and hope would be restored. But with every round, that hope became a little more brittle, a little less comforting. How much more could they take?

At the end of the hall was the master bedroom. The other investment brokers Matt worked with had nice homes, nice cars, vacations in Hawaii—the works. But he and Maddie were still living the lifestyle of college kids. Two and a half years ago they'd received notice that their apartment complex was selling off the units as condos, and they had the opportunity to buy without a down payment. They liked the area and couldn't afford anything better, so they decided to transition from renters to owners without needing a U-haul. They liked the idea of earning equity and painting the walls any color they chose, but it was still an apartment, with cheap fixtures and an unimaginative floor plan. Instead of indulging in the luxuries their taxes proved they could afford, they had put all their money into making a baby—forty thousand dollars so far.

Matt opened the door to their bedroom. Maddie wasn't there. He checked the guest room and found the door locked. Big surprise. He went to bed alone but found sleep hard to come by.

It will happen, he told himself, trying to believe it as the thoughts spun and whirled through his head. He didn't often dwell on the situation they were in, choosing instead to focus his energy on furthering his career and having faith that their waiting would soon be over. But he couldn't escape it tonight. He ached for a child, for the new life it would give his marriage, for the joy he and Maddie would find in becoming a family.

But one reason in particular haunted him tonight. A reason all the more powerful because it was the only one his wife knew nothing about.

It seemed silly even to him, but deep down he believed that if he could create a child with the woman he loved, the woman he was sealed to, it would make up for his misuse of intimacy all those years ago. Maybe it was his idea of what the Catholics would call absolution. He just felt it would somehow make it right—proving to himself and to God that he was a man, ready to be responsible, ready to do things right this time. Yet the one thing he felt could shut the book on that chapter of his life continued to elude him.

Alone, in the dark, with one more disappointment wrapping around him, it made no sense at all. At times like this, when the memories were raw, he wished he'd told Maddie in the beginning what he had done. He'd come to realize that she likely would have forgiven him when their love was new and fresh and their future looked rosy. But it was too late. Their marriage wasn't strong enough to support a confession like that now. It would only serve to hurt her, and he couldn't add to her pain or give her reason to pull further away. He'd felt it wise not to burden her with the whole truth back then, and he *had* repented and done everything possible to repair what he'd done. But his mistake continued to lie between them, whether she knew the reason or not, and keeping it to himself became more and more uncomfortable with each failure they faced.

Finally, he put a pillow over his face and groaned, his frustrations demanding an outlet. *This is not the way life is supposed to be.*

He removed the pillow and stared at the dark ceiling, glad Maddie had slept in the guest room after all.

★　★　★

The next morning, Maddie came out a few minutes before Matt left for work. His company kept East Coast hours, and he arrived at the office by 6:00 A.M. every day. Maddie worked for a company that developed meal plans for hospitals, day cares, and anyplace else that had to meet mandated dietary standards. She worked from nine to five and didn't often wake up before he left. Maybe she wanted to see him—or maybe she wanted to fight about the phone call last night. He couldn't be sure. He pulled her into an awkward hug; it seemed as if they'd forgotten how to touch each other this way. She didn't hug him back.

"How was the game?" she asked, pulling from the embrace and heading into the kitchen. He sat down at the small table and continued putting his shoes on.

"Okay, I guess," he said, watching her every movement. He wanted to make all his thoughts of last night up to her somehow, but that didn't make sense. "I'm sorry for being so brusque on the phone, Maddie," he added. "If I'd known . . ." His voice trailed off as he realized that he didn't know what he would have done or said if she'd told him.

She didn't look up, just shrugged as if it were no big deal.

"Are you okay?" he asked.

"Not really."

"Do you want to talk about it?"

For a moment she paused. "Maybe it's time to think about adoption."

"We agreed, Maddie," Matt said with frustration. Every now and then she would bring up adoption, and it made him angry for reasons she didn't understand and he had no intention of explaining. With last night's thoughts and frustrations still very much on his mind, it was harder than usual for him to have this discussion. She might change her feelings about adoption, surrender to what seemed to be the easy answer to their problems, but he wouldn't give up. "We already decided that wasn't our Plan B."

"I feel the same way—I don't want to adopt either. But Plan A isn't working."

He let out a breath. "We agreed on three in-vitro fertilization treatments."

"Yes, we did," she said with a sigh and turned to the pantry without further argument.

She looked so sad, it made his stomach tighten. He was her husband; he was supposed to make things better. It was a horrible, hollow feeling to be so helpless. "Is there anything I can do to make this easier for you to deal with?"

She turned from the pantry with a box of Wheaties in her hand and met his eyes. "Not really." They held each other's eyes for a moment, until the alarm on his watch beeped twice, his signal that he needed to be out the door in order to get to work on time. It broke the spell, and Maddie looked away again.

"You better get going," she said as she poured the cereal into a bowl.

"I can stay."

"No, you can't." Her voice held just a hint of the bitterness he felt sure was roiling within her, waiting for him to say the wrong thing so she could unleash her anger on him. He almost wished she would. Her anger was easier to deal with than her sorrow. "We have another in-vitro to pay for."

He vacillated for a few more seconds but couldn't deny that her real message was, "I don't want you here." He nodded and finished getting his things together. "How about we go out to dinner tonight?"

"I thought you had clients coming into town?"

"Oh yeah," he said, deflated. "How about tomorrow?"

"Whoa," she said with mock sincerity, holding her hands up, palms facing him, as if in shock. "Let's not plan too far in the future. Who knows what clients, meetings, Jazz games, or other excuses tomorrow might bring. I'd hate to get my hopes up."

"That's nice, Maddie. I'm just trying to—"

"Whatever." She dropped her spoon on the counter with a clatter that seemed to echo through the tension. She looked at him, staring him down, her face tight. "Go to work."

CHAPTER 3

*T*he school bus backfired as it pulled away from the gravel drive-way. *Eight o'clock already?* Sonja asked herself. She burrowed deeper into the blankets.

After half an hour of trying to go back to sleep, Sonja gave it up altogether. She was stretching her long brown arms above her head, noting that the room was cold and she needed to turn up the heat, when someone knocked on the front door of the trailer.

Pulling a large Corona T-shirt over her head, she muttered about who could be out there at eight-thirty on a Thursday morning. When she opened the door, the UPS man was standing on the second step, eye level with her bare legs. It was cold outside, even for January, but she didn't react to the affront of frigid wind, watching the man instead. By the time his eyes reached her face he was blushing. Few women on the reservation would be so forward, but Sonja put little stock in the modesty and decorum handed down from woman to girl in the Navajo clans. She preferred to stand out—and she always did.

"Good morning?" she said, cocking her head to the side and

enjoying his discomfort. She leaned her back against the door frame and smiled down at him. Sonja Begay Hudson was only twenty-six years old, but she hadn't aged particularly well. Her hair was no longer shiny, her face too round to be striking, and fine lines had sprung up around her eyes and mouth. But she was still slender, if not a little too skinny, and her legs continued to be among her best features. She liked it when people noticed.

"Uh . . . good morning, ma'am," he said, averting his eyes as he handed her a rather large box. Heavy too, she realized as she took it from him. Once unencumbered by the package, he hurried back to his vehicle, and in a blaze of dust and gravel from the rutted dirt road his big brown truck was gone, heading through the nothingness toward Twin Lakes a few miles farther north and only ten miles or so past the border of the Reservation. She was likely his first delivery of the day—but one he wouldn't forget too soon.

Sonja smiled to herself and went back inside, slamming the flimsy door too hard and causing the whole trailer to shudder.

The box was addressed to Mrs. Begay, causing Sonja to furrow her brow. Her mom had been dead for over six months. You'd think anyone who cared enough to send her a package this big, expensive for shipping alone, should have known that. She shrugged. When her mom died, Sonja got the trailer and the old truck. This would be hers too, by default. She hoped it would be something good.

The package was taped up like Fort Knox, and it took some effort, a kitchen knife, and several curse words to get it open. When she pulled the box flaps back she found a single sheet of paper at the top.

Dear Mrs. Begay,
I hope this package finds you and Sonja well. We haven't been in
contact for so long we can only hope this is still your address. We're
moving to a smaller place now that the kids are grown, and in

cleaning out the spare room that Sonja and the other girls we fos-
tered had used, we found a box in the closet with her name on it.

Sonja smiled to herself. Apparently it was hers after all—no
default ownership needed. She kept reading.

We didn't have the heart to throw it away. We're hoping you could
get it to her. We wish both of you the best and hope you'll give
Sonja our love.

> *Sincerely,*
> *The Petersons*

Sonja snorted. Their love. Their Christian, or better yet, *Mormon*
duty was more like it. Her mom had enrolled Sonja and her two
older brothers in the Indian Placement Program, better known as the
Lamanite program, when Sonja was twelve years old. Her brothers
went to the same home in Provo. She went to a different one in Salt
Lake. For the next four years she traveled to the Peterson home for
the school year, returning to the Reservation every summer. Her mom
had fallen hook, line, and sinker for the Mormons and all their little
programs—at least for a while—and took full advantage of everything they offered. Sonja had been baptized too, but like her
brothers, she never put her heart in it. At first she had thought going
to Salt Lake would be an adventure, but she'd felt like a fish out of
water and hated it, begging her mom to let her come home after a
month. However, with the three of them farmed out, her mom had
only Sonja's younger sister at home and wasn't about to give up her
freedom just because Sonja was uncomfortable. It wasn't until Sonja
was sixteen that she managed to come up with a plan to keep her
from ever having to go to Salt Lake again.

The Reservation held no great attraction for her; Sonja had as
much respect for the Navajo traditions as she did for the Mormon
ones. But at least she had friends and could do her own thing on the

Rez. And Garrett was there. He was nineteen, Anglo—which made him a forbidden fruit—and lived in Gallup, New Mexico, a few miles off the Reservation. They had become pretty serious the summer before her sophomore year of high school. She'd been furious about leaving him, sure he would find someone else while she was gone. The idea had festered like an ulcer.

Sonja put the letter aside and dug through the packing peanuts, smiling as she pulled out some dance pictures. The Petersons hadn't let her go to dances until those last few months, after she had turned sixteen, but she'd been popular with the boys back then, pushing aside the traditions of her people in order to have much more fun.

Under the photos she found a buckskin dress—it wasn't even Navajo, but the Anglos in Salt Lake didn't know the difference. She'd bought it at a summer powwow comprised of several different tribes and taken it with her to Salt Lake that last year. People were always asking her about Indian stuff, and they oohed and ahhed over the treasure. The animal-skin dress fit their Native American perceptions better than the long, multicolored skirts Navajo women really wore. She couldn't imagine how anyone could stand wearing buckskin, even for the ceremonial dances. She thought the dress smelled like roadkill, and ten years in a box hadn't helped any. Wrinkling her nose, she threw it aside.

Digging into the box again, she found a pair of jeans she'd hated even then and a few books she couldn't remember reading. Halfway through the box she came upon a spiral notebook, and whatever might have lain beneath it was suddenly of no concern at all.

She had assumed this notebook was history.

The journal was supposed to contain her feelings about the topics taught in her seminary class each day. When she realized the teacher would never check what she chose to write—privacy and all that—she began writing her rampages against the society she was forced to live in for nine months of the year. She hated the continual looks she got, the awkward questions about the Navajo traditions, and the way she never quite fit in with everyone else. She missed the Reservation's wide openness and laid-back pace, the friends she'd known all her life, and her mother's low expectations. The journal became her outlet, and it was where she'd recorded the last two weeks she'd spent in Salt Lake.

Garrett had done the right thing when she had informed him she was pregnant a month or so after getting back to the Rez. Though marriage was optional, she insisted, and he agreed. Once she had the forty-dollar ring on her finger, they moved to Phoenix. Garrett had a job at first, but he lost it and had a hard time getting another one. He eventually found work in New Mexico—right after the baby was born. They named him Walter, after Garrett's dad. Sonja refused to move back to New Mexico, so she remained in Phoenix, and Garrett came back on weekends as much as he could.

Garrett had proved to be an okay husband, and he'd gotten her away from her mother's house and spared her the treks to Utah. But he was dead boring. When Walter was two, Sonja began seeing other men to relieve the tedium of being alone all the time. When Garrett found out, he filed for divorce. Now and then the Navajo Nation Division of Child Support Services (DCSS) would catch up with him and garnish his wages for all the back child support he owed, but then he would disappear again.

Sonja hadn't expected things to turn out quite like they did, and although the Bureau of Indian Affairs (BIA) gave her financial help, it wasn't enough—she still had to work in order to support herself. When she was forced to move back in with her mother on the Reservation, she wished she'd kept the seminary journal. It was the only place where she'd thought to keep track of the boys she'd hooked up with—her insurance plan for getting pregnant and therefore getting Garrett. But chances were good that Garrett wasn't Walter's biological father. In fact, she felt pretty certain he wasn't, which meant someone else was. If she could have found the real father, she might have had a chance of getting more money than the BIA gave her. But she couldn't remember their names, even that of the one guy who told his bishop. She'd actually had to talk to the boy's bishop and promise him that she wasn't pregnant—it had been so humiliating. Of all the guys she'd been with, she ought to remember *his* name, thanks to all the trouble she'd gone through to assure him he was free of any obligation to her. But she couldn't remember it any better than she could remember what she had eaten for breakfast two Tuesdays ago. There had been a lot of men since him. Without the journal, there was no way to track any of those boys down.

Or so she'd thought.

Now, the spirit of the ancients—if you believed that stuff—had brought the notebook back to her. With a little luck, she might be able to get child support after all.

She looked at the list of names and wondered where those boys were today.

Matt Shep

Zack Lawson

Jack Bernstein

Tim Thompson

Greg Vander—something

Then she shrugged. Didn't much matter where they were or what they were doing, they had to be better off than she was. She'd call her caseworker at the DCSS office tomorrow and see what she could do with this information.

She couldn't help grinning as she went to the small refrigerator. She needed a beer to celebrate. Better yet, a whole six-pack.

CHAPTER 4

*K*nock, knock," Maddie called out as she pushed Kim's front door open. She was three steps into the room before her sister-in-law appeared from the hallway with her coat in hand. It had been only a week or two since Maddie had seen her, but her pregnant belly looked like it had doubled in size since then. Kim was the only woman Maddie didn't resent for having babies—well, not as much, anyway. But she knew the coals Kim had walked across to get where she was, and that knowledge made it impossible for her not to share in Kim's joys.

"Hey there," Kim said. Her ash-blonde hair was long and pulled back into a ponytail, as it was most days. Even without makeup, her smile lit up her face, and her blue eyes were welcoming. She put her arms in her coat as she crossed through the kitchen. "Aren't you supposed to be at work?" she asked.

"They had upper management meetings this afternoon. Those of us low enough on the totem pole of corporate politics got to leave early. I brought those movies back." She laid the two DVD cases on the counter in the kitchen.

"Oh, thanks. I forgot you had them. We're going for a walk; want to come?"

"Um, sure," Maddie said. She followed Kim, now pushing a stroller that had been hidden by the counter between them, out the back door and down the ramp Allen had built last summer. Maddie didn't remember her older brother being all that handy when they were growing up, but he apparently had a knack for putting boards together.

Once outside, Maddie zipped up her leather coat before leaning over to say hello to Lexie, Kim's two-year-old daughter. Lexie's cheeks dimpled as she said hi and waved her gloved little hands at her Aunt Maddie. She had a book in her lap and, after her greeting was finished, turned her attention back to it, pretending to read.

"It's too cold for a walk." Maddie pulled the coat collar up to her chin and pushed her hands into her pockets.

"It's the warmest day we've had in weeks," Kim said as they turned from the driveway to the sidewalk. "We've got to get our exercise in while we can."

"Whatever you say," Maddie replied, wishing she hadn't pinned her hair up today. She'd have liked the insulation of hair covering her neck. But she *could* use the exercise. Though she avoided the scale, her clothes told her she was at least thirty pounds heavier than she had been when she and Matt got married. She hated the puffy look it gave her, and knew she should try to drop those pounds, but there were so many other things to worry about.

As if reading her mind, Kim said, "It wasn't until Jackson was in the hospital that I lost the extra weight I gained with him." Maddie was surprised at the candor. Jackson was Kim's son from her first marriage. Almost four years ago, right after Matt and Maddie had gotten married, he'd spent weeks on life support before he finally died from injuries suffered in a car accident. He'd been seven years old, and the loss was devastating. Kim didn't talk about him very often, at least not in a casual way like this, and Maddie felt uncomfortable with it somehow. "I'm not getting any younger," Kim added as they rounded the corner.

"Neither am I," Maddie said. She let out a breath, noticing she couldn't see it. Maybe it wasn't that cold after all. She just wasn't used to being outside.

They were silent for a minute or so before Kim spoke again. "How was the shower Wednesday night?"

"Horrible," Maddie said, not wanting to relive it, yet anxious to tell someone how it had felt. But she couldn't find the words, so it was a fruitless moment of excitement to think she could somehow unburden herself.

"I talked to your mom this morning. She's worried about you."

Maddie let out a breath. "She's always worried about me."

"As any good mother should be," Kim said.

They turned another corner and were now walking with the wind at their backs. Lexie started singing "Twinkle, Twinkle, Little Star," and Maddie smiled at the sound, even though it made the constant ache just a little stronger.

"I know. Mom wants so badly to help me," Maddie said. She remained silent for a moment, weighing out how far she wanted to go with this conversation. "I told her not to ask me to go to showers anymore. It's the third in four months—I can't take any more."

"So you'd rather not be invited at all?"

Good point, Maddie thought. Kim had a way of keeping things annoyingly logical. Maddie knew she would feel left out if she wasn't invited. She groaned out loud. "I'm so tired of this, Kim. I want a new story; I don't even care what it is, but I'm tired of telling this one."

"Are you still against adoption?" Kim asked. "I mean, if you really want to move on, it's a good option. Four years is a long time, and you've tried everything else."

Again, right to the heart. "I don't want to adopt—neither does Matt. But like you said, things aren't working, and I've been thinking more about it," Maddie admitted. "But I tried to bring it up a few days ago, and Matt shut it down."

"Well, maybe it's time for him to get over it."

Maddie considered that as they walked in silence for a minute or two. Kim made it sound so easy. Maddie watched other moms pushing their own strollers while kids played outside, enjoying the warm day—well, warm for January, anyway. Once again she felt left out.

"You know the worst part?" Maddie asked a few seconds later. She didn't give Kim a chance to answer as the internal dam that had kept all these things held inside began to creak and groan under the pressure. "The way one dream after another keeps dying. You give up having to plan a vacation around a possible pregnancy. Then you give up making a special announcement dinner for your husband, since it's all you two talk about anyway. Soon after that, or maybe before, I can't remember, you give up being intimate for the fun of it. Then you give up the vacations to pay for the treatments. Every Christmas you get pictures of your friends' kids, and each year they grow and change. Matt and I don't even have family pictures. What's the point?

"Meanwhile you blame your partner—until you find out you can only blame yourself. You become bitter toward other people's pregnancies and feel guilty for it. In time the images you've had of pushing swings and tying shoes fade. You can't see yourself holding your own child anymore. After a while you stop talking about it because you're tired of sympathy. You stop having sex with your husband because it's a worthless waste of energy. Your entire future seems paused, while everyone else's keeps going forward. Then you start to wonder about unsticking that pause button by taking someone else's child. What if I resent the child because it isn't mine? That scares me to death. Adoption seems so obvious to everyone else, but it's hard for Matt and me to even feel excited about it."

They had stopped walking sometime during Maddie's monologue, but Maddie hadn't noticed. Kim stared at her in silence, and Maddie felt a blush creep up her cheeks. It wasn't like her to unload her feelings. She looked away just as Kim stepped closer and wrapped her arms around Maddie's shoulders. The gesture took Maddie off guard. "I'm so sorry, Maddie," Kim said against Maddie's coat. "I can't even imagine."

Tears filled Maddie's eyes as well, and soon she was crying on the sidewalk, oblivious to the cold or to Lexie's stream of chattering. Kim continued to hold her, to cry with her, and Maddie realized how much she needed the support of her friend. After almost a minute, Kim pulled back and wiped at her eyes. She held Maddie's hands and looked her in the eye. "I know you hate it when people say this, Maddie, but the Lord has a plan for you. It's not what you thought it would be, and I know you feel cheated, but there is a plan in this."

Maddie did hate it when people said that kind of thing to her, but she knew Kim was trying to be helpful. She shook her head and wiped at her own eyes, wishing she'd opted out of mascara today like Kim had. "I've always had a hunger for children. I've had names picked out for my kids since junior high. I lived a good, clean life, served a mission, waited for the perfect man, did everything I was supposed to do to get to this point in my life where I could have the right family at the right time with the right guy. All I ever wanted to be was a mom. Yet here I am, a career woman—like it or not. I feel more than cheated, Kim. I feel lied to."

"I know," Kim said. "I've been there. Not exactly as you are now, but I've shaken my fists at heaven. I've wondered where I went wrong, why God was so angry with me. But life went on, and the plan for my life has continued to unfold, like yours will."

"But why would God give me such a strong desire and then pull the rug out from under me time and time again?"

"Maybe you're *supposed* to adopt."

Maddie let out a breath and looked away. "So why would He give Matt and me such adamant feelings against adoption?"

"Maybe you did that yourself."

A stiff breeze blew wisps of Maddie's hair around her face, and they started walking again. Maddie looked at Kim, offended by the comment, but unsure why. There was truth in those words. Certainly everyone wanted to have their own children. Had she and Matt taken the desire too far?

"I have some good friends who adopted their son," Kim continued. "They don't resent him, they rejoice in him—maybe even more than other couples because it was such a trial for them. They don't feel ripped off, they feel they received an amazing gift."

"But the real mother is out there somewhere. Someday the child will probably look for her. That would kill me."

"*You* would be that child's mother. The baby would be yours: named by you, rocked to sleep by you, sealed to you. It would call *you* Mom, it would paint *you* pictures at school, and it would be your child, in every way but genetics. Yes, another woman would give birth for you, but it doesn't negate who you would be to your baby."

When she said it like that, it made sense. But Maddie was still hesitant—very hesitant—to embrace an idea she and Matt had been so opposed to. Besides, genetics *were* a big deal. How many people charted which of their child's features took after their own? How many personalities were explained by "Just like dad" or "My mom's the same way." She didn't want to give that up and settle for something less. "I don't know," Maddie said. "Matt's more adamant than I am. He won't even talk about adoption."

Kim was quiet for a few moments. "Are you guys okay? I mean, other than this—are you guys okay?"

Maddie shrugged. What did *okay* mean? "There isn't anything but this," she said. "This whole infertility thing is who we are—it defines us."

"Wow," Kim said. "That's scary."

She stopped walking, and Maddie turned to her. Scary? What did she mean?

"You and Matt are married, Maddie. You're a team. This is only one play in the game. It makes me nervous that you think this is all there is between you guys."

When she put it that way, it did sound scary, but Maddie couldn't see any way around it. She was starting to feel like the lecture was going too far, though she couldn't deny that Kim had her best interest at heart. "We just want this so bad. We got married to make a family, and we can't. It's a pretty major hurdle in our relationship. Matt blames me, I know he does, but he won't say it. It simmers between us all the time. I can feel it."

"Have you told him you feel this way?"

"What's the point? He'll just deny it. He'll say there's no distance, no blaming. But I live with it every day—the little part of him that won't let me in."

"He loves you, Maddie. The fact that you aren't talking to him about your feelings is wrong, and he might surprise you. He needs to know your thoughts, and you need to know his. Babies are hard. They test you in a whole new way, and you need to be solid, strong with each other before you step up to the challenge. That means you have to trust one another with your feelings."

"I don't know how. Strong—solid—those sound like pretty big words." She didn't say out loud that she believed a baby would fix everything. Not having one was why it had all fallen apart, so why wouldn't having a baby put the pieces back together?

"Tell him what you're feeling," Kim said. "Open your mouth and let the words come out. He loves you; he'll listen."

Lexie started to whine about wanting to get out of the stroller, and Kim started to walk again. Maddie followed a step or two behind. They didn't say anything more about it, the moment lost. But the words were not forgotten, and Maddie found herself stewing in them all the way home.

She wanted more from her marriage than what she and Matt had—she wanted what they'd started with. They had once been best friends, longing to be together every minute possible. At some point their friendship had become a partnership centered on this one goal they both had, and then the partnership had become strained. She tried to remember when things had started to change, but there didn't seem to be a single transitioning moment. It had just happened. She found it hard to believe that making it better wouldn't just happen too. Regardless, she suspected Kim was right. She and Matt had to make things better. She just didn't know how.

CHAPTER 5

*M*addie frowned as she pulled in next to Matt's car. He usually arrived home around 3:30, yet, since she'd gotten off early today, she hadn't expected that he would be there already—another symptom of how disconnected they were from one another. She had hoped to have some time alone to consider the things Kim had said. Then again, maybe putting it off would do no good. "Tell him what you're feeling," Kim had said. Maddie took a deep breath and stepped out of the car. She could do that much, couldn't she? If it didn't work, she could always go back to the silent sorrow she'd become so good at.

Matt was sitting at the kitchen table working on his laptop when Maddie came in. "Hi," he said without looking up. "You're home early."

"Management meetings." She pulled a chair out from under the table and sat down. He stopped working on the computer in order to write some checks and punch numbers into the calculator as if she weren't there. She surmised he was paying bills. There was a subtle tension between them, a bubbling beneath the surface, and it saddened her. Matt was usually the first one to reach out, and she was usually the one turning her back on his offerings. It was sick and twisted and yet comforting in a strange way to feel so much power. The thought made her heart drop. Had things gotten so bad?

Looking up, she took advantage of his distraction and really looked at her husband. His light brown hair had darkened during the winter, and though cut short, it needed a trim to restore the style. His strong jaw framed his face, and the hint of a five o'clock shadow showed across his chin. He was a good-looking man in many ways, but his best feature was his eyes. He had the most beautiful dark blue eyes—navy eyes, a stark contrast to her brown ones.

"I hope it has your eyes," Matt would say when they talked about what their child would look like—a topic they'd spent hundreds of hours discussing over the years.

"No way," she'd counter. "Your eyes are so blue—like the ocean."

Thinking about those conversations brought a lump to her throat and tears to her eyes. All those discussions seemed so silly, so petty, and so sad. When Matt placed his hand over hers, she jumped. Looking up, she met his eyes and saw the same pain, the same heartache reflected there. Her first impulse was to pull away, to stomp out from the room and regain her composure, but Kim's words echoed back. She took a deep breath and said a silent prayer that she would be up to this.

"It all feels so final this time," she whispered, the words hard to get out. She had made it a habit over the last year to not share her feelings with Matt. In a way it felt like a betrayal to trust him with her thoughts.

"It seems stupid we could have felt so positive about it after all the disappointments we've had," Matt said. "I feel like an idiot."

His candor disarmed her, and the emotions she'd unloaded on Kim began to roll forward again, sweeping her away with them. "I'm so sorry, Matt," she said with her eyes overflowing. "You could have all the kids you want," she whispered, so quietly that she thought for a moment he didn't hear her, since he didn't respond. Admitting it out loud, however, made it hurt even more.

Several seconds stretched by before he took her face in his hand and turned her to look at him. "What I want is you," he said softly.

The words sent a shiver down her spine. He meant what he said, she could feel it, and part of the wall she'd built cracked upon its foundation. "But look at us," she said, wiping at her eyes. "We can barely stand spending time together, and after all the stress and frustration, I can't have your child. Sometimes I think you must hate me for it."

"Hate you?" Matt said, his tone shocked. "I love you for trying so hard. This isn't your fault, Maddie. I've never thought that."

She shook her head, feeling childish for saying it out loud, but not taking it back. How could he not be angry with her?

He didn't flinch, his face as soft and open as it had ever been. "I love you, Maddie, and we're in this together. I promise I have never blamed you."

"But I can't get pregnant. We've tried so hard and nothing has worked—it might not ever work. We have to face that fact."

"It's not a fact," Matt said, his voice a bit stronger than it had been thus far. "We're going to do the IVF one more time."

"And if it fails like the others did?" Maddie asked, disappointed he was still holding on to the hope, yet wanting to feel hopeful herself. "Are we going to keep doing this? I don't know how much more I can take, Matt."

"One more try, Maddie," Matt said, his tone begging her to agree. "Just once more. If it doesn't work then we'll . . . talk about our options."

Although the words he used were the ones she wanted to hear, the look in his eyes told her the issue was far from resolved. The alternatives were second-rate to him. If they couldn't have the child they'd been seeking for so long, would there be anything else left for them to build a marriage on? She wiped at her eyes and nodded, unwilling to push it anymore today, glad to have made this much progress.

"One more try." Matt leaned forward and kissed her forehead. His lips lingered against her skin, and she closed her eyes, inhaling the scent of his cologne, relishing the closeness. He lowered his face and looked at her. "One more try," he said again, like a mantra he was determined to memorize. "And if it doesn't work, we'll start looking into adoption."

"Really?" Maddie said, shocked he'd said it out loud. They had both been against it for so long, but she'd been feeling herself soften, and the chance that he too felt the same way gave her hope.

"We'll have the money to start the IVF process in a couple weeks. Let's see this one through to the end before we start losing our focus, okay?"

"Okay," Maddie said, wiping at her eyes.

"And let's go to dinner tonight," Matt said as he returned to his bills. He acted as if there had never been a problem, making her wonder if the strain between them was wholly her fault. She actually liked that thought. If it was her fault they had become so distant, then she could make it better.

"That would be nice," Maddie said.

Matt looked up at her and winked in a way that made her heart melt. How long had it been since she'd looked at her husband and seen the man she loved? Their relationship had become so insecure. Maybe Kim was right. Maybe there was a plan, and maybe all she'd needed to do was talk to her husband again.

CHAPTER 6

*M*onday afternoon Matt came home from work and grabbed the mail from the box nailed to their building. He reflected on the weekend as he sorted through the letters and climbed the steps. He and Maddie hadn't done anything special, just watched TV and made dinner together, but they'd both wanted to be there and they hadn't argued—much. It was the most connected Matt had felt to his wife in months.

There seemed to be equal amounts of bills and junk in the stack of mail, and he reflected on how much fun it had been to get mail when he was a kid. Nowadays, good news rarely awaited him. A small pink envelope addressed only to him gave him pause. *Who sends a man a pink envelope?*

After letting himself into the apartment, he dropped the mail on the counter and put his laptop case on the floor. With a butter knife he took from the dishwasher, he slit the pink envelope open, removing the card inside. On the front the card said, "Thinking of You."

Odd, he thought to himself. When he opened the card, a pink, folded paper fell out, but he ignored it for a moment and read the preprinted words stamped inside the card.

> *It's been a long time*
> *But I wanted to say*
> *That I am thinking of you*
> *And have a nice day*

He read the signature and his smile fell. The name *Sonja* was scrawled across the bottom of the card. He folded the card shut as his heart dropped to his toes. Then he noticed the pink paper that had fallen to his feet. With hesitation he picked it up and unfolded it. It was a photocopy of a sheet of college-ruled paper, the kind he used to carry around in a Trapper Keeper ten years ago.

> *Well, I'm finally goin home. I finished everthing I wanted to do and with a little luck I'll never come back heer. I can't wait to get back to the Rez. I've missed Garrett sooooooooooooo bad. He'll be so syched when he learns about the baby—I just know it. His mom won't be able to say much then. Ha ha.*

Matt swallowed and kept reading, not wanting to know what else she had written about but unable to stop himself.

> *I timed it perfect, tracked everything, I found my last guy over the weekend, he's Michaela's friend, she would freak. But anyway, they all have blue eyes and light hair like Garrett—I made sure to cover my bases. If I'm not pregnant then there must be something wrong with me. For posterities sake j/k:*
> *Matt Shep*
> *Zack Lawson*
> *Jack Bernstein*
> *Tim Thompson*
> *Greg Vander—something*

Not bad for a little Indian girl? We'll see what happens. I hate this class!! Journaling is so dumb. Two more weeks and I'm gone!

Matt swallowed again and let out a breath. His whole body tingled, and he crumpled the paper in his hand, wanting nothing more than to get rid of it. He recognized two of the other names—the type of guys someone would expect to be on a list like this—not like Matt Shep. His stomach burned, and yet he felt a bit relieved knowing he wasn't the only one.

With the paper pressing into his palm, his mind went back to that Memorial Day weekend. It was so long ago, and yet as clear as if it had happened yesterday. High school graduation had been right around the corner, and Michaela Peterson, a girl in his group of friends, offered their family's cabin for Memorial Day weekend. Her family had already been planning to go and said it would be fine to invite some friends to join them. Matt hadn't met Michaela's parents before, or the foster daughter they took in during the school year. Michaela didn't like the girl, Sonja. She had said there was something odd about the Navajo girl—calculating and strange for a sixteen-year-old. She blamed it on the Indian blood in her veins. Matt thought Michaela's judgment was a little harsh and found Sonja to be nice enough, pretty, and shy.

Saturday afternoon Matt sprained his ankle while they were all out hiking. With the help of two friends, he made it back to the cabin and put some ice on it. He assured his friends he would be fine being there alone, that he didn't want to spoil their fun, and they went ahead while he rested his leg. Sonja declined the invitation to go with the other kids, and when her foster parents said they were leaving to get some groceries in the nearest town, thirty miles away, Sonja volunteered to stay with Matt. At first it was fine—a little uncomfortable, but fine. He found himself flirting with her a bit in hopes of getting her to open up—and then she sat next to him and put her hand on his thigh. Suddenly it wasn't fine anymore.

Matt knew how to keep within the moral boundaries when it came to dating, but he'd never prepared for what happened that day in the cabin. Even now he couldn't put the pieces together in a way that made sense. She had gone from demure and soft-spoken to aggressive and seductive in mere seconds. The term "coming on strong" was an understatement, and though he protested at first, he was soon pulled along with the intensity. He'd wondered since then if the stress of graduation had made it harder to resist, or the fact that he'd been sluffing seminary and ignoring his scriptures.

When everyone returned from the hike, he told them he thought he should go home and get his ankle checked. He'd been shocked at what had happened, and yet intoxicated by it as well—but he knew he had to get away from Sonja, who acted as if nothing had occurred.

When he first got home from the cabin and locked himself in his room, he told himself he could work it out alone—humiliated to admit to anyone what he'd fallen victim to. But as soon as he knelt to pray for forgiveness, he knew that what he'd done was not that simple. After less than 24 hours of internal agony, he called the bishop, who met him at the church within the hour. The bishop had him call Sonja. Two weeks later, just days before she was to return to the Reservation, she and Matt met with the bishop together, where she assured them both that there was no way she was pregnant. Matt couldn't even look at her. It was one of the lowest moments of his life, and yet the relief was indescribable. Because she wasn't pregnant, Matt might be able to serve a mission—a goal he'd had all his life. Those two weeks of waiting and wondering had been horrible, and he had begun to learn then just what a broken heart and contrite spirit were as he realized the magnitude of what he'd done.

The last he'd heard of Sonja was when Michaela told him that Sonja's mom had called a few weeks after she returned to the

Reservation to tell them Sonja wouldn't be coming back next year. He felt horrible for likely helping her come to that decision, and yet he was relieved that he would never have to see her again.

Though he would turn nineteen in November, he and the bishop decided he needed to put off his mission for several months. He enrolled in the fall semester at BYU and did everything he could to fulfill the requirements of his repentance and prepare to serve a worthy mission. For good and bad, he'd been irrevocably changed by the experience. He did not take his sin lightly and knew he had lost something precious, had broken promises that changed who he was forever. What he'd done was wrong, very wrong. But it had been the catalyst for a real and burning testimony of the gospel plan, the power of repentance, and the true presence of his Father in Heaven. He'd wondered since then if he would ever have understood what the gospel was about if he hadn't felt the chasm his sin had created in his life. More than once he'd expressed his gratitude to the Lord that he'd been able to make it right, that he'd been able to serve his mission and become the man he should have been in the first place.

However, his repentance didn't make the sin go away. And it didn't make this unexpected note any easier to swallow. Matt closed his eyes, slumping into a kitchen chair. He'd lived his life since then in hopes of one day banishing the experience from his mind forever, of never being that boy again. Yet here it was, crushing him beneath the burden of his transgression. He read the note again to make sure he'd read it right the first time. Despite her assurances to the opposite, she had gotten pregnant. She'd lied. Had she told the truth back then, his whole life would have been different—in ways he couldn't imagine. He read the note a third time and then just sat there, trying to think what could possibly come next.

CHAPTER 7

*W*hen Maddie got home a little after six, she found a note from Matt saying he'd gone to the gym. Mail was stacked on the counter, and she wondered why he hadn't sorted it. Most days he went through the mail and paid any bills as soon as he got home. He liked being on top of things. She sorted it herself, putting his things on the counter and taking care of the items pertaining to her. The J. Jill store at the Gateway Mall downtown was having a sale. Maybe she'd stop in after work one day.

She was a little disappointed Matt wasn't here—the weekend had been so nice. But she didn't mind having the evening to herself. She heated some leftover spaghetti for dinner and watched the news. To support her recent goal to lose a few pounds before they started the next round of IVF, she did a one-hour yoga video, all the while expecting Matt to come home. She was more tired than usual when she finished and looked at the clock. It was nine o'clock, Matt's usual bedtime. She wondered why he was so late. Four hours at the gym was masochistic.

When she woke up at six-thirty the next morning, he was already gone. She wouldn't have known he'd been there at all except that the covers on his side of the bed were messed up. She'd slept like a rock. When she got to work, she called the doctor's office and made an appointment to get the initial blood work done next week. If everything looked okay, she would start the hormone treatments a week or so later. The hormones would prepare her one remaining ovary for the egg retrieval, and then a few days later the fertilized eggs would be implanted in her uterus. It was an emotionally and physically draining process. She felt guilty for not being more positive, but it all felt like a waste of time. Still, what were her options? She needed Matt's support, and he was insistent they do one more round of in-vitro.

The receptionist said Dr. Lawrence would be leaving on vacation in the next week and his schedule was booked, but she'd see what she could work out. As Maddie sat on hold, she couldn't help but wonder how much of that vacation she and Matt would be paying for. With the IVF running $15,000 each round, not to mention the artificial inseminations before then, and the medications she'd taken the year before that, they had doled out a lot of money. They'd stopped keeping track a long time ago.

Maddie came home to find a note telling her Matt had gone to a hockey game with James—he would be home late. Maddie thumped it back on the table, taking a deep breath. Two nights in a row—ridiculous. So much for making strides in their relationship.

Determined to wait up for him, she cleaned up the apartment before turning on the TV. Since Matt worked so early in the morning, he almost never stayed up past ten, but at eleven he still wasn't home.

She wasn't sure what woke her up, and it took her a minute to orient herself. All the lights were off, as was the TV, and she had been covered with a blanket. Matt must have come home. The clock on the microwave in the kitchen said 3:12. She went into the bedroom—

sure enough, there he was, sleeping like a baby. She crawled in next to him and snuggled up to his side. Even with the two evenings apart, the connection they'd established last weekend was still in the air. She would talk to him in the morning, though, to make sure everything was okay and that he wasn't avoiding her on purpose.

Matt left before she woke up again—making it two full days since they had even spoken. Her compassion from the night before disappeared. She picked up the phone and called his cell phone.

"This is Matt," he said when he answered.

"Matt," she said and found herself at a loss for words. What had she planned to say? Finally she just said what she was thinking, "Are you okay?"

"I'm fine, just busier than usual. Sorry."

"Oh," Maddie said, feeling stupid for even calling. "I . . . uh . . . made an appointment with Dr. Lawrence for next Thursday. They'll get the blood work, and we can go over the schedule with him. Will that work for you?"

"What time?"

"I made it at four so you wouldn't have to take work off."

Matt was silent for a moment. "Of course I'll be there." His voice was soft, sweet, and she smiled. Maybe being nice was all it took. Maybe it was more powerful than nagging. She might be on to something.

"Good," she said, still smiling to herself. "I didn't want to go alone."

"I'll see you tonight," he said. "But I've got to get back to work right now."

"Okay. Love you."

There was another pause, and when Matt spoke she could barely hear him, but his sincerity melted her heart all over again: "Oh, Maddie, I love you too."

★   ★   ★

Matt came home that night and every other night for the next week. He had high hopes for this IVF and determined to be a better husband than he had been. The letter from Sonja had thrown him into a shock, and he'd taken a few days to get his bearings, but he was feeling better now. The only decision he had come to regarding Sonja's note was that he wasn't willing to do anything about it right now. It haunted him, and he wasn't sure what it meant, but he didn't want to destroy the fragile reconciliation he and Maddie had made for something that might be unfounded.

It was hard to quiet the guilty voice in his head, but he decided if he got another note from Sonja, or anything else related to the situation, he would tell his wife. For sure. It made him feel better knowing he was taking it seriously but not burdening Maddie. Besides, it was so nice to be getting along with his wife again. He didn't want to mess it up.

CHAPTER 8

*T*hursday afternoon Maddie left work early and drove to the doctor's office. Matt arrived a few minutes later. He kissed her hello and she smiled, remembering that up until this last week it hadn't been their routine. She liked it. They chatted for a moment, and although Matt seemed a little distracted, he also seemed to hang on her every word, and she liked that too.

"Madeline Shep," the receptionist called out.

They stood and walked to the desk. Usually, Dr. Lawrence's nurse called them back. The receptionist smiled an apology when they reached the counter. "I'm sorry, but Dr. Lawrence was called away this morning. He had hoped he'd be back by now, but he was called in on an emergency surgery for another patient at the hospital. He phoned a few minutes ago to say he won't be making it back."

Maddie let out a breath. It was nice to be a patient of such a renowned fertility specialist. But there were drawbacks. "I guess I need to reschedule then," Maddie said.

"Not necessarily. The nurse can do the blood work. When you

make your follow-up appointment we'll extend it to allow for consultation time, unless you *want* to reschedule and do the consult at the same time as the blood work."

"No," Maddie said with a smile, "I'd rather not waste this appointment." She collected the urine sample first and put it through the little door. After washing her hands she rejoined Matt, rolling up her sleeve in preparation for the blood draw.

"I was hoping we could talk to Dr. Lawrence," she said as they waited for the nurse to stop fiddling with things. "I always feel better when I know the plan."

Matt put his arm around her, rubbing her shoulder. "Yeah, me too."

"Maddie," the nurse asked, interrupting them. "Have you had a period since your last IVF?"

Maddie thought for a few moments. "Yeah, it's been three months—two cycles," she answered at last, assuming the nurse wanted to make sure everything was operating as it should. "I was supposed to get this going last month but put it off." She looked at Matt, and he squeezed her knee. They'd put it off because they'd thought she was pregnant, and then she wasn't.

"Huh," the nurse said. She opened a cupboard and pulled something out.

"Is something wrong?" Matt asked.

"Well, hang on a minute."

Matt and Maddie exchanged another concerned glance, though what bad news could be uncovered by a urine test was yet to be known.

Another minute passed, and the nurse looked up at them smiling. "You're pregnant."

Maddie blinked, but the instant hope was quickly smashed. "No, it's the hormones from the last round."

"I don't think so. The hormones only give false positives for a few weeks at most. You're pregnant."

Maddie stopped breathing and stood up, hurrying to the counter and staring at the two tests, both showing the pink plus sign she'd seen over a month earlier on the test she'd taken at home.

"We always do a mandatory pregnancy test before we start any medications or blood work," the nurse said, looking back and forth between the two of them with a huge grin on her face. "The first one came back positive, so I ran it again to make sure."

"But I had a period three weeks ago," Maddie said.

"Was it lighter than usual?"

Maddie had to think for a second. "Well, yeah. It only lasted a day or so, but—"

"It's not uncommon for a woman to have a short period early in the pregnancy."

"I can't believe this," Maddie said, stunned and unsure how to react. They had waited so long for this, and yet she felt she needed someone to jackhammer it into her head in order for her to understand what was happening.

"And there's no way it could be wrong?" Matt asked. He'd come to stand behind Maddie, and his voice showed as much shock as her own had a few moments earlier. He put a hand on her shoulder, and she reached up, squeezing it.

"Well, there's always a chance," the nurse said with caution. "But let's get a blood sample. If I can get it to the lab right away, we can have your results in about an hour."

Matt and Maddie sat in the waiting room without speaking. They were in shock and afraid to talk about the possibilities. Maddie had never been so nervous. In all the years of trying, this was the closest they'd come to a confirmed pregnancy. She had to fight herself not to get too excited about it. The nurse had told them they could go home and she would call, but they'd decided to wait. It had been the longest hour of Maddie's life.

At five minutes to six, the waiting room empty except for them, the swinging door separating the exam rooms from the reception area opened up.

"Congratulations," the nurse said with a huge grin.

For a few seconds there was total silence as the words sunk in. Then Maddie screamed and Matt picked her up, swinging her around and around. When he put her down, she was crying and he was laughing. She ran to the nurse and hugged her too. "Really?" she asked.

"I'd have to be the cruelest person on earth to be teasing you at this point."

"Oh my gosh!" Maddie squealed, looking at Matt in shock. They hugged again, Matt still speechless.

"Now, you'll want to come in on Friday for a confirmation test. We'll check to make sure the ACG levels have doubled, a sign of a healthy pregnancy. We don't have any ultrasound appointments available that day, and the doctor is leaving town for a week on Saturday. Hmm." She went around the desk and moved the computer mouse, making faces at the monitor. The receptionist had gone home at five-thirty. "You can either get an ultrasound from another doctor, or wait until Dr. Lawrence gets back."

Matt and Maddie looked at one another. "This ACG test on Friday, it will let us know if everything's going well?"

The nurse nodded. "For the most part, yes."

"Then if it doesn't matter, I'd like to wait until Dr. Lawrence comes back. He's been through everything else with us."

The nurse chuckled and nodded while typing on the keyboard. "How about a week from Monday. It's Valentine's Day and his first day back. I can wiggle you guys in at one o'clock."

They'd both have to take off work, but Maddie knew Matt

wouldn't mind, and she wasn't about to complain. "Sounds fine to me," Maddie said, beaming up at Matt. He gave her shoulders a squeeze.

"Okay," the nurse said, hitting one final key with a flourish and looking over at them. "One o'clock on the fourteenth."

"Perfect."

They hugged before deciding to meet at a restaurant to celebrate. All through dinner they chattered and laughed as if there had never been any strain between them.

"Clay if it's a boy," Matt said before putting a bite of steak in his mouth.

"Clay?" Maddie said with dismay. "I like Zane."

"Zane the insane?" Matt questioned. "I knew a Zane growing up—we can't name him Zane."

"How about McKenzie for a girl," Maddie suggested. They hadn't had name conversations for months, and she'd forgotten his suggestions—but was still partial to the ones she'd held on to since junior high school.

"There are only about thirteen McKenzies in our ward—we need something more original. Like Naomi."

"Naomi?" Maddie said, wrinkling her nose. "As in Naomi Judd?"

They continued to argue and banter, returning home as if floating on air. A baby—all their own. She'd always known the feeling would be glorious. But she'd never known just how sweet it would really be. *Thank you, Lord,* she said in her mind over and over throughout the evening.

"I just have to check my e-mail. Justin was getting me some background on a new fund," Matt said when she asked if he was ready to go to bed at nine o'clock that night.

"Promise?" she asked with a smile.

"Promise," he replied with a smile and wink.

"And then you'll pack up the laptop and come to bed?"

He nodded, clicking on an e-mail and beginning to read.

Maddie picked up his laptop case from the floor and rested it on the table.

"What are you doing?" he asked as she started to unzip the case.

"I'm helping," she said, flipping open the top.

Matt jumped up and grabbed the case, causing Maddie to pull back. "I'll do it," he said.

"Okay," she said, stepping back with her hands up as if caught in a searchlight. "I was only trying to help."

"I know, sorry. I have everything organized just right." He smiled, leaned forward, and gave her a quick, light kiss. "I'll be right there," he said.

Maddie accepted his apology with a nod, not wanting to ruin this day by getting angry about his weird behavior. "I'll be waiting."

★　　★　　★

Matt watched her walk into the bedroom, and then he opened the laptop case and stared at the pink envelope he'd thrown in there last week. He picked it up and hurried outside, hoping she wouldn't notice he was gone. Less than two minutes later, with the envelope in the dumpster, he turned off his computer and headed down the hall. He chose not to dwell on what he'd just done, reminding himself of all the good things the day had held.

CHAPTER 9

"Ta-da!" Sonja called out as she threw open the door of the trailer. Anna, her sixteen-year-old kid sister, looked up from the stove, where she was stirring what smelled like mutton stew. Anna had gotten into traditional Navajo cooking over the last year, but Sonja would have just as soon heated up a frozen pizza. Walter was watching TV.

"Ho, ho, ho," she sang out again, then staggered in and put down the bags she was carrying. She shouldn't have had so much to drink, but she was celebrating, and it was a half hour drive on rutted roads back from Gallup—the closest Wal-Mart and bar. As far as she was concerned, Operation Child Support was a slam dunk. She'd given all the information to her caseworker, and the woman had said she would take it from there. Sonja had taken her BIA check and splurged.

Anna and Walter didn't say a word; they just looked at her. "Well," Sonja said, flopping into a chair and lighting a cigarette. "Aren't you going to say hello?"

"Hi, Mom," Walter said, sitting back against the couch but eyeing the bags.

"Hey," Anna said. She opened the only cupboard that still had a door and removed some spices. Sonja wondered why they didn't just remove the door altogether—then the cabinets would all match. Cabinets with doors were a waste of effort. "I got something for you," Sonja said, turning her blurred eyes to look at her son.

"You did?" he asked.

"Yup, come get it." She began digging in the bag, and when she pulled out the box, Walter's eyes went huge.

"A Game Cube," he said with reverence. Then he looked at her face. "For me?"

"You betcha," Sonja said with a nod. She took a long drag on the cigarette and kept fumbling in the bag, pulling out three different games one at a time. Anna had come up to stand behind her.

"Where'd you get this stuff?" she asked as Sonja pulled out a new pair of stiletto heels and some cheap, very un-Navajo jewelry.

"Can't you read the bag?" she said. "I got it at Wal-Mart."

"Where'd you get the money?" Anna asked, picking up the shoes to inspect them.

Sonja slapped the girl's hand, causing the shoes to fall back on the table. "None of your business," she said. Then she looked at Walter, who was shredding the box in an attempt to open it. "We're celebrating," she said.

"Celebrating what?" Walter asked. Anna had gone back to the stove, and though Sonja knew she was pouting, she didn't much care. Their mother had left the trailer to Sonja, and it was out of the goodness of her heart that Sonja had allowed Anna to stay.

Sonja leaned forward. "I may have found your real dad," she said.

Walter stopped fumbling with the package and looked at Sonja. "Garrett?" he said. Sonja never let him call Garrett *Dad;* it bugged her that even after ditching child support he should get the title. Now she was proud of herself for not letting him do so. She'd been thinking ahead and didn't even know it.

She shook her head. "Not Garrett. He's not really your dad."

"He's not?" Walter asked. He looked at the floor, and she rolled her eyes.

"Now don't get all dramatic," she said. "It's not that big a deal. You know how all this stuff works. Anyway, I think I know who it is. I met with an attorney today, and we'll be getting child support soon."

"I'm going to go to Grandmother's," Anna said from behind Sonja. She turned off the stove and grabbed her jacket from the hook by the door. She started saying something to Walter in Navajo but stopped when Sonja turned and shot her a look. Sonja had never learned Navajo, and she hated it when Anna or Walter spoke the little bit they had learned from school and from Grandmother. The only reason they spoke it was so Sonja wouldn't understand, and it aggravated her to no end.

"Don't be such a prude, Anna," Sonja spat. The cigarette had burned down, so she smashed it into the ashtray and lit another one.

"I don't think he needs to know this," Anna said quietly, opening the door and letting in a cold gust of air.

Sonja whipped around, making herself dizzy, and glared at her little sister. "I didn't ask you, did I?"

"I'll go with you," Walter said, looking at Anna and jumping to his feet.

"No!" Sonja roared, the alcohol intensifying her anger. "You're going to stay here and play the stupid game I bought for you!" Walter sat back down, but his pleading eyes were on Anna. "Now play!" Sonja ordered.

Anna was waiting at the door. Sonja turned toward her and told her to get out, following it with a few choice expletives. The door banged shut behind her, and Walter ducked his head. He didn't touch the box, and Sonja's anger boiled over. Of all the spoiled, ungrateful things!

"Play it!" she screamed.

CHAPTER 10

*T*he week following the confirmation that Matt and Maddie were having a baby was wonderful. Maddie went into the doctor's office for the ACG test on her way to work, confirming everything was going well. The nurse said she would call and let her know the results. On her way out the door, Dr. Lawrence came out of an exam room and congratulated her. She'd had a perma-grin for three days and thanked him for all he'd done. The office called that afternoon, confirming that levels were within normal range. Maddie thanked them and called Matt right away.

That night they called their parents, siblings, and close friends, not the least bit hesitant to share their good fortune now that they were certain. Everyone was ecstatic for them, and Matt and Maddie loved finally sharing good news.

Their evenings centered on detailed discussions of their plans. They suddenly had so much to talk about. First on the list was choosing a regular OB/GYN for the rest of the pregnancy.

The following Thursday, after a week of walking on air, Matt went home and got the mail. There was a form telling him he had a certi-fied letter from the Navajo Nation Division of Child Support Services waiting for him at the post office. He drove to the post office in order to collect the letter. In the car, he opened the official envelope and started reading. When he finished, he started at the top again as his arteries and veins seemed to stop the flow of blood through his body. He'd received a Service of Process and was being asked to supply a blood sample to test for paternity of Sonja Begay's son, now nine years old. Matt had thirty days to comply, at which time he would be taken to court and likely forced to obey.

Matt was sure his heart had stopped beating as he read the letter a third time. This could not be happening. In a daze, he drove back home. Inside the apartment he picked up the phone and called the local lab listed in the letter. He almost hoped it was James or some other friend pulling a sick joke on him. But no one knew about Sonja. This had to be real, even if it did seem impossible.

"Uh, yes," Matt said when the call was answered. "I need to make an appointment for a . . . uh, blood paternity test . . . Monday morn-ing would be okay." It was the same day they would get the ultra-sound for Maddie. His stomach turned.

He hung up after confirming the appointment, leaving his hand on the phone and staring at the kitchen counter. Now what? He'd promised himself he would tell Maddie if he got any other corre-spondence from or about Sonja. But the idea of telling her was even more unattractive now than it had been two weeks ago. After all their joy and closeness, revealing this now was out of the question. She definitely didn't need the extra stress now that she *was* pregnant.

But not to tell her? What kind of reflection was that on their rela-tionship? No, not on them, on him. He'd kept his secrets for so long, making it that much harder to face up to them now.

He dropped his head in his hands, raking his fingers through his hair and letting out a long, deep breath. *It's not for sure,* he told himself. He was only one possibility—there were four other guys on the list. Thinking about that further disgusted him. He slipped from his chair and knelt on the floor. As he begged and pleaded for this child to not be his, he realized that the boy's paternity had already long since been established. The Lord couldn't change it. But Matt begged anyway. He begged that this would not be another roadblock for him and Maddie. He pleaded that the paternity test would come back negative. By the time he said "Amen," he was in tears. There was no doubt that should this test come back positive, he was in big trouble. The sheer magnitude of the trouble terrified him.

He had dinner with clients after work and drove around for an hour afterward, hoping Maddie would be asleep when he got home. Last week's euphoria, when they had learned their child was coming, had been all but squelched. He had to find a way to get it back. But until he got the test results, he knew he would be more tense than ever. He prayed in his heart to have the strength to do what was right, but even when he felt impressed to go home and tell Maddie right away, he resisted. Surely tomorrow would be better than today—next week better than this week. He needed time to absorb it himself, find a way to put the words together. Again he felt the urge to go home and get it over with, but again he pushed it aside. *Not yet,* he told the little voice inside him. *I'll do it, but not yet. This isn't the right time.*

CHAPTER 11

addie was having a bad day on Friday. Matt was gone
by the time she woke up, which worried her since he'd come home
after she'd already fallen asleep the night before. But the newness
they had before them was enough to keep her from analyzing it too
much. As she sat up, her stomach churned, and she lay back down,
unable to keep from smiling.

Maddie had been feeling a little nausea for weeks, but since she'd
been certain she wasn't pregnant, she had ignored it. Now that she
knew the cause, it seemed worse, and she didn't mind it a bit. Kim
had been the perfect cheerleader and told her to eat small meals during the day and drink peppermint tea. Maddie followed those
instructions to the letter, and yesterday the nausea had gone by the
time she left for work. She followed the same advice today, and by
eight o'clock she was feeling pretty good. Her mother called to see
how she was doing just as she was heading out the door. Her mom's
exuberance made Maddie grin.

She and Matt had already decided Maddie would keep working

until about six months along in the pregnancy. They hoped they could sell the apartment and be in a house by then. Without having to pay for all the treatments and IVF, they could have an excellent down payment. Her salary would go into savings from here on out. When she quit her job, she could then work on getting the house ready. She was so excited she could hardly stand it, and yet it was unbelievable too. After all this time it was hard to accept. All the sorrow and bitterness seemed ridiculous to her now. All she could feel was gratitude and incredible joy.

At lunch her stomach was rolling and she had a headache. She decided to take the afternoon off, and her supervisor was accommodating. At home she changed into flannel pajama bottoms and one of Matt's T-shirts before curling up on the couch and falling asleep within moments.

She woke up when Matt came in from work. She blinked a few times and sat up.

"Maddie," he said in surprise when he realized she was on the couch. "You're home early."

"I was too sick to work," she said, unable to wipe the smile off her face. She rolled onto her stomach and propped her chin on the arm of the couch. "How was your day?"

"Good," Matt said. He shrugged out of his coat and put it on the chair before coming to the couch. She scooted over for him, then laid her head in his lap. He hesitated for a moment and then began stroking her hair. She closed her eyes and felt her body relax from head to toe.

"I love you, Maddie," he said a few minutes later, as she was drifting off. She opened her eyes and looked at him, wondering at the concerned look on his face.

"I love you too. Are you okay?"

He bent down and kissed her forehead. For a moment it seemed as if he was going to say something, but he settled on a smile. "I just love you."

Maddie grinned and sat up, wrapping her arms around his neck. He returned the embrace, and she molded into him, wondering how it was that they had ever had the distance of just a few weeks ago. Things were working out. She'd never been so happy. Next week, on February sixteenth, they would celebrate their fourth wedding anniversary. It would be a sweet celebration—the best one yet.

★   ★   ★

They got online that night and started researching the area and houses they were interested in. Matt already knew the approximate price range they could afford, and they found several that seemed perfect.

Saturday they spent the day driving from house to house. They knew they were getting ahead of themselves—they hadn't even listed the condo yet—but it was fun dreaming and getting ideas for where they wanted to live. Several neighborhoods stood out to them.

When they returned home, they wrote out all the financial ramifications, determining what price range they wanted to shoot for. They were feeling rather wealthy without the monkey of fertility treatment bills on their back. They could do this.

When they finished going over the minute details, Matt put all the fliers and listing information in a file they could reference later. "I'll call someone about listing the condo on Monday," he promised.

Maddie agreed and they enjoyed discussing it throughout the evening. When they went to bed, Maddie fell asleep almost instantly. As the day had worn on, her back had begun to ache. It wasn't bad enough to do anything about, other than take some Tylenol, but she determined she needed to take it easy. Spending all day on her feet wasn't a good idea anymore.

Sometime during the night she was awakened by a dull pain. It wasn't in her back this time, but on the side, lower in her abdomen. She began to panic, but told herself that not ever having been pregnant before, she didn't really know what was normal. She recommitted to never spend so much time on her feet again. The pain didn't go away, though, and she got up around five A.M. Moving around seemed to help a little, and she took some more Tylenol. Sitting on the couch, she stretched her arms above her head and twisted from side to side, thinking maybe she had a kink somewhere. After a few minutes she felt better and went back to bed.

Around seven A.M. she was awakened again. She couldn't fall back to sleep and tried different positions to relieve her discomfort. Kim had gotten a bladder infection when she was pregnant with Lexie. Maddie hoped that wasn't what she had. She got up, with Matt still oblivious in bed, and drank a glass of water. A few minutes passed, and she convinced herself the drink had helped.

Matt got up at eight and found her on the couch. "You okay?" he asked.

Maddie nodded. "My side's hurting me. I think I might have a bladder infection."

Matt's eyebrows shot up. "Well, let's take you in."

"No," she said, waving it off and sitting up ever so slowly. "It's Sunday and I've got to teach my lesson. I'll call Kim and ask her what I should do."

But she didn't call Kim right away, and by the time she did, after Matt's continual harassment, Kim wasn't home. The pain was worse than ever. She looked at the clock. Church was in half an hour. *I'll just lie down for a little bit,* she told herself. Matt watched her every movement. She kept perfectly still on the bed for ten minutes and was sure she felt better. Sitting up, she took a deep breath and stood. Maybe she could walk it off somehow. She took one step forward and the most intense pain she'd ever felt exploded within her. She felt as if she'd been cut in half and heard herself cry out before falling back on the bed. Matt had been in and out of the room the whole time, watching her with concern. He was at her side within moments.

"What?" he asked, brushing her hair back and doing a horrible job of hiding his worry.

She could barely breathe. "I think you better—" she moaned and bent over as another wave of pain radiated throughout her body. She felt dizzy and sick to her stomach.

Matt carried her to the car as she started to cry. Something was very wrong.

CHAPTER 12

*M*att and Maddie pulled up to the hospital within ten minutes. Maddie was doubled over in pain and sobbing. Matt slammed the car into park in front of the ER and ran inside to get some help. He returned with orderlies and a wheelchair to help get her inside. She was taken through the double doors as Matt explained what had happened. A doctor met them and began assessing Maddie while a nurse asked Matt for her name and address. The doctor felt Maddie's belly, causing her to tense up and moan again. Matt didn't like the look on the doctor's face as he ordered an ultrasound and called for an OB. Things seemed to be happening at warp speed.

Matt answered the nurse's questions for Maddie's chart while another doctor came in and did the ultrasound. Maddie's face was contorted in pain. She was crying and her whole body seemed rigid. After what felt like forever, the doctor turned to face Matt and Maddie.

"I'm sorry to tell you this, but we believe you are suffering from an ectopic pregnancy."

"A what?" Matt asked. He was holding Maddie's hand, and her grip tightened.

"A pregnancy that has attached itself to her fallopian tube. When the embryo reaches a certain size, the tube often ruptures, spilling fluid into the abdominal cavity."

"Fluid?" Matt asked, trying to keep up and having a hard time making sense of things.

"Blood. Your wife's abdomen is hard, which is a definite sign of internal bleeding. You say it's been about twenty minutes that she's been in pain?"

Matt nodded, holding on tight to Maddie's hand—as if they could somehow make this better if they were together. "She said it started hurting this morning, but then got bad really fast."

"If that's the case, she is likely bleeding quite a lot. We have to get her into surgery."

"No," Maddie said, shaking her head, her eyes clenched shut. Matt looked over at her. Hadn't she heard what the doctor said? She was bleeding inside.

"I'm sorry," the doctor continued. "I know this isn't what you were hoping for."

"Can you save the baby?" Matt asked, certain that in this day and age there were options.

The doctor looked at him as if Matt should know the answer. "We're prepping a surgical room, and I've ordered blood for a transfusion. But we need her to sign these forms before we can proceed."

The doctor held the clipboard out to Maddie, but she wouldn't take it. Her sobs filled the room. Matt took the clipboard in a daze as Maddie tucked her chin to her chest and pulled her knees up even higher.

The doctor waited, the anxious look on his face intense. When neither Matt or Maddie moved, he repeated that surgery was their only option.

"You'll take the ovary and the tube," Maddie said between her tears, holding Matt's hand in a death grip. "I'll never have a baby. I want Dr. Lawrence." Maddie lifted her head to look at Matt with pleading eyes. "Call Dr. Lawrence."

The OB doctor—Matt hadn't even caught his name—cleared his throat and spoke. "Ma'am, there is no time for another doctor. Your life is in danger here, and every minute we waste increases your risk. We will do all we can to keep the ovary intact, but the sooner we get in there, the better our chances are of saving it. We need to get this going, and you've got to sign the paperwork in order for us to proceed."

Matt looked at Maddie, and she shook her head. "I'm not signing anything until I talk to Dr. Lawrence."

The doctor clenched his jaw and looked at Matt. "I'd like to talk to you outside," he said.

Matt nodded but stood with reluctance, not wanting to leave Maddie's side. Another round of pain seized her, and she clenched her teeth and curled around herself once again. "Don't," she managed to say as Matt turned to leave.

"We will save what we can," the doctor said once they were in the hall. "But your wife is bleeding inside. She's in shock as well. Just since her arrival here, her abdomen has distended. She *is* bleeding to death right in front of you. Pretty soon she'll lose consciousness, at which time you can sign these forms and hope it's not too late. The OR is prepped, but we can't do anything without permission, and as long as she's conscious, it's her permission we need."

"But—"

"But nothing," the doctor said with irritation. "Is it worth losing your wife all together? Surgery is the *only* solution."

Matt swallowed the lump in his throat and realized he had no choice. Taking a deep breath, he entered the room again and placed the clipboard on the bedside table. Maddie looked so small in the hospital bed, still curled in a ball, her body shaking and yet tense, her face pale. Matt pulled a chair up to the bed so he was at eye level with her. The doctor stood in the doorway, tapping his foot ever so slightly—the only sign, other than his expression, that he was anxious about the delay.

"Maddie," Matt said, his voice shaking as he tried to keep his own emotion and heartache at bay for the moment. She didn't respond, so he reached out and put his hand on her shoulder. She flinched and lifted her head enough to look at him. Then her whole body tensed, and she moaned in pain. "Maddie, you have to sign the forms," he said. He'd never felt so small and powerless in all his life. If there were *anything* he could have done at that moment to make this better, he'd have done it. His eyes filled with tears, and his stomach clenched. It wasn't supposed to be like this!

She shook her head. "I can't," she said between clenched teeth.

Reaching out, he took her head in both hands and turned her to look at him as his own tears overflowed. "Maddie," he whispered in a shaky voice. "You have to let them do this. You're bleeding inside. This will kill you." He choked on the words as the full weight of the situation descended. He began to panic but didn't want to freak out and make things worse. He also didn't want to be the one signing those forms, for fear she'd never forgive him for it. He could see she was losing strength. The thought was paralyzing.

She clenched her eyes shut and tried to shake her head again. Her eyes were swollen, her entire face drawn and grey. With his thumbs he wiped her eyes, smoothing back the hair from her face until she opened her eyes again and looked at him with such torture that he had to choke back a sob. "No," she whispered, her chin trembling and the tears still falling. "Matt, no."

"I'm so sorry," he whispered, nearly unable to speak, still

smoothing her hair as tears ran down his face. "But we made promises to be together, no matter what. You can't back out now. You're more important than anything else."

She closed her eyes again, clenching every muscle as she cried out in pain. The doctor stepped up and tapped Matt on the shoulder. Matt stared at the clipboard as if it were a serpent. He took it from the table and held it out to Maddie. The doctor handed her a pen.

"You have to," Matt said once more. He placed a hand on the side of her face, and she turned into it. "Please," he begged with tears falling.

With a shaky hand, she signed her choppy signature on the line.

Before the doctor and nurses could get Maddie out the door of the room, she had lost consciousness. Matt stood in the hallway and watched them run her gurney down the hall and around the corner. He stared at nothing for several seconds before dropping his chin and giving in to the devastation he'd been holding back.

★　　★　　★

Matt sat next to the bed Sunday evening, waiting for his wife to wake up and wondering how he would find the words to tell her what had happened. It had taken seven units of blood to restore what she'd lost before the surgeon was able to clamp the broken vessels. Both the tube and the ovary had been removed. If she'd come in a few hours earlier, before the rupture, they may have been able to save the ovary and graft it to her tube on the other side. Had she come half an hour later, she'd have bled to death. As far as ectopic pregnancies went, this one had been severe.

Being so close to losing Maddie had left Matt in shock. Yet he couldn't focus on his own emotions too much because when Maddie woke up, he'd have to tell her what had happened. The truth would be almost as devastating for her as the close call had been for him. It would feel like a death sentence to her. For all these years and through all their trials, faith had been their only solace. Now, along with the physical parts necessary to make a baby, that faith had been ripped from them too.

Both sets of parents had come to the hospital, as well as Kim and Allen, but Matt had asked them to leave before Maddie awoke, knowing he needed to tell her what had happened and not wanting an audience. He was grateful for their understanding and had spent the hour since their departure trying to find the right words.

It was several minutes from when she first began to stir until she was conscious enough to ask for a drink. He poured water from the pitcher beside the bed and helped her sip it through a straw. He stroked her hair and held her hand, using all the strength he had left to keep from laying his head on her chest and sobbing like a child.

"What happened?" she asked in a scratchy voice.

Matt forced a smile. "You lost a lot of blood, and they had to—"

"What happened?" she demanded, and he knew that beating around the bush would do no good.

"I talked to Dr. Lawrence, and he said that having him there wouldn't have made a difference," Matt said as tenderly as he could. "It wouldn't have changed anything."

"What happened?" she demanded a third time, this time trying her best to give him a hard look, though she seemed to have a tough time focusing. Her chin began to tremble before he could answer.

"They had to take the ovary too. Honey, I'm so sorry." Her shoulders began to shake, and he placed a hand on her arm. "I'm so sorry," he repeated, feeling inadequate. In reply she buried her face in the pillow and began to sob. For several minutes he stayed there, smoothing her hair, rubbing her arm, desperate to comfort her and not knowing how. When the nurse came into the room, Maddie was shaking, sobbing, and struggling to breathe as Matt tried to calm her down.

"She needs a sedative," said the nurse, hurrying out of the room.

She returned a few moments later with a syringe and injected its contents into Maddie's IV line.

"This will keep her down for a few hours," the nurse said as they watched Maddie's eyes flutter closed, her breathing equalizing and her jaw falling slack, though her face was still flushed with emotion and streaked with tears. "You may as well go home and get some rest. There's nothing more you can do for her right now, but she'll need you tomorrow."

Matt drove home in a daze, opening the front door to the empty apartment only to stand in the doorway, oblivious to the cold behind him. The apartment was just as it had been when they left: his cereal bowl on the counter, her scriptures and lesson manual stacked on the kitchen table waiting for them to head out the door to church. It was all so familiar, so untouched, yet their lives were forever changed. Stepping over the threshold seemed to symbolize a certain level of acceptance—a joining of the hopes and dreams formed within these walls to the bitter reality that those dreams were dead. They would not have a child—not ever.

And all day, in the back of his mind, had been the reminder of his appointment tomorrow to get the blood paternity test done. In the middle of the mourning and realization that certain things were now gone forever was the continual reminder that other things were far from over. Yet, what could he do to change anything? What was done was done—there was nothing to do but move forward. He wished he knew how he was supposed to do it.

The wind blew against his back as he let out a breath he felt he'd been holding for hours and stepped inside.

CHAPTER 13

$\mathcal{M}$onday was the worst day of Matt's life. He'd returned to the hospital around four in the morning, unable to sleep at home. Maddie woke up around six, but the nurse kept her meds pretty high, so she wasn't fully coherent. At nine o'clock Maddie's mother, Trisha, arrived, and Matt asked if she would stay while he took care of a few things at work. She said she would, sharing her sympathy, which he had to shake off to avoid more tears. He still couldn't believe this had happened. It had never crossed his mind that they would be asked to face something so overwhelming and final.

He wanted to forget about his appointment for the paternity test, to put it off for a week, or a month, or a year. But he knew he needed to get it over with. Maybe then he could focus on accepting what had happened.

The lab was located in downtown Salt Lake, not far from his office. The waiting room was decorated with pink streamers and heart cutouts stuck to the wall, reminding him that it was Valentine's Day. How perfectly awful that he should be submitting to this test, behind his wife's back, while she recovered from surgery, on the holiday of love and romance. Some other hopeful couple had likely already taken the appointment Matt and Maddie had scheduled with Dr. Lawrence for this afternoon. They probably thought it was a good omen to have gotten in so easy.

As the blood was drawn from his arm, Matt reflected on what lay ahead. For more than a week he'd put off telling Maddie about the paternity test, and he couldn't tell her the truth now. He couldn't imagine when or if he ever could.

"How long until we know the results?" he asked a minute later as the attendant taped the cotton ball on his arm. He'd watched enough *CSI* to believe it could be fast, but he was smart enough to know that TV shows couldn't always be trusted. The shame cut deeply, and he wanted to run away and never see these people again—but he needed answers first.

"This is actually part of a series of tests and has to be done in a specific, court-approved lab. The sample will be going back to . . . New Jersey," she said, reading the paperwork. "About three weeks." She smiled, and it seemed odd that she didn't understand the magnitude of this in his life.

"How do I find out the results?" he asked.

"You'll want to ask whoever ordered the test. I don't know those details." She handed him a paper. "Here's your receipt," she said. "For your records."

Records, he echoed in his mind. Just the family history he wanted to keep around. He crumpled the paper and shoved it in the pocket of his jeans. He felt sick and exhausted and drowning in guilt and regret.

When he returned to the hospital, Maddie was asleep. It shamed him even further to be glad he didn't have to try to comfort her again.

"Did you get your work done?" Trisha asked, standing up from the chair beside her daughter's bed.

What a loaded question. "Uh . . . yeah," he said, taking Maddie's hand and wanting to plead for forgiveness right there on the spot. "Thanks for staying with her."

"Sure," Trisha said. For a few moments she watched him. "Are you okay?"

"I don't know how we're going to get through this one," he replied. He felt numb by everything and hadn't the first clue how to move forward.

"But you will," Trisha said with a nod. Matt looked at her, surprised to realize she believed her own words. Their whole lives were built around the family they wanted to have. How could she be so sure they would get over that? And she didn't know that Matt might have a child. The thought made him sick all over again. He could have a child he didn't know—let alone want to have anything to do with—and Maddie was barren. What a pretty family picture that would make.

The two waited for another half an hour, but Maddie was still out.

"Why don't you go home and take a shower?" Trisha offered. "I can stay longer. She was lucid for a little while this morning, and I'd like to wait for her to wake up again, see if she needs to talk or cry or whatever."

Matt didn't care about the shower as much as he wanted to get away from there. He needed to sort things out, though he didn't think he would ever find the peace he wanted. "I haven't had one since this started," he said.

"Then go," Trisha said with a smile. "Take a nap if you need to. I'll be here until you get back. Your parents called a little while ago. They're coming this evening."

Matt thanked his mother-in-law, went home, and threw his coat over a kitchen chair. The apartment was so quiet, so sad. He turned on the shower and stood under the hot water for a long time. Life suddenly felt like play dough, only it wasn't his hands forming it into shapes. He felt out of control and without direction. He tried to think about tomorrow, next week, next month, but it was like an endless blank canvas. Somehow he had to become strong enough to support his wife through this while preparing himself for what might be the greatest challenge of all. He had no idea where to start.

★　　★　　★

When Matt returned to the hospital Monday night, after his shower and failed attempt to take a nap, he recognized a familiar face—well, a familiar head. Maddie's older brother, Kim's husband, had shaved his head years earlier when the first signs of male pattern baldness had begun. He had a tendency to stand out.

"Allen," Matt called out from twenty yards away.

Allen turned, smiling recognition with that sad, hesitant smile Matt was getting used to. Matt caught up and they headed for Maddie's room together.

"I'm glad you're back," Allen said. "Maddie's been waiting for you. She wants a blessing. I thought I'd hang around long enough to assist."

Matt stopped. It took a step for Allen to realize it, then he stopped too. He had to turn around to face Matt. "She wants me to give her a blessing?" Matt asked with a lump in his throat.

"Uh, yeah, you're her husband," Allen said with deep curiosity in his voice.

What do I do? Matt asked in his mind. Of course he *wanted* to give her a blessing, but he'd just given blood for a paternity test his wife knew nothing about. Whether he was worthy in God's eyes wasn't the issue as much as whether he was worthy in his wife's eyes. If she knew, he was certain she would not feel he was in any position to give her a priesthood blessing.

"What's up, Matt?" Allen asked, and Matt recognized the tone right away. Allen was a psychiatrist, and he'd mastered the even, uncalculated tone years ago. It was the tone that made his patients feel safe. But his patients weren't married to his sister.

"Uh . . . is anyone else here?" Matt asked, shoving his hands deep into his pockets and looking at the floor. "I mean, who could assist you in the blessing?"

Allen looked at him long enough to double Matt's discomfort, something that, given the day's events, Matt would have thought impossible to do.

"Your wife needs you in this. I know it's hard, that you have peace to make with this thing, but she needs your guidance. Especially now."

Matt looked up after a few more moments of silence. "I can't do it, Allen." He wanted his voice to sound strong, but it sounded scared.

"You're her husband. This is why you have the priesthood—to bless your family."

Matt closed his eyes and raked a hand through his hair. "Allen," he said with frustration. "You're right—I need to make peace with things, but I haven't yet. I can't give her a blessing."

"Maybe you need a blessing too," Allen finally said. Matt looked down and shook his head even though he knew Allen was right. If he'd ever needed comfort and direction it was now, but the fear of what might be said was more than enough reason to resist. Allen let out a breath. "Will you at least assist me with Maddie's blessing?"

Again Matt shook his head. Allen placed a sympathetic hand on Matt's shoulder, but didn't say another word. After a few seconds, he turned and went into Maddie's room. Matt went the other direction and hid in a waiting room for over an hour. No one came to find him—not that they knew where he was anyway—and he spent the time with his head in his hands reliving all the moments leading up to this one.

When he returned to Maddie's room, she was asleep, and only her mother was in the room with her. Trisha put a finger to her lips and ushered him back outside.

"We missed you for the blessing," she said, but Matt didn't detect any suspicion in her tone. "It was beautiful."

Matt nodded. He wondered how Allen had explained his absence and who had assisted in the blessing—though he assumed that Dale, Maddie's dad, had come. Trisha continued, "They gave her a sleeping pill, and she'll probably be out all night. I was just about to leave."

"I'll stay," he said. He made to move past his mother-in-law, but she put a hand on his arm and held him back. "The blessing promised her strength to weather what was ahead, if she would support you and stay close to the Lord. I hope when the newness of all this wears off, she'll remember that."

Matt held back the tears and nodded. He hoped she'd remember it too. "Thanks for staying. I'm sorry I wasn't here for the blessing."

"We all grieve in our own way," Trisha said, patting his hand. "Your parents want you to call them when you get a minute."

She left a few minutes later, and Matt sat in the chair watching Maddie sleep for hours. He didn't call his parents back, not wanting to talk to anyone. Around midnight Maddie seemed restless, turning her head back and forth on the pillow, and moments later he found himself hurrying down the hall. The fear of facing her was too much. Once again he was running away. What a man he'd turned out to be.

CHAPTER 14

"Hi, Mom," Walter said, bounding through the front door as the bus drove away. He was in third grade at Twin Lakes Elementary School and took the bus since they lived almost five miles out of town.

Sonja was at the kitchen table, reading legal papers and fighting a headache. She waved him away, but he stood there with a huge grin on his face.

"What?" she asked a few seconds later. She'd slept until noon, but last night's hangover was a stubborn one and she wasn't feeling well.

His smiled faded, and he finally shrugged and went into his room. At least he wasn't playing that annoying video game. The noise drove her crazy, and she was tired of him complaining when she made him turn the sound off. Walter didn't come out until Anna's bus pulled up a half hour later—her high school was in Navajo city, forty miles away. Walter ran to the front door and opened it, waiting at the threshold. Sonja looked at him and shook her head. It drove her crazy how much Anna babied him.

Sonja went back to the papers, aggravated that so much made no sense at all. She looked up again when she heard Anna singing happy birthday—the Navajo version of the white man's song. Walter's back was to Sonja, but she could tell he was smiling again. *His birthday.* How did she forget? She clenched her teeth in annoyance. Anna reached the door and gave Walter a big hug.

"Did you have a good birthday?" Anna asked. She went to the small fridge that was as old as the trailer and pulled out some beans she'd been soaking overnight. Sonja watched her sister and felt the familiar but unwelcome envy well within herself. Few people believed they were sisters—half-sisters, actually. Anna's skin was lighter than Sonja's because Anna's dad was Anglo. It made her look much more like Walter; they could have been siblings. Anna was sweet and demure, studious, and she believed in the stupid Navajo traditions. She was also young—a sin that was growing in its power the older Sonja got. Sonja would give anything to be young again, to have her life back. But instead she was stuck here with her son and kid sister. Sonja had realized it was time to find a job again since the child support still wasn't coming in and the BIA money didn't cover the expenses. That didn't better her mood any.

"I had a real fun day," Walter said with a huge grin. "My class made me cards, and I got to choose the game we played at break."

"I'm glad. I got something for you too," Anna said. "But you can't open it until after cake."

"You made me a cake?" Walter yelled.

"I'm about to," she said. Sonja kept reading—choosing to ignore them since they were doing their best to ignore her. The long words in the documents were making her head spin. She lit a cigarette in hopes it would improve her mood.

Anna did make a cake, and they had a traditional Navajo dinner of fried bread with beans. Afterward, Anna gave Walter a new backpack with Spiderman on it.

"Wow, cool!" he said, putting it on. "What did you get me, Mom?"

Anna turned to look at Sonja, and Sonja resisted wiping the accusatory look off her face. "I got you that Game Cube last month," Sonja said with a shrug.

"I thought that was to celebrate his new daddy," Anna said. Then she quickly got up and went to the sink, avoiding the slap she must have sensed was coming.

"It was both," Sonja said with a look that told them not to push it. She didn't have to put up with this. She stood up from the table, stuffing the papers back into the folder they had come in. "I'm going out. I'll be back. Probably tomorrow."

They didn't say a word, and she fumed about their ingratitude all the way to Gallup—until she found peace at the bottom of a shot glass.

CHAPTER 15

*I*t was three days before Maddie was released from the hospital. Their fourth wedding anniversary, two days after Valentine's Day, went by with only a bouquet of daisies blending with the other flowers well-wishers had sent. They didn't talk about the four years they had spent together or the lifetime ahead. Matt didn't even buy a card. He knew Maddie wouldn't care. With the loss of her only ovary, she'd been forced into what the doctor called surgical menopause and had started hormone replacement therapy in hopes of avoiding the side effects of no longer having her own estrogen production. It was one more daily reminder of all she'd lost. The tension was high and the sadness overwhelming. Forcing a celebration was the last thing on their minds.

She came home on Thursday and spent the next four days sleeping and watching TV. Matt hovered over her, desperate to help in any way he could. After two days, she asked him to give her space. How could he say no? Her mother came every day, and Kim stopped in a few times, but Maddie wasn't much up for visitors. She seemed to have locked herself into her sadness and didn't want anyone to try to rescue her from it.

Matt went back to work the following Monday, grateful for the distraction but hoping that Maddie would be okay alone. He wanted to be there for her, to be everything she needed, but the secrets were overwhelming. She seemed unable or unwilling to let him help her anyway. He accepted the condolences of his co-workers and was grateful for a week's worth of work waiting on his desk. Anything to keep him from thinking about all the things going on outside the office.

★　★　★

Maddie woke up hours after Matt had left for work and slowly walked into the kitchen. It would be her first day alone. She wandered, straightening up here and there, before deciding to take a shower. Her movements were careful, her head foggy from the pain medication, and her belly still throbbing. Maddie ran the shower and took off her clothes. She caught her own reflection in the bathroom mirror, and for a moment she stared at herself, studying the body that had let her down. A scripture came to mind: "The spirit is willing, but the flesh is weak." It was very fitting. She'd ached and longed and wanted so badly to have a child, yet she was trapped—a willing spirit in a broken body.

She ran a hand above the incision on her belly and faced the fact that it would never swell as her child grew within her. Her breasts would never nurse a baby. She would never have stretch marks; she would never give birth or try to lose the baby fat—all those things women bragged about in their complaints. She was a woman, her body was designed to reproduce, and yet it wouldn't. *It's over,* she said in her mind. Then she met the reflected Maddie's eyes in the mirror and said it out loud. "It's over."

The words seemed to bounce off the walls in the small room,

echoing in her head. Reality descended like air being let out of a balloon. She hadn't cried since those first few days in the hospital—she'd been too drugged, too empty, and too lost. But as she stepped into the shower, and the water ran over her head and face, the tears started to fall again. The pursuit of parenthood was over. Soon she was shaking from the sobbing and wondering what she would do with the rest of her life.

She stayed in the shower until the water ran cold, then stepped out, got dressed in clean pajamas, and took her pain meds before lying down on the guest-room bed. She'd told Matt she preferred to sleep in the guest room for a little while, so he didn't wake her in the mornings, but mostly she needed the distance. Being around Matt made it harder, as if she had to digest all this for them both when she could barely take it in herself. She was glad he hadn't fought her over where she slept—but she wished things were different. For all the progress they had made, things weren't as they should be. They no longer shared the dream that had made them better. Still shivering from the icy shower, she pulled the blankets up to her chin and stared at the blank wall.

Each failure thus far had been followed with a step sheet for the next phase. Another test, another treatment, months of savings before they started again. But there was no solution this time. There was no way around it or through it or past it. It was what it was. *How long will it take before I get used to this?* she wondered. Would she feel like this for weeks, months—years, maybe? Forever?

As the tears rose once more, Allen's blessing came back to her, bringing a glimmer of peace. She'd felt the Spirit that night, even through the layers of pain she'd been entrenched in. She knew he had spoken the words her Father in Heaven wanted her to hear. But she hadn't been ready to listen. Now the words of the blessing spilled forth from the corner of her heart where they'd been waiting. The blessing told her how loved she was by her Heavenly Parents, her earthly parents, and her husband. She'd been told to cleave to him, to keep her heart close to his, and to let the Spirit guide them through the trials they faced. It had been a beautiful blessing. But she didn't know how to apply it.

The blessing had also promised her children. Though she knew now that they wouldn't be her own, the Lord had made her a promise. She had to find a way to have faith in it—that despite her doubts and her failed expectations, the promise made to her in the blessing would bring her the joy and peace she'd been seeking. She wished she felt better prepared. Everything was different now. They would have to make peace with adoption—somehow. She didn't know where to start and couldn't imagine that her feelings could change enough that adoption would ever feel right.

The ringing phone startled her, shaking her out of her thoughts. Rather than letting it ring, like she wanted to, she picked it up and placed it to her ear.

"Maddie?" the voice asked after she said hello. "It's Dr. Lawrence. I wanted to call and see how you're doing."

Maddie pushed herself up on her elbow, wincing only slightly. "I'm okay," she said, but her tone wasn't convincing even to herself.

"Somehow I doubt that," he said. "And I know I can't make things better, but I wondered if you had any questions I could answer. If there was anything I could do."

It was on the tip of her tongue to say no, but she stopped herself. "There are a few things," she said, willing the tears to stay back and forcing herself to move forward. "I'd like to know what happened."

For the next ten minutes Dr. Lawrence explained everything, filling her in on all the details. She listened intently, asking questions here and there—letting things sink in.

"I want your honest opinion," she said when he finished. "If we'd have waited for you, is there even the slightest chance it could have been different? Those doctors weren't specialists; they weren't trained like you; they didn't know me or my history. They pushed everything through so fast. I can't help but think you could have at least left me the ovary. Then it could have been grafted into the tube on the other side."

"If you had waited, you would likely have bled to death, or had blood poisoning from all the internal bleeding—possibly a stroke. The pregnancy likely ruptured before you'd even left for the hospital. The rupture was at the top of the tube, right near the ovary itself, which is why the ovary couldn't be saved. I spoke to the surgeon, who *is* a specialist, and he explained the details. I promise I could have done nothing beyond what they did, and I'm certainly glad I didn't have to explain to Matt why his wife was facing death due to the extra wait."

"It was that serious?" Maddie asked.

"Yes," he said. "It was. We live in a modern world, but women still die from ectopic pregnancies. Those who don't die face the same outcome you did. It's devastating, but at least they live to tell about it."

"But most started with two ovaries," she pointed out. "They don't hit a dead end like I did."

"That's true," Dr. Lawrence agreed.

The simple acknowledgment that he understood softened her, and Maddie started crying—again.

"Are you ready to discuss options?" Dr. Lawrence asked a few moments later.

Maddie groaned and wiped at her eyes. "Didn't you just tell me I didn't have any?"

Dr. Lawrence laughed. "I never said that. I've got two minutes until my next appointment needs me—I'll give you a crash course, and we can discuss it at length when I see you for your post-op appointment next week."

"Okay," Maddie said with a sigh, exhausted by the conversation already. "But I don't think I can take much more than two minutes."

★   ★   ★

Matt stopped to grab a pizza on the way home. His mom and mother-in-law, as well as some ward members, had provided meals for the last week, but Matt was in charge of dinner tonight. That meant they were having pizza.

Maddie's favorite pizza parlor was next door to a floral shop, so he ducked in while the pizza was cooking. When he walked into the apartment with a pizza in one hand and a bouquet of lilies in the other, Maddie was on the living-room couch. As it had all week, his stomach dropped a little upon seeing her, and yet he felt such a yearning to be with her. The secret paternity test was always at the front of his mind, yet he accepted that there was no solution. If the test came back negative, he might be able to put it behind him then.

She smiled at him, and he wanted to take a picture. It had been so long since he'd seen her smile, even a small, sad one like this.

"Hi," he said, "I brought dinner home."

"And flowers," she pointed out.

Matt smiled. "Yeah, and flowers."

"They're beautiful," she said, smiling again and stopping his heart with the softness he saw on her face. The hope bubbling in his chest was powerful. He put the flowers in water and then came to sit on the other side of the couch. He turned to face her. "How are you feeling?"

She shrugged, slowly turning so she was leaning against the arm of the couch. "Dr. Lawrence called," she said, looking up at him. "He explained everything to me, how the outcome was inevitable."

"I'm so sorry," Matt whispered.

"I am too," she said, tears in her eyes again. She sighed in frustration and wiped at them. "He was determined to tell me what our options were," she continued.

Matt furrowed his brow. Options? They had options?

"I still have a uterus, and I can take daily hormones and have a donor egg implanted. I'd have to have those horrible shots every day and get tested three times a week through the pregnancy, if it takes. But he said it might work."

"Really?" Matt said, trying to stifle his excitement.

"Yeah, but it costs over twenty-five thousand dollars, and since the other IVFs didn't work, there is no way of knowing if this would either—in fact it probably wouldn't."

"Oh," Matt said, glad he hadn't given in to the hopefulness. "What do you think about it?"

"I think I'm done," Maddie said as she let out a breath. Her chin shook, showing how hard it was for her to say these things aloud. "I thought about it all afternoon, and I'm tired of living on hope, or for hope, or in hope of hope. It's hard for me to say this, but it's just a tiny relief not to wonder anymore. No more counting days in my cycles, no more carefully calendared sex, no more wondering and worrying and stressing and hoping for it anymore. I can't imagine spending another six months saving up for something with so little promise. I feel like everything is telling us to give it up." Her chin trembled, but she tried her best to hold back the tears.

Matt bit back the argument. He wanted to say that at least the baby would be his, and it would grow inside her, but shattering the veil of relief on her face was too much risk for him to take right now. He nodded and felt the last tendrils of hope seep away from him. "And the other options you discussed with him?"

"Surrogacy and adoption."

"Surrogacy—when another woman carries the baby?"

"It would be your sperm, her egg, we pay all the expenses, and I adopt the baby after it's born. It's not legal in Utah, though. We'd have to go out of state, and it's even more expensive than the donor egg situation."

"I can't imagine another woman carrying my baby," he said, and then almost choked on the words.

"Yeah, I'm not sure I could handle that," Maddie said with a nod.

"Which leaves us with . . . ?"

"Adoption."

The word hung heavy in the air. Too heavy. Matt didn't respond. He should be ready to discuss this, but he wasn't.

"But I think we need to take it slow," Maddie added. She ran a hand through her hair. "It's going to take time for us to get used to the idea. Dr. Lawrence suggested we get some books, read up on it for the next few months. He gave me some titles to check into."

Matt nodded. He wanted to feel different, but adoption still seemed second-rate—yet he felt guilty for that, too. A child was a child, wasn't it? Wasn't any baby a child of God? Shouldn't he be grateful enough to have a family to forget his hesitation?

"Anyway," Maddie said with a smile, "it was good to talk to him. Kind of like closure, I guess."

Matt leaned forward and took her hands, resting his forearms on her knees. "I'm just so sorry, Maddie," he whispered, unable to keep the quake out of his voice. It was hard to see her give up the fight, to know he had no choice but to give it up too. But he could feel the finality, the necessary abandonment of all those dreams.

"Me too," Maddie whispered, and her voice was shaking like his. She put her legs down, and he pulled her into an embrace. Within a few moments he could feel the wetness from her tears through the dress shirt he'd worn to work. It wasn't the angry, rage-filled crying from the hospital, but a cleansing grief—the kind of tears people shed when they have accepted a loss but still mourn the "what could have been." He pulled her closer and felt his own tears fall. There was a certain eagerness to enjoy this closeness now, knowing the clock could be ticking on just how long he would have it. A week had passed since he had taken the paternity test. That meant there were only two weeks left before the official result.

If the test was positive, he'd have to tell her, and it would be horrible. But if the test came back negative, he had all but convinced himself never to tell her. He kissed the top of her head.

"I love you, Maddie," he said into her hair.

"I love you too," she said with a sniffle. They sat in silence, enjoying what they *did* have—each other.

CHAPTER 16

I don't care about all the legal stuff, I just want my money. It's been weeks!" Sonja yelled into the pay phone in Gallup. She'd just finished her shift at The Hogan café, where she'd been working for two weeks. She had her first paycheck in her pocket, but it wasn't enough to pay the bills, and the tips were paltry. Though many Navajo managed to survive on very little money, she wasn't about to try to live off the land, nor did she have—or want, for that matter—family and clan support like some natives did. Her mother had lived away from the Reservation for many years and had four children with four fathers, only two of whom were Navajo. The traditional family unit had become broken while she was away. If not for the free housing, her mother never would have come back to the Rez—that was why Sonja had come back after her divorce as well. She looked forward to a day when she could leave it for good. But that meant money—and she needed more of it.

"The samples are at the lab, but it will be a couple more weeks.

If the putative father disputes it in court, then it could be months. I told you it would take time."

"Putative father? What does that mean?" Sonja asked. She hated all these long words. They made her feel stupid.

"The *putative father* is the man we prove to be the biological father, but who hasn't yet been deemed as the *legal* father. Because Garrett Hudson was married to you and signed the birth certificate, he is still the legal father until we prove someone else to take his place. I do have good news, though," she continued. "We were able to track down Garrett in Montana, and he agreed to voluntarily relinquish his rights as legal father. That will ensure that the process is much smoother than if we had to prove it without him."

Sonja didn't care about finding Garrett—that was their job. "I really need the money," Sonja said. Even though she remembered the caseworker telling her these same timelines at the beginning, she'd assumed it was an exaggeration. In this day and age it seemed ridiculous that it could take weeks to determine who the real father was.

"I'm sorry," the caseworker said. "I'll let you know as soon as we find out."

"Fine," Sonja said as she slammed the phone down. She went to the old, beat-up truck and drove to the closest bar. A man—Hispanic, she thought—bought her a drink. She raised her chin and crossed one long leg over the other. He smiled back and moved closer. The day took a turn for the better.

CHAPTER 17

*W*ednesday afternoon, ten days after the surgery and a week since getting home from the hospital, Maddie sighed in frustration when yet another talk show came on the TV. She hadn't watched daytime TV in years and found it vastly unsatisfying. She lay back on the couch but knew she wasn't going to fall asleep. The last few days had her feeling a lot better—she had turned the corner everyone kept talking about, at least physically. Emotionally she still felt like she had tumbled off a cliff and was stuck in perpetual freefall.

She'd gone online to find some books on adoption last week but couldn't bring herself to buy anything. If she bought them, she'd have to read them, and that was an overwhelming prospect. Dr. Lawrence had told her to take her time, get comfortable with each step, and she felt it was good advice. Matt hadn't said another word about it since their initial conversation on Monday, but she was grateful he'd at least accepted the idea. It was their best option. Her eyes moved to the lilies he'd brought home the other night, and she smiled. Matt had been very attentive, and his care was helping a great deal. Being cherished and having continual reminders that he loved her made things a little less painful.

The sound of a key in the lock startled her until Kim poked her head inside. "Hey," she said, finding Maddie with her eyes and smiling as she entered with a grocery bag in each hand. "I borrowed your mom's key so I didn't have to make you get up if you were sleeping."

"I'm supposed to be on my own these days," Maddie reminded her friend, but she wasn't the least bit bothered.

"Yeah, well. I needed an excuse to stop in. Didn't want you starving to death."

Maddie smiled. "Thanks," she said. "Where's Lexie?"

"At my mom's," Kim said, then, as if anxious not to talk about children, she changed the subject, though her very pregnant belly was impossible to ignore. "How are you feeling today?"

"Good," Maddie said. "I'm getting around better. I even did the dishes last night."

"I guess it has been a week and a half."

"Yeah," Maddie said, refusing to dwell on the self-pity filling her heart. A week and a half ago she was planning paint for a nursery. She'd already decided to stop feeling so sorry for herself—still, it was hard.

Kim stayed for over an hour. She did some laundry and fixed dinner, but they also talked, and even though Maddie cried a little bit, she didn't get into the anger and bitterness. She was tired of burdening everyone with her feelings, and she did want to heal from this. Dinner was in the Crock-Pot as Kim put her jacket back on and tried to zip it up. Her belly was too big, and she sent an embarrassed look in Maddie's direction before giving up. She was due in just over a month, but had delivered early with her other babies. Maddie looked away and tried to push the jealousy from her mind.

"Oh, I forgot the last load of laundry," Kim said as she started shrugging out of her jacket again.

"I can get it," Maddie said, already standing. It had been a welcome gift to have Kim, her mom, and Matt's mom popping in to help her out, but she wanted to reclaim her independence.

"It just needs to be folded," Kim said, fiddling with the zipper again. "You sit. I can get it if you're sure you're up to that."

"I'm up to it," Maddie said with a nod as she sat back down. In fact, she was much too excited about having something to do. Kim disappeared down the hall and returned with a basket of warm laundry just removed from the dryer. She placed it on the couch and handed a paper to Maddie.

"I found this in the pocket of Matt's jeans. It looked like it might be important—but I threw away the candy wrappers."

Maddie took the paper and chuckled. "I wish I had a nickel for every time I told him to throw the wrappers away rather than shoving them in his pockets all the time."

"After four years you might want to give up."

"Yeah, I'm considering that." She looked up at Kim and smiled. "Thanks for coming today. I appreciate the help."

"You look good—and you sound *really* good. I'm glad."

Maddie shrugged. "I said I wanted a new story, didn't I?"

"I don't think this is what you meant." Kim sat down across from Maddie, the movement awkward due to her size. Apparently she wasn't leaving yet.

"It wasn't," Maddie said, shaking her head. "But the blessing Allen gave me in the hospital has stayed with me. I will have children. I've been told that before, but now I realize just how much promise it is. It's been a lifeline—even if I can't make myself look into it yet. At least I know it's there. It's something to work for. I can do this."

"I know you can," Kim said. "And how is Matt doing?"

"He seems okay," Maddie said. "I know he's sad and disappointed, but it's hard to fault him. We're talking about things and enjoying one another's company. That's enough for now."

Kim smiled and stood up, bending down for a final hug before reminding Maddie to call if she needed anything. Once she left, Maddie turned the TV back on and started folding the laundry.

When she finished folding, she took the basket, ever so slowly, to the master bedroom and put the clothes away. It took nearly fifteen minutes to complete the chore, but at least she was doing something. Only when she returned to the couch did she see the paper Kim had handed her earlier.

Whatever it was had been crumpled at some point, and it seemed that Kim had flattened it out and folded it. Maddie opened it up and discovered it was a medical form of some kind. *Odd,* she thought when she read Matt's name at the top. She was the one with an inch-thick folder of medical forms.

She inspected the paper, noticing that it was from a lab company she'd never heard of. The office was downtown and the form was dated last week. She couldn't recall him mentioning anything. Would he tell her if he was sick? Or would he not want to worry her? Either way, she didn't like being in the dark. The test type was a PATB4592, whatever that meant.

She stretched out on the couch and placed the paper on the coffee table as fatigue overcame her. Her belly was beginning to ache, telling her she'd done enough for the day. She would ask Matt about the paper when he got home.

CHAPTER 18

*M*att's early dinner meeting went well; he landed the account. It had taken weeks to convince this man to invest, and Matt was excited to have closed the deal. But the success didn't mute his continued worries. The closer he got to the apartment, the more he realized how impossible it would be to keep the paternity test to himself much longer. It seemed to permeate his thoughts more and more every day. The little voice telling him to " 'fess up now" was getting louder by the hour. The thought of telling Maddie, however, made him want to run his car into a tree. Facing his already heartbroken wife and breaking her heart all over again made his blood go cold.

Maddie was watching TV but turned it off when he came in.

"You can keep watching," Matt said as he put his planner and laptop on the counter. He avoided meeting her eyes, wishing he could just forget this stuff. He couldn't remember his own parents' birthdays; why couldn't he just not think about this too?

Maddie rested her chin on the arm of the couch and smiled. "I think my brain is melting. This stuff is pathetic."

Matt chuckled and lifted the Crock-Pot lid. "This looks good."

"Kim brought it over."

"How are you feeling?" he asked as he replaced the lid and removed his coat.

"Pretty good," she said with a smile.

"I'm glad."

"And how was your day?"

Matt shrugged and hoped she wasn't picking up on the tension he felt was choking him. "Long—but not too bad. I landed that New York guy."

"Congratulations," Maddie said. "I folded a whole basket of laundry all by myself."

Matt laughed, enjoying the banter. It had been a long time. He kept waiting for all this normalcy to help clear his mind.

"Oh, Kim found this when she was doing the laundry."

Matt turned and looked at what she was holding. He recognized it right away, and his heart stopped. His eyes jumped to Maddie's face, but it took a moment to realize she wasn't looking at him with suspicion. However, he felt sure his face was showing his guilt. After a few moments, Maddie's brow began to furrow, and he felt the last few sands sift through the hourglass of his secrecy.

"Matt?" she questioned. She looked at the paper she was holding in her hand and then back at him again. "What is this?"

The moment had arrived, and not in the least bit how he expected it. He had two choices. He could lie to her and put this off for another week, or he could tell her the truth. Before they married, he had promised himself that if she ever directly asked him, he would tell her the truth. Even then, straight-out lying to her had been impossible. That was as true now as it had ever been. The moment had arrived, and the realization was devastating.

"Matt," Maddie said, this time with a sharpness in her voice—a demand for answers.

"Oh, Maddie," he sighed as tears rose in his eyes. He couldn't imagine what her reaction would be, but he could feel the pain that was coming and found it hard to breathe.

"What?" she asked, and her face was beginning to show her panic. She was sitting up now, and he knew she was trying to imagine what would have him acting this way. He could almost hear her thought processes spinning.

He took two steps forward and sat down in the chair next to the couch. He tried to say a prayer in his mind, but couldn't find the words. He'd known weeks ago that he needed to tell her then, and he'd ignored the internal prodding. He was a selfish fool to expect help now, when the timing was as horrible as it could be. "There's something I need to tell you," he said after a few more seconds ticked by.

Maddie didn't say a word; she just stared at him.

Matt swallowed and took the form from her fingers. He looked it over and took a deep breath. Staring at the paper, he wished he'd remembered to throw it away. If he had, he wouldn't be doing this right now—maybe not ever. "Back in high school . . . I . . . messed up."

"Messed up?" Maddie echoed when he didn't expound. "What does that mean?"

"There was a girl," Matt said. "And I . . . uh, she and I . . . slept together." It was like battery acid on his tongue to say this, and he couldn't meet Maddie's eyes. She said nothing, and when he looked up, the shock on her face drove home what a surprise this really was.

"You what?" she whispered, leaning forward.

"I slept with her," he repeated. The words stung as badly as they had the first time. Maddie pulled back. "I'm sorry I didn't tell you,

Maddie. I went to the bishop. I fixed it, so I didn't think it was . . . necessary."

"Not necessary?" Maddie said, her voice shaking. "That's crap, Matt. I had every right to know."

"Part of repentance is living your life as if the sin didn't happen. The bishop encouraged me to live my life that way," he explained, wishing it didn't sound so trite to his own ears. "I took his counsel seriously."

"What does that paper have to do with it?" she demanded, pointing at the form he'd forgotten he was holding.

"Um . . ." He hung his head. He did not want to do this to her. Not after everything that had happened. When he spoke, his voice was shaky, and the words came out as if in slow motion. "I found out recently that the girl had . . . a baby, and I had to take a paternity test to find out whether or not it's mine."

Maddie was silent for several seconds. He couldn't even hear her breathing and didn't dare meet her eye.

"You have a kid?" she finally said. The edge in her voice raked down his spine like fingernails on a chalkboard.

"I don't know," Matt hurried to say, wanting her to hold on to the hope that it wasn't his. That hope was a lifeline to him. He wanted it to be a comfort to Maddie as well. He looked up. "There are four other guys being tested."

Maddie recoiled and put a hand over her mouth. He realized how horrible it sounded. That he was one of five men who had been with this one girl was disgusting to him, but even more so to her.

"Maddie, it was a mistake—such a big mistake. I went to the bishop, and she promised both of us she wasn't pregnant. She promised, Maddie. I did everything I could to make things right. She was from New Mexico. I had no idea she had a baby—I've never seen her since the meeting with the bishop. I was eighteen years old and it was such a stupid thing to do, I risked everything in my life and future—I just . . . I'm so sorry I didn't tell you."

"Oh my gosh," she said, and she stood up, wrapping her arms around her midsection and closing her eyes. He reached out to her, but she slapped his hand as soon as it touched her. "I can't believe this." She wiped at her eyes, looked around the room, and walked toward the front door.

"Maddie," Matt said, standing and turning to keep her in sight. "I'm so sorry. I can't believe it myself, and I feel horrible, and I wanted to tell you and didn't know how and was so scared that—"

"When did you find out?" Maddie suddenly asked, turning to face him again.

He paused and swallowed. "A few weeks ago," he muttered.

"And you didn't tell me?" she asked. "You knew this was coming, and you didn't tell me? If I hadn't found this paper, would you have lied to me forever?"

Right now, if he had believed he could have kept it from her, he would have. But it was past that point, and he now knew why he hadn't told her this sooner. "I didn't lie to you," he said. "I never told you I was a virgin."

"Oh yes, you did," Maddie spat between clenched teeth. "When my old roommate called me to tell me they canceled the temple ceremony and had to be married by a bishop—you agreed it was horrible."

"That was different—I had repented and I'd been forgiven and I had no reason to believe there was anything more I should have done."

She glared at him and continued as if she hadn't heard a word. "We've talked about how immoral the world has become and how grateful we were to have the gospel as a lifeline through it. We've been very open on this subject for four whole years, Matt, and you've worked hard at making me believe you were someone you most certainly are not. You served a mission, Matt—that's supposed to mean you're a certain kind of man."

"I repented, Maddie. If I'd known she was pregnant, I realize everything would be different," he said, willing her to understand what that meant. "But repentance is also part of the lifeline of the gospel. Because of my sin, I came to understand how powerful the Atonement is. I made such a horrible mistake, committed the kind of sin that could have ruined my life and the one after this—but then I went to the Lord, Maddie. I'm a better man for having learned so much. It was wrong, and if I could go back in time it would never have happened—but it did. Part of the man I am today is because of that mistake and the way I made it right."

"Don't patronize me and try to tell me this was a good thing," she said. Her chest was now beginning to heave as she cried harder. "And don't try to justify this. You knew what I believed, and you let me believe you were something you were not—that's a mean, terrible lie! And then you didn't even tell me when you found out about . . . this." She stepped forward and slapped at the paper he still held in his hand. Matt watched it flutter to the floor.

Her words were like a thousand swords. There was no explanation other than he didn't want to hurt her—but he had to try anyway. "I should have told you when I got the first notice. I know that, but the timing was bad and—"

"And this timing is good?" The emotion made it hard for her to breathe, and he tried again to reach out to her. She backed up and went to the coat closet. "My whole world was just flushed down the toilet, and now you're telling me that not only are you not the man I thought you were, but you might be a father to some other woman's child? You've lived a life you didn't deserve—didn't earn." She pulled her coat from the closet. Her movements were slow, reminding him how unhealed her body was. She couldn't be thinking of leaving?

"Maddie," Matt begged.

She put her coat on, slipped her feet into a pair of sandals at the bottom of the closet, and headed for the door.

"Don't go," he said, trying to hold back the sobs rising in his chest. "Please don't leave. Let me explain."

She turned to look at him once more. The anger, the betrayal, and the sheer sadness in her eyes burrowed into him. "I've heard enough," she spat as tears coursed down her cheeks. "Don't you dare tell me how I'm supposed to handle it."

The slam of the door echoed through the apartment. Matt slowly sat back down. He dropped his head in his hands. How *could* he do this to her? All his justifications and excuses were brittle and crumbling. What kind of man allowed these things to happen? He felt small and worthless and wished he could disappear.

He considered calling Allen and asking him for the blessing he'd offered at the hospital, but couldn't do it. Having just lived through Maddie's reaction, he wasn't ready to steel himself for another one. He'd ignored the promptings the Lord had given him. It was impossible to feel as if he were still entitled to guidance.

CHAPTER 19

*M*addie drove and drove, eventually finding herself at the same lookout point she had gone to six weeks earlier after leaving the baby shower. It was the first time she'd driven a car since the surgery, and she was glad her meds had decreased enough that she was able to. Staying in the apartment with Matt would have been more than she could stand. She had to get out.

A light snow was falling, and she parked the car so it faced the city, turning off her lights. There weren't many tears once she left the apartment. She was too angry, too shocked, and too beaten to cry over yet one more tragedy. She kept repeating their conversation over and over, feeling smaller and sicker and more useless every minute. It was hard to decide which part hurt the most. That he'd lied to her? That he'd been with another woman? That he could be a father—that was it. That was the hardest part. The irony was piercing: Amid all their attempts to have a child, he may already have one. But the rest was no less cutting. *How could this happen?* she kept asking herself over and over again.

Maddie had had serious relationships before Matt, and she'd always been the one who had broken them off. She had been picky—and then she'd started dating Matt. He seemed so perfect. He was the poster child for everything she'd ever wanted in a husband—kind, sensitive, generous, and absolutely devoted to the gospel. She'd always felt she knew him inside and out—and yet he wasn't who she thought he was. How could she be so stupid? What else didn't she know about him? If he could lie about this, what other lies had he led her to believe?

There were a million questions she wished she had asked. Who was this girl? When had it happened? How could he allow it? Why hadn't he found out before now about the child? How could he convince himself it wasn't necessary to tell her? And most of all, what were they going to do now? *No*, she corrected herself, *not us, him*. What was *Matt* going to do now? She'd survived the loss of her pregnancy, the chance to be a mother, but this—this divided them. Matt could be a father. The future, already so vague and empty, looked darker and blacker than ever. There was no voice in the back of her head egging her forward, calling out encouragement.

A lesson given years earlier came to mind: "When you feel least like prayer is when you need it the most." Instantly she rebelled against the idea. When she'd awakened after the surgery, she'd been angry and felt at the lowest point a person could go, but that paled in comparison with this. At least back then she felt she still had a husband to depend on and grow with. Now that was gone too. Where was God in any of this? If He loved her, like she'd always believed, how could He allow this to happen? After everything else, why *this*?

The words of Allen's blessing came back to her, the admonition to cling to her husband and support him. *Is this mess what the blessing was referring to?* If God had wanted to prepare her, had really wanted her to stand by her husband through this hell, He should have prompted Matt to be honest in the first place. Or helped her be more liberal in her views of right and wrong. She had always believed that premarital sex was a sin and a sign of weak character. Now that belief seemed to be working against her. She felt like the butt of a cruel joke, the only one left out of what everyone else already knew. Matt's explanations came back to her, tempting her to consider that he'd sought forgiveness—but she refused to soften.

The emptiness was overwhelming, and yet she couldn't ignore the habitual instinct to pray. She'd always been a prayerful person, and with nothing else to cling to, she leaned forward and rested her forehead on the steering wheel. She took a deep breath and began to speak, though the anger still rolled within her.

"What did I do to invite these things into my life?" she whispered as the tears began to fall once more. "I've lived right, I've kept my covenants, and I believed I would be blessed for those things. I believed I would avoid heartache by following Your footsteps, and yet I'm drowning in things I never imagined." She paused, waiting for a lightning bolt to strike her down or perhaps for a burning in her bosom to push her forward—something to remind her of her Heavenly Father's love for her.

She felt nothing and raged inside at being ignored right now, when she needed comfort the very most.

"I don't know what to do," she continued, her hope for an answer fading. "I feel as lost and alone as I ever have." Still she felt nothing. He wasn't listening, was He. Had she always prayed to such nothingness? She'd had spiritual experiences before. Had they been in her head? She'd never needed solace like she did now, and it wasn't there. Perhaps all the other comfort she'd received had been a figment of her imagination after all. "Answer me!" she demanded, slamming her fist against the dashboard. "Give me something to work with!" Nothing happened. With a heavy sigh, she wiped her eyes and sat back up, staring through the water spots of melted snow covering her windshield.

Their wedding day came to mind, and she pictured Matt's face as he'd knelt across from her at the altar. Life had been so wide open back then. Yet he'd been keeping such a horrible secret from her all along. The multiplied reflections in the sealing room were an eternal symbol, and the hope of generations yet to come. But there would be no future generations—at least not from her. She'd been trying to make progress in her feelings toward adoption, the lifelong sharing of the child she raised with another woman who would do the one thing she couldn't—give birth. But now she also had to somehow reconcile that Matt might have a child without her? It made her stomach burn to think about it. When was enough, enough?

She lowered the seat and curled around herself as the tears started again.

"What am I supposed to do with the rest of my life?" she whispered amid the sobbing. The heater hummed, and the snow covered the windows, closing her in. She shut her eyes and let out a deep breath, wishing she would fall asleep and never wake up.

If infertility was supposed to be her destiny, did she have to have her face rubbed in it like this? How could she embrace that and move forward after being lied to and betrayed by the one person who, until now, she'd felt was part of the solution to her sorrows? Why had she tried so hard to live right if she was just going to end up paying for Matt's sins? Nothing made sense. She reached forward and turned up the heater. If this was the life God wanted her to live, He should have prepared her for it.

★ ★ ★

She woke up with a start, not knowing where she was, feeling a great deal of pain. It took a moment for her to realize she was in her car. The snow had obscured the view out of her windshield. The clock on the dashboard said it was after three in the morning.

Her belly was killing her, but she'd left her meds at home, and she didn't want to go back there. She considered going to her mother's, but trying to explain this to her was impossible. Maybe Kim's—but that was an equally bad idea. Kim might be Maddie's best friend, but she was also Matt's sister. Maddie wasn't ready to tell anyone what she still hadn't made sense of herself. The sheer humiliation of telling people what Matt had done made her face heat up with shame. She turned on the windshield wipers, relieved that there was only an inch or so of soft powder. She needed her pain pills, and there was nowhere else to go but home.

★   ★   ★

Matt had paced and cried and tried to pray the whole time Maddie was gone. He picked up the phone a dozen times to call Allen or his dad, but put it back each time. He didn't know what he would say.

The conversation replayed over and over in his head. He'd handled it badly; he'd said it wrong. But then he never could come up with the right response. He kept walking out to the parking lot, hoping to see her car, wishing the snow would stop, and then coming back inside. He waited for the phone to ring, Maddie telling him she was never coming back, or the police to tell him she'd had an accident. He put away dinner, tried to clean, even tried to work, but after a few minutes on one task he was up and pacing again, sick at heart for what he'd done and trying to brainstorm any possible solutions. As the hours ticked by and he realized how unfixable this was, his anxiety increased.

When he heard the front door open, he turned to face it, and relief washed over him. Maddie didn't look at him as she limped inside, her sandals tracking in snow and her face pinched. He froze for a few seconds, so glad to see her, and then sprung forward, wanting to hold her and tell her a million times how sorry he was.

"Maddie, I was worried sick."

"I need my pills," she said.

Matt filled up a glass with water while she opened her pill bottle with shaking hands. She swallowed the tablets and walked slowly to the couch with her hand on her abdomen. She winced as she sat down. Matt watched her anxiously, wishing he knew what to say.

"What are you going to do?" Maddie asked. She looked beaten and exhausted. He wished he could ask her to wait another day for them to talk about it.

"I don't know," he said, standing in the kitchen and looking at the floor.

"Surely in all the weeks you've known about this, you've thought about what you'll do," Maddie said, her voice laced with judgment.

He couldn't meet her gaze. "Not really," he said. "I mean, I'll have to get an attorney, but I don't know what I'll do. I don't want to think about it."

"And what about us?" she whispered.

"What do you mean?" he asked, looking up.

Maddie shrugged as if the question were a casual one. "What's left for us, Matt?" she said with sorrow and fatigue in her voice. "You're not the man I thought you were, and I'm not the woman you thought I was when we got married. Neither of us signed up for what we're facing."

"Maddie, you're everything I ever wanted. From the moment we met, I had no doubt you were the woman I wanted to spend my life with."

"But you couldn't trust me enough to tell me the truth?" she replied, shaking her head and staring at her hands in her lap. "And you only showed me the parts of yourself you wanted me to see— you didn't give me a fair chance. You should have followed up with this girl better—and you shouldn't have gone on a mission and tried to pass yourself off the way you have. Do you realize that?"

"So if you'd known what I'd done, even though I repented, even though it only happened one time, even though this girl had promised me and the bishop that there was no pregnancy, even though I was forgiven for doing what I did and even though I *did* get to serve that mission, you wouldn't have married me?"

"I don't know," she said. "But I would have liked the chance to decide it for myself rather than being tricked into it."

"I didn't trick you," Matt said, his eyes filling with tears as his heart sank even lower. "I was forgiven. It was as if it hadn't happened."

"Don't give me that," she spat. "It *did* happen and it's part of who you are. You obviously didn't make things right if you never thought out the consequences of what you'd done. You could have been a carrier for a sexually transmitted disease, Matt. I deserved to know about things that very much affect my future."

Matt was speechless, surprised by her lack of understanding, her discounting of all he'd done back then to overcome his mistake. For a brief moment he wondered if *he* had been wrong about *her*, and yet she was right—but still missing the point. He *wasn't* the same person who had slept with some girl he didn't even know. He *had* left it behind him.

"I can't ever have your children, but someone else could and someone else quite possibly did. We don't have what we used to have, Matt—or what I thought we used to have. Maybe that distance is okay with you. Maybe you've always felt it, since you didn't think I could handle the truth. But it's not enough for me. I want what I thought we had when we started out, and I don't know if it's even possible."

Matt felt like he'd been hit in the face with a baseball bat. "We don't know if this kid is mine," he said. "I know that's only part of it, but what we have is worth saving. It's worth fighting for. I was wrong, I know I was. But it doesn't make all the good things null and void."

"Why not?" Maddie said. She was so diplomatic about it, almost cold. "What is it you see between us that I don't? Because all I see are two people unequipped to meet one another's needs who have been very unhappy for a very long time."

"I love you," Matt said with tenderness.

Maddie snorted and shook her head. "That's not enough, and you know it."

Matt blinked. "It's something to build on."

"So is trust and having a family—but those things are done. How about factoring child support into our budget? What about me being forced into playing stepmom to your child? How will I ever know if you're telling me the truth about anything?" She paused. "When we make love, do you think about this girl? Do you daydream about where she is, what she's doing? Is she the one that got away, Matt, the happy place you go to when life gets tough?"

Cold washed over Matt. "I have nothing but anger and pity for that girl, now more than ever. I don't think about her. I don't think about it at all, not ever. Other than this one thing, I've always been honest with you."

"This one thing," Maddie asked, raising her eyebrows. "You treat it as if you skipped a tithing payment once. This is huge. More than huge."

Matt looked down, holding back the tears. He didn't know what else to say. He just shook his head. "I'm so sorry," he whispered. "And I do love you—so much."

"Matt," she said, pushing herself to her feet and looking hard at him. There were no tears in her eyes, and he wished she would cry. The coldness was worse than the anger and sorrow. At least when she was crying and yelling, he knew what was going on inside her. "I don't know what to do with all this. In some ways you feel like a stranger, with a whole other life you kept from me."

"I was eighteen," he said.

"I was eighteen once too," Maddie said, heat in her voice now. "But I kept my covenants, and I never gave you any reason to believe I wasn't a virgin. You never gave me any reason either, but you weren't. You've known about this test for weeks, and you didn't tell me.

"I want to feel like I'm in love with you, like I'm safe with you. I want to honor you and respect you, but I'm not sure I can do that anymore. Our lives are different now. You might have to go to court hearings and custody battles. Our chances of adopting might be affected. This . . . girl could be a part of our lives now, and her kid. I'm having a hard time convincing myself I want a life like that."

"Maddie, I'm so sorry," he said, moving toward her, but stopping when she stepped back. "I never wanted to hurt you, never. But all those things you've said assume I'm the father—we don't know that."

She paused. "When will you know?"

"Sometime next week, I think."

Maddie stood there for several moments, staring at the floor. "I can't stay here."

"What?"

"I'll go to a hotel for a few days to think things out. I don't want to be with you."

"Maddie . . ."

There were tears in her eyes when she looked up at him. "Don't tell me how to handle this, Matt," she said, her voice shaking. "I need to do this my way if I'm going to do it at all. If you fight me, I'll leave and never come back."

Matt was shocked. "Don't say that."

"Then don't push me," she retorted. "You've had plenty of time to figure this out. Ten years, in fact."

Matt closed his eyes and took a deep breath. Then he nodded. "Will you tell me where you're staying?"

She didn't answer his question. "I'll call you in a few days.

Hopefully by then you'll have decided what you're going to do, and I'll have reached a conclusion myself."

"I love you, Maddie," he said, wanting to get that in as many times as he could.

She turned and walked down the hall. "I'll leave tomorrow—well, today," she said. He heard the door to the guest room close, and a moment later the lock clicked into place. He stood there alone, and finally fell to his knees. He pleaded with the Lord that she would stay, that they could fix this. A little voice in his head reminded him that he'd been told to tell her long before now. He found himself trying to justify his actions in his prayer and then stopped. The Lord knew. He knew everything, and He'd given Matt a warning—several, in fact. Matt had ignored them all.

Matt opened his eyes and stared across the room, looking at nothing. Consequences. Such a small word compared to what it meant. He'd always been taught he could make any choice he wanted, but couldn't choose the consequences. Here he was, overwhelmed with consequences. His marriage was on the line, and his wife was crying herself to sleep behind a locked door. He dropped his head once more and begged for forgiveness—not for the sin so many years ago, but for ignoring the help he had asked for and for hurting his wife. He could only hope that he could be forgiven of those things and that the consequences would be something he could live with.

CHAPTER 20

*M*addie checked into the Iron Blosam Lodge at Snowbird the next afternoon, glad to be out of the house and away from reminders of the life she shared with a man she felt she didn't know anymore. The room had a kitchenette, a fireplace, and a queen bed that she would sleep in alone. The view from the balcony looked over the snow-covered mountains, still dotted with skiers getting the most out of the record snowfalls. While unpacking her suitcase full of sweats and T-shirts, she came across the manila envelope Matt had left out on the counter that morning. Though tempted to leave it there, she'd thrown it in the suitcase at the last moment. The envelope was the same kind her teacher used to send her artwork home in at the end of the semester when she was in elementary school. On the front of this envelope, Matt had written a note in magic marker.

Maddie,
Here are all the letters and other correspondence I've received about
this as well as my own explanation—the one thing missing is the
first note. I threw it away but wish I'd have kept it now. I hope it

doesn't make things worse, but I haven't had the chance to explain
how everything happened, and I don't want to keep anything from
you anymore. I'm so sorry. I do love you.

Matt

She put the envelope in a dresser drawer. For now she needed the
distance. Once unpacked she bundled up and walked slowly to
the small grocery store located a quarter mile up the mountain. By the
time she got back with some cereal, Cup o' Noodles, and bread, she
needed a nap.

For the next three days she slept and spent a lot of time looking
out the window, watching the skiers and falling snow. She stepped
away from her emotions and made several different plans for her life,
most of which didn't include Matt. She could start a new life without him, and maybe then she would be happy. David in accounting
had been left with two kids when his wife walked out last year.
Someone like that would be perfect for her. She could fill the gap in
their family. She could belong to them and find part of the dream
she had lived for all her life. As it was, there were more gaps than
filled-in spaces with her and Matt.

Perhaps she wouldn't find anyone else. Maybe she'd be alone,
spend her life being the best she could be all by herself. It had to be
better than this. Maybe the burning desire she'd always had for a
family was a sick game someone was playing with her. There were
lots of women who didn't want kids. Why couldn't she be one of
them? Why couldn't she feel the drive for a career instead? Or travel,
or politics—something that had nothing to do with being a mother?

None of her ideas sounded all that tempting. They weren't what
she wanted, but then the life she had wasn't what she wanted either.
She was glad she wasn't home. Being there made her feel too angry,
made her want to punish Matt, and that didn't deserve her energies
right now. She just needed to think. She needed to face the different

futures she had, and she couldn't do that with Matt watching her, begging for her forgiveness.

Forgiveness. What did that mean, anyway? It wouldn't change anything that had happened or what was going to happen. Wasn't it showing him that what he'd done was okay with her? It wasn't okay. The more she thought about forgiving him, the angrier she became.

On the fourth day she opened her scriptures. Up until a month ago she had read every day, at least a chapter. The scriptures had always brought her comfort—though she couldn't help wondering now what good it had done. But it was a habit, and as habits go, it wasn't broken easily. No matter how much she tried to talk herself out of it, she was drawn to them.

She turned to where the silver ribbon marked her place and picked up where she had left off in the Doctrine and Covenants. She read off and on all day. The TV tempted her several times, but an inner prodding kept her turning pages. It had been so long since she had felt an inner anything that she didn't dare ignore it. There was no divine inspiration or wondrous peaceful feeling, but her heart and her mind agreed that if she wanted solace, she had to turn to God somehow—even if she felt He'd let her down. She'd been unable to pray since the flat prayer in the car Wednesday night. But something within her craved a connection to things greater than herself, and so she turned page after page, reading word after word in hope of . . . something.

Around nine o'clock she came to section 58. When she hit the second verse in the section, she read, "*For verily I say until you, blessed is he that keepeth my commandments, whether in life or in death; and he that is faithful in tribulation, the reward of the same is greater in the kingdom of heaven.*"

She tossed the scriptures on the bed as even more anger overwhelmed her. So much for solace. She had kept the commandments, all of them. No, she wasn't perfect, but she had always done what she was supposed to do. She followed the Spirit; she kept her covenants. This very scripture promised her blessings. For a few more seconds she fumed, but then her eyes went back to the book, now lying on the bed. She picked it up again and read the next verse, despite the anger still raging inside.

"Ye cannot behold with your natural eyes, for the present time, the design of your God concerning those things which shall come hereafter, and the glory which shall follow after much tribulation."

Her eyes began to fill as the Spirit touched her, finally. She still felt a little rebellious. She didn't want glory in the hereafter, she wanted peace now. But something inside her had awakened, and she kept reading. *"For after much tribulation come the blessings. Wherefore the day cometh that ye shall be crowned with much glory; the hour is not yet, but is nigh at hand."*

A life of misery sounded like a high price to pay for joy on the other side. Was her life meant to be full of sorrow and regret? She knew it wasn't.

"So why is this happening?" she asked out loud. In the next moment she was taken back to a woman she had taught on her mission—a woman she hadn't thought about in years. The woman was in her forties and had struggled with addiction, abusive men, and a lot of poor choices for most of her life. But she was humble, and when Maddie and her companion knocked on her door one morning, she invited them in. After a few lessons she became confused, wondering why, if there was a God who loved her, she had endured so much suffering. Maddie had felt it was due to her bad choices, but her companion had turned to section 122 in the Doctrine and Covenants. Maddie turned there now to reread what her companion had read that day. Back then it was powerful, but now, when she looked at herself through the words, she knew she had never fully appreciated the message before.

"And if thou shouldst be cast into the pit, or into the hands of

murderers, and the sentence of death passed upon thee; if thou be cast into the deep; if the billowing surge conspire against thee; if fierce winds become thine enemy; if the heavens gather blackness, and all the elements combine to hedge up the way; and above all, if the very jaws of hell shall gape open the mouth wide after thee, know thou, my son, that all these things shall give thee experience, and shall be for thy good.

"The Son of Man hath descended below them all. Art thou greater than he?

"Therefore, hold on thy way, and the priesthood shall remain with thee; for their bounds are set, they cannot pass. Thy days are known, and thy years shall not be numbered less; therefore, fear not what man can do, for God shall be with you forever and ever."

Maddie wiped at the tears on her cheeks and read the final verse again. The word *priesthood* stood out to her as if it were bold and highlighted with neon arrows pointing it out. She picked up the phone and dialed a number.

"Mom?" she said, trying to control her voice.

"Maddie," her mom said with relief. "I've been calling all weekend and keep getting the machine. We were just talking about coming over to see you."

More tears fell, and she swallowed her embarrassment. "I'm not home, but I need some help. Is Dad there?"

To her parents' credit, they didn't ask many questions. Within half an hour they were knocking on the door. She'd had time to feel silly for calling, and embarrassed for her reasons, but the power of those scriptures had stayed with her. In her own way she was staring into that pit, she felt as if the heavens were going black, and the jaws of hell were waiting. It didn't compare in circumstance to Christ's hour of Gethsemane or Joseph Smith's ultimate test, but she felt pain unlike anything she had ever faced or expected to face in her life. She knew she couldn't claw her way out by herself.

Maddie opened the door, and her mother enveloped her in a hug only a mother could give. A hug, Maddie realized, she herself might never give. Her father shut the door behind them and placed a comforting hand on Maddie's shoulder.

"What's happened?" her mom asked when Maddie pulled back. For a moment Maddie worried that she couldn't find the words to tell them, but she opened her mouth, and it all came tumbling out. The shock on their faces barely fazed her.

"I don't know how to handle this," she said between sobs several minutes later. Her mom was sitting next to her on the bed, and her dad had pulled up a chair. Her mother's hand in hers gave her strength to continue. "I keep trying to think what to do, and the only solution I can come up with is to leave him and start over."

"What Matt did was wrong," her dad said. "But he's a good man."

"I can't seem to convince myself of that," Maddie said with a shake of her head. "But I want to believe it. I want to find peace."

Her father stood, and Maddie took his seat. Then he walked to the back of the chair without another word. Her father's hands resting on her head relaxed her. "Madeline Marie Jackman Shep, by the power . . ."

She tried to listen to each and every word he spoke, but before long they blended together. Her father's love and her Heavenly Father's love burrowed into her soul and released the valve holding in all the anger and hurt. Allen's blessing of a few weeks earlier had calmed her, but this blessing helped to remove the burden of Matt's sins from her heart.

"You are not being punished," her father's voice said, though she knew the words were not his. "You are being challenged and will be helped as you choose the future ahead of you." She was told how much Matt loved her and reminded that he had been forgiven of these sins long ago.

When her father closed the blessing and removed his hands, she opened her eyes. Her mother was crying. Her father was too, but Maddie's eyes had dried.

She looked at her hands, not able to deny the peace and comfort she felt. "I feel better," she said. "But I don't feel like I got an answer."

"Sometimes," her father said as he came around and sat on the bed across from her, "it's not about getting an answer as much as making a choice. Your Father in Heaven doesn't want you to make a choice that will bring you agony any more than your mother and I do. But if you go back to Matt, you will have to make the choice to do so—the choice to forgive him and accept what may lie ahead."

"What if I can't?"

"Then you will have made another choice," he said. "You will have chosen to leave him to face it alone, to turn your back on the covenants you made to God and to Matt. He *did* repent, Maddie—he was an honorable missionary and has been a good man and a good husband. Leaving him because you can't forgive what the Lord has already forgiven would be a heavy burden for you to carry."

Maddie met his eye. "You think I should stay?" she asked, disappointed and wondering if they understood how she felt. Then she realized they couldn't understand, not completely. No one who hadn't sat right where she was could see things from her perspective. No one, that is, except Christ. He had not sat where she sat now, but He knew. Hadn't she just received His words, through her father?

"You need to decide for yourself," her dad replied. "When Christ atoned for the sins of mankind, He also took upon Himself the pain caused to others through those sins. It doesn't make what you're going through *easy* to bear, but it makes it *easier*—bearable. It's a big choice, a life-changing choice, whichever path you follow."

They were silent, and Maddie stared at her hands in her lap as she considered his words. It didn't feel like this was something she could bear, but she'd been taught about the power of the Atonement all her life, and she couldn't ignore it now.

113

"Do you still love your husband, Maddie?" her mom asked after almost a minute of silence.

She'd been wondering when they would ask that. She considered saying that she wasn't sure, or that she didn't know anymore, but it seemed silly to lie about it. She did love Matt. That was why this hurt so much. She finally nodded, still looking at her hands.

"Most people expect forgiveness to be a feeling or an event, Maddie—something that comes over them and allows them to let go. But it's not that way. Forgiveness is a choice you have to make. It will be the decision to go home, love your husband, and support him through this, while allowing him to comfort you. It won't feel better or even right all at once. But if you choose to do this, and lean on the Lord to hold you up, you will grow into it, and one day it won't sting quite as much as it does now."

"And if I choose not to go back? If I decide, along with everything else we can't have, this is too much?"

"Those things won't necessarily feel better or right, either. They will also be hard and painful. I would hope that one day they, too, would lose their sting. The difference is that you once promised to love and support Matt in all things. You promised God, and I can't imagine you would find the same peace in a choice that breaks your promises." She paused, and Maddie stared at her hands in her lap. "And something you're probably not thinking about very much right now is how hard and painful this is for Matt—*all* of this. He needs you and your love and help to get through this, just as much as you need his."

Maddie's first instinct was to argue again, but she couldn't. The words cut deep, and she didn't have the pride left within her to find an argument worthy of the energy it would take to dispute her mother's words.

Her parents stayed for another hour, talking it out, helping her see the big picture. She'd never had such a discussion with them, and she found safety in their words. They loved her, she knew it, and they wanted to help her make a choice that would give her the greatest joy. Their insight helped her see beyond herself—a little. When they all ran out of words, her parents begged her to come home with them, and when she refused that, they offered to stay with her at the hotel.

"I'm okay," Maddie said, feeling stronger thanks to their help and the blessing. "I feel like I need this time to myself." She had to repeat it several times before they gave up trying to convince her otherwise.

"You'll call if you need anything?" her mother asked at the door.

"I promise."

They left, and Maddie pulled a chair next to the window. It was almost midnight. A full moon illuminated the snow, making the night look more like early morning. She wondered what Matt was doing, if he was looking out the window thinking about her. She missed him, and the realization surprised her. Wasn't she too angry to miss him?

Do I believe in forgiveness? she asked herself. Yes, she knew she did. *Even for a serious sin like Matt's?* This one was harder. She had talked to many people on her mission about forgiveness, and she had believed it then, for them. But did she believe that the same forgiveness applied to Matt? *Not really,* she admitted. He was supposed to be better than those people. He knew better.

It took another hour to boil down her feelings to one solid truth: All she had ever wanted was to be happy. That was the core reason behind having the perfect little family. "Men are, that they might have joy." Might she also find it? She had always expected she would. But could she find it now? After all this heartbreak? Could she have the faith to look at her life and make joy from the pieces she had left? It seemed overwhelming at the moment.

Maddie went to the dresser and pulled out the manila envelope Matt had sent with her. She opened it and, one by one, read through the different letters and correspondence he'd received in regards to the paternity test. She found his explanation, written on two pieces of paper. He explained who Sonja was, how he knew her, and how it had happened. He also explained the hours and hours of study, the heartfelt prayer, and the dedication he gave to the gospel because he knew what it felt like to lose the Spirit, and he never wanted to feel that again. He apologized over and over, explained the timing of the letters, the desire he had to protect her from this if he could. But he also said he knew he was wrong.

She could read it only once before putting it aside and continuing with the letters from the attorney. The last letter in the stack was still in the original envelope. It confirmed that his blood sample had been received by a lab in New Jersey.

By next week they would know whether Matt had a child. The thought made her stomach sink, but she ignored it for once. As she folded the paper, she noticed there was something else in the envelope. She pulled it out and looked upon the photo of the boy who may or may not belong to her husband.

He had light brown skin and long, dark hair that hung to his shoulders. It was unkempt, and his smile revealed he would need braces in the next few years. But his eyes captured her attention. Her breathing slowed. For almost a minute she stared at the picture, seeing so many similarities between Matt and this boy while talking herself out of them at the same time. This boy couldn't be Matt's son. How could the Lord allow Matt to serve a mission if he knew Matt had fathered a child? Then she looked at the scriptures still lying open on the bed. She considered reading again, but she was too emotionally and physically drained. She picked up the triple combination and closed the book, smoothing her hands over the textured leather. The scriptures had been a gift from Matt on their first wedding anniversary. The name *Madeline Jackman Shep* was embossed in silver across the cover.

Remembering that night, she realized that Matt *was* the same man now as he had been when he had given her the standard works that shared his name. He was the same man now as he had been when she had promised to love and cleave to him for eternity. Maybe the reason he hadn't told her the truth about his past was because he feared she would react just as she had reacted. Perhaps her own piety exacted the price of his secrecy.

Her eyes were drawn to the boy's picture again, and she propped it up against her scriptures on the nightstand. She turned off the lights and climbed into bed, thinking about the boy in the picture for the first time. In the attorney's letter they referred to him as "the child." But this child was a boy without a father, a boy who could change her whole life. Another thought, not entirely welcome, came to mind. She and Matt had prayed for children. For years they had begged the heavens to make them into a family.

She asked herself for a moment why she wasn't spending time thinking about the possibility that this boy wasn't Matt's—but she knew the answer. In the darkness, she could just make out the face in the photo. She stared for several moments and tried to talk herself out of the understanding that was dawning.

★　　★　　★

The next morning Maddie showered, dressed in a light blue jogging suit, and went down to her car. She didn't check out of the hotel—she wasn't ready to go home for good—but there was something she had to do.

It was almost ten when she let herself into the apartment. Matt's dishes were in the sink, and his scriptures were open on the counter.

The boy's picture was in her purse, and she took it out, stared at it for a few seconds, and put it on the coffee table. She went to the bookshelves where the photo albums were kept. Two years ago she'd done a scrapbook of their lives to that point as a Christmas gift. She flipped pages until she found the one she wanted, then returned to the couch. She placed the scrapbook on the coffee table and put the photo next to it. For a few seconds she looked back and forth between the two smiling faces. They were about the same age, and there was no denying the similarity. It would be easy to overlook if you were a casual observer. However, Maddie was not a casual observer. Matt was fair and freckle-faced, his hair light brown and cut short. But the eyes of both faces were the same dark blue, with the same shape, and framed by the same powerful brow line. Even the snaggly smiles, with the gaps and partially grown-in teeth, were similar.

Maddie let out a breath and cupped her hands over her mouth as she realized with absolute certainty that the paternity test was a waste of time. The evidence was right there, smiling back at her with the innocent abandon of youth.

She had a choice to make. She slid off the couch and onto her knees.

"Lord," she whispered, still in disbelief over what she'd discovered, "what would you have me do?" In contrast to the similar prayer she had uttered in the car five nights ago, this one was sincere. She was beyond humble and felt prepared to do whatever it was He wanted her to do. Still on her knees, with only the ticking of the clock to be heard, she opened her eyes and looked at the photos again. She turned several pages in the scrapbook until she found the pictures from Matt's mission. He had served an honorable mission, and she knew he was a better man for it. Yet his child had paid the price for it. Was that fair? Her mind was suddenly impressed with the fact that it wasn't her job to figure that part out—that she should leave that issue in hands bigger, wiser, and far more capable than her own. What she needed to do was have faith. Faith that she *did* know the man she loved, and that God knew him too. She turned to another page, their wedding day, and stared at the naïve and love-struck couple. She knew what she was supposed to do.

If her Father in Heaven wanted her here, she would stay. Yet she knew it would not be easy. She turned back to the picture of Matt as a little boy, and the photo of the boy who was his son. She touched the little brown face in the photograph. She and Matt had longed for a child. It deeply hurt her to know that another woman had created him, that Matt had taken for granted back then the same intimacy they shared as husband and wife. But Matt did have a child, and, as his wife, so did she. She looked at that face again and felt a connection, a kinship, and for that instant she was at peace with it. There was a method to the madness that had put them here.

This boy was part of that.

CHAPTER 21

*M*att went to the gym after work—anything to avoid returning home to the empty apartment. But it couldn't be put off forever. He pulled into the parking space and let himself in a few minutes after six. The eerie stillness of the apartment depressed him, and he felt the need to turn on the TV and fill the room with sound. The open scrapbook on the coffee table stopped him. It took only a second to assure himself he hadn't put it there as he hurried toward it. Then he saw the other photo. He felt the anger and guilt and despair rush through him, but he picked up the photo and stared at it. When it had come in the mail, he'd only glanced at it before shoving it into the envelope. Now he really looked. Could this boy be his son?

"Maddie?" he called, though he knew she wasn't here. Knowing she had been here, however, made the apartment feel more like home. He sat on the couch and looked at the scrapbook. His brow furrowed, and he looked again at the photo in his hand and then back at his own grade-school picture. Then he took a deep breath and laid the pictures side by side. He noticed a single piece of notebook paper lying beside the scrapbook, and when the initial shock passed, he picked it up.

I'm in room 722 at the Iron Blosam Lodge. Will you meet me there for dinner at 6:00? We need to discuss some things. Bring the picture.

Maddie

He looked at the clock and leapt to his feet. It was 6:08. He was late!

He jumped in the car and sped to Little Cottonwood Canyon. As he drove, he called the Iron Blosam's front desk from his cell phone and asked to be connected to Maddie's room, but was told her line was only taking messages. He left a message and continued to drive as fast as he dared, winding up the canyon roads with his heart thumping in his chest.

It was 6:40 when he pulled into the parking lot. He was too anxious to wait for an elevator, and only while taking the stairs two at a time did it occur to him that she might be planning to tell him she didn't want to see him again. His steps slowed, and he was still trying to catch his breath when he knocked on her hotel room door seven flights later. It seemed to take forever before the door opened.

Maddie peeked out at him through a four-inch gap, her expression blank. "I didn't think you were coming," she said. Her curls were pinned up, and he thought she had a little makeup on. Would she dress up to give him bad news?

"I hate going home knowing you won't be there, so I went to the gym," he said between deep, sucking breaths. "I got here as fast as I could, once I got the note."

She stood to the side, inviting him in. He passed her, but her hand on his arm stopped him. He turned to look at her and noticed tears in her eyes. "I love you, Matt," she whispered. "I'm still mad, and hurt, and scared—but I love you, and I want us to do this together if you'll let me."

"Let you?" Matt choked. Wasn't it obvious that having her was the only thing he wanted? Tears began to course down his cheeks as he absorbed her words. Until a couple of weeks ago he could have counted on one hand the times he'd cried as an adult. Now, between nearly losing Maddie's life and then losing her love, he couldn't seem to stop.

Maddie continued. "I've been hard on you," she said, now wiping her own eyes. "For a long time, for a lot of reasons, and I'm sorry for not being the kind of wife you could share things with."

Hearing her apologize broke his heart, and he shook his head. "Don't apologize to me," he said, wanting to pull her into an embrace but sensing it was too soon. "I'm the one who did this. I'm the only one who needs forgiveness. I'm sorry for everything, but mostly that it happened in the first place. You deserved better, and you were right when you said that I should have told you. I just didn't want to be anything less than what you wanted me to be—but I wasn't fair to you in the process. I'm so sorry."

"Maybe it's wrong for me to be so hurt. Maybe it was my own judgments that made you not trust me enough to tell me, but I needed that apology. Knowing that you were with someone else . . ." Her voice trailed off, and she shook her head as if chastising herself. "Did you see the pictures?" she asked, releasing his arm as she changed the subject. He nodded. "Where is he?" she asked.

He, Matt thought to himself. It was so real. Matt removed the photo from his back pocket and handed it to her. She took it and walked to the counter, where she opened the back of a small silver frame. Then she placed the frame on the counter. Matt looked from her to the photo and back again. She was making a point. It hit him like a rock in the chest.

Maddie held his eyes as he forced himself to take a deep breath.

"What you did was a mistake," she said in a soft voice. "We both know that. But for two people who have worked so hard to make a baby, this boy is not something to apologize for anymore."

Matt straightened, confused at how accepting she was, but not wanting to argue. He knew her acceptance hadn't come easy. The look in her eyes was one of absolute sadness. But she was working past it. Could he do the same? "I'm sorry," he whispered again.

Maddie took a step forward, put a finger to his lips, and shook her head, though her chin was trembling.

"No more apologies," she whispered. She didn't remove her finger until he nodded his agreement.

They went downstairs to the Wildflower Restaurant for dinner. They didn't know enough about what lay ahead to make any grand decisions, other than that Matt needed to hire an attorney, but Matt was relieved they were at least working on it. They were both tense, and as the meal progressed the conversation slowed down and finally stopped. It was like discussing a terminal illness—necessary, but heartbreaking.

When they finished their meals, he walked her back to her room. She stopped in the hallway outside her door and turned to face him. "I'd like to stay one more night," Maddie said. "I'll come home tomorrow."

"Can I stay with you?" he asked.

Maddie hesitated and looked at the floor. "I need one more night," she said.

He didn't understand, but he nodded anyway. If she needed one more night, he would give it to her. It was the least he could do. He pulled her into his arms and then pulled back, resting his forehead against her own. It felt so good to be close to her, to smell her and feel her. He raised a hand and brushed his knuckles along her jawline. "I love you, Maddie," he said. She turned her head, allowing him to kiss her goodnight. He let his lips linger, still hoping she would change her mind and let him stay with her.

After a few seconds, she pulled back and turned to put the key in the door. "I love you, too," she said with her back facing him, emotion thick in her voice.

★　　★　　★

Once inside the room, Maddie put her back against the door and dropped her head into her hands as the tears came. Despite all the spiritual assurances and conscious choices she'd made, it had been so hard to keep her feelings to herself, to not scream and rage against all that was happening. She slowly sank to the floor, crying, sobbing, wanting to let out as much as she could. This was the right thing to do; she knew that. But it stung and burned and hurt like nothing she'd ever felt before. She had hoped that seeing Matt and making this choice would help her feel better. But it was still so hard. She was reminded that nowhere in the scripture stories she'd been raised on did it say that doing the right thing didn't hurt. She hoped as time went by it would be easier. She clung to that hope and tried to focus on why she was doing this. Why wasn't she driving to Mexico to open a small café? Why wasn't she going through the Yellow Pages taking notes on good divorce attorneys? Why was she subjecting herself to something so painful?

Because I love him, Maddie told herself. *And because it's the right thing to do*. A warmth filled her chest and reminded her that she hadn't made the decision alone, and she wouldn't have to press forward alone either. *This is an occasion to rise to*, she told herself, taking a deep breath and wiping at her cheeks.

It was time to rise.

CHAPTER 22

*M*addie came home on Tuesday and moved into the guest room. She was home, and she was committed, but she had yet to come to grips with certain aspects of the situation. She was also still healing, physically and emotionally, and needed space. Matt hadn't argued about the separate rooms, and she was glad. She didn't want to explain.

Matt walked in the door after work Thursday evening holding the mail. Maddie was making cookies, and when she saw the mail in his hand, she stopped. They had gone through this exact routine the two previous afternoons.

"Is it there?" she asked, looking from the mail to her husband.

"I didn't look yet."

"Well, look," she said, wiping off her hands on a dish towel as she turned to rest her hips against the counter. Getting so much rest over the weekend seemed to have helped her healing a great deal. She was taking Motrin to control the pain and was feeling better every day. She had medical leave for two more weeks, but had talked to her boss about coming back part-time next week. She worried about spending two more weeks with nothing to distract her. Emotionally she was still running the gamut of ups and downs. One minute she felt ready and peaceful, and the next she was mad again, feeling ripped off and bitter. She longed for it to even out—so did Matt.

Maddie watched Matt's hand move one letter at a time as he sorted through the stack. Then he stopped, and her heart seemed to stop with him. He looked up and their eyes met.

They seemed to take a breath in tandem, and then Matt pulled a butter knife from the drawer and slit the envelope open. Even though Maddie knew the results were positive, she couldn't help but hope she was wrong. It would be so much easier for them to *not* have this complication. They could be like Abraham and Isaac, taken to the very moment of obedience, only to be let off the hook. She hoped and prayed for that as Matt's hand pulled the paper from the envelope.

"Well?" Maddie asked after watching Matt scan the paper for several seconds. Matt shook his head. Did that mean it was negative? Without meeting her eyes, he put the letter on the counter and went out the front door, slamming the door behind him. That was pretty much his answer. She picked up the paper and read it, though she wasn't surprised. Her heart began beating again. She looked at the door where he'd just exited but wasn't in any state to catch up and comfort him.

She baked another pan of cookies, but the apartment began feeling rather claustrophobic. Leaving the hot cookies on the counter, Maddie grabbed her coat and went out for a walk. Matt's car was in its parking space, so she circled the apartment complex, scanning the area for her husband. She also watched the kids playing, the moms chatting, and the cars moving past. Her life was about to change—it was a powerful thing to face. Surprised with herself, she realized she wasn't feeling angry or resentful, just apprehensive for now.

After a while she sat down on a bench across from the small park and watched the people come and go. Some boys were kicking a soccer ball back and forth, enjoying the snow-free March weather. They looked about nine or ten, the boy's age—they still didn't know his name. A shiver went down her spine, and she let out a breath. It was difficult to imagine this was for real. But she was calm, and she was at peace, and she knew those two things—especially right now—were a gift.

When Maddie got back to the apartment, almost an hour had passed. Matt had beaten her home and picked up where she'd left off with the cookies. She sat across the counter and watched him remove the cookie sheet from the oven.

"You okay?" he asked in a careful tone. He was always careful when he spoke to her these past few days. Even though she hadn't said as much, he knew she was here because she'd chosen to be, not necessarily because she wanted to be.

She shrugged and picked up a cookie from the rack. It was still warm and she broke it in half, popped a piece in her mouth, and looked at him, "Aw oo?" she asked with her mouth full.

He shrugged as well. "I was still hoping, I guess."

"Yeah, me too," she said once she'd swallowed. "But I feel bad about that. I mean, it's not his fault."

Matt's mouth tightened, and he nodded.

She realized that her statement also implied that it *was* Matt's fault. "I didn't mean—"

"It's okay," he said. He removed the cookies from the sheet. "It's just so . . . I don't know . . . embarrassing, disgusting, unfair, weird." He took a breath. "You were right—I've lived a life I didn't deserve. I should never have served a mission. I shouldn't be here at all."

Maddie agreed with what he said, and yet . . . "For whatever reason you had the chance to serve, we'll never know or understand why—but we can still be grateful for it."

Matt nodded but said nothing.

"Now what?" Maddie asked after a few moments. "We need to tell your folks, talk to my folks, and the bishop."

Matt started dropping balls of cookie dough on the cookie sheet. "I know," he said. "I'm almost looking forward to talking to the bishop and getting his advice, but my parents . . . and yours . . . I don't know how I'm going to do that."

Maddie didn't either, and she didn't want to be there when he told them. Her parents already knew, of course, and she'd told Matt so. But he still needed to talk to them himself. Thinking about other people's reactions made her stomach tighten up. She imagined his parents looking at Matt and then at her, the blasted pity in their eyes. Then hugs and platitudes and evil looks at Matt. She wouldn't mind the evil looks toward Matt so much. Then again, maybe they would be achingly compassionate toward Matt—that might be worse.

Matt slid another pan in the oven, and Maddie knew she needed to change the subject or leave the room. She could feel the emotion building but didn't want to lose it right now. She was saved from making a decision when the phone rang.

"Hello?" she said, after the second ring helped her find the cordless phone on the couch.

"Maddie," Allen said, a sympathetic tone to his voice. "How are you?"

"I'm fine," she said, forcing a smile while thinking how much more sympathetic he would be if he knew the whole hardship she was trying to deal with. "How are you guys?" She hadn't talked to Kim, or anyone other than her mother, for almost a week. Things were too weird.

"Well, Kim had our baby this morning," he said. She knew he was curbing his excitement for her, and she was both grateful and irritated by the consideration.

"Congratulations," she managed to come up with. Maddie had

been at the hospital shortly after Lexie had been born, back when she and Matt were grateful Matt had finished school before they'd gotten pregnant. It hadn't been so hard to accept the Lord's will back then, and they were sure that within a few months they would make their own announcement. Kim had been so happy, she'd told Matt and Maddie to get on with it, make a best friend for Lexie. It seemed lifetimes ago.

"Maddie?" Allen asked. "Are you okay?"

"I'm fine," she hurried to say, putting on a smile for Matt's benefit and raising the level of her voice in hopes to put her brother at ease. "I'm really happy for you guys."

"Well, thanks," Allen said. But she knew he could feel her lack of enthusiasm. He probably regretted having called her, much like she regretted having him call. "I better call the grandmas," he said after another awkward pause.

"Okay." Maddie hung up the phone. The worries about telling other people what she and Matt were facing were paled by a sudden onslaught of emotion. This was the baby that would have been her child's playmate. They might have even been in the same grade at school. The pain was forced front and center—again. Her eyes started to fill, and things were getting heavy. Matt took the phone from her and pulled her into a hug.

"What a day," Matt whispered as he stroked her hair.

"I think I'm going to go lie down," Maddie said. She made to move away.

"Actually—why don't we go out instead?" Matt suggested. He stepped back but remained holding her arms.

"I'm not in the mood." The bed was calling to her. There were tissues there and chocolate in the nightstand drawer. Her incision ached. She was exhausted and depressed and wanting nothing more than a pain pill and a dark room.

"Exactly," Matt said. "Neither am I. But we're going to go through this for the rest of our lives, and we need to find a way to deal with it better. So let's find a way to make these things less painful."

"Like how?" she asked, reluctant to dismiss her feelings, and clueless as to what could make this less painful.

"Well, what's something we can do for ourselves? A reward—something we've wanted to do for a long time?"

"The only thing we've wanted to do for a long time is have a baby," Maddie said. She looked at the floor and wiped at the first tear.

"Surely there is something else we want out of life—anything."

Maddie searched her thoughts but could come up with nothing. "I can't think of anything else."

Matt looked crestfallen. "Me neither—that's kind of pathetic."

Maddie forced a smile and nodded. It was pathetic. They'd been married four years. Most couples had possessions or activities they enjoyed or saved up for. But not them. They didn't plan trips or get excited about saving up for a really big TV. They used to, before fertility treatments had overwhelmed their life. But making a baby had replaced everything else. It was the only thing they wanted. The chocolates in the nightstand drawer started calling louder.

"Remember when we went to Liza's wedding in Logan, and we stopped at that steakhouse at the bottom of the canyon."

Maddie thought a minute. "Mad Dog?"

Matt couldn't help but laugh. "Maddox, I think."

Maddie nodded. It had been a couple of years ago, but she remembered.

"They had that bison steak you loved."

"And real mashed potatoes," Maddie added, pushing the self-pity away a little bit.

"And that pie thing, with raspberries. And those rolls."

"Oh, those rolls were good."

"Should we go?" Matt said. "Celebrate our infertility?"

Maddie's stomach sank and her eyes narrowed. "That's not funny," she said.

Matt shrugged. "It could be funny if we'd let it be funny."

"No, it can't," she said stubbornly.

"How many couples with kids can drive an hour on a Thursday night to get dinner at the best steakhouse in the state?"

"I'd rather have kids to bathe and put to bed." The self-pity was making a strong comeback.

"But we don't—yet—so let's find a way to make other people's success less heartbreaking by making ourselves have a good time."

Maddie pondered the idea. It felt like a betrayal somehow, but she wasn't sure what or who was being betrayed. She didn't want to go, and she didn't really want to be with Matt right now. But she hadn't wanted to come home from the hotel, either. She'd made the choice to do it because it was the right decision. She could do it again.

"Let me change my clothes first," she said.

Matt smiled, and she smiled back. It was a step in the right direction.

CHAPTER 23

he next day Matt called an attorney, who would then call the caseworker in New Mexico to get the ball rolling. Matt met him and signed the initial paperwork that afternoon, planning to meet again as soon as the attorney had been brought up to speed. It was in this meeting that they learned the boy's name, Walter Begay Hudson. *Walter?* Maddie had thought when Matt told her. Who named a baby Walter? But she said it over and over again, trying to get used to it.

On Sunday morning Matt met with the bishop. "How did it go?" Maddie asked when he came home. She could tell Matt had been emotional, though he was now subdued. She was lying on the couch reading a John Grisham novel—one of the few authors she enjoyed who never mentioned babies or pregnancy in his books. She'd been rereading his books all week long. The women's fiction that she had always loved was still too hard.

"Pretty good," Matt said as he loosened his tie and undid the top button of his shirt. "He assured me that feeling guilty about not being in the child's life and having served a mission wasn't necessary—I'd done everything I could do on my end. That made me feel better. We talked for a long time, and he made a point of letting me know that all I can do now is do my best from here on out. I also asked to be released from my calling with the Young Men."

"Why?" Maddie asked, laying the book on her lap. "You went through the steps, it isn't a worthiness issue—even the bishop emphasized that." She was impressed with herself for being able to see it, and gave herself a little mental pat on the back.

He came and sat down on the other end of the couch. Lifting the blanket covering her legs, he took one foot in his hand and began to massage it. The debate swirling in her head faded fast, and she relaxed despite herself.

"I think my energies would be better served somewhere else." He looked up and met her eyes. "With you, perhaps."

She didn't respond—wasn't sure what to say. He loved his calling, and the young men he served with loved him back. He looked at the foot in his hand and continued. "The boys need someone who can be a role model, show them the right path to take. I don't see how I can give them that right now. There is so much ahead of us now, so many things to prepare for."

So many things ahead of them was right. They had to tell their families, and they had to prepare for the possibility that Walter might come for the summer. They'd been in this ward for three years. The members knew them. They were their friends. She imagined the looks, the continuous questions, the humiliation—and her heart sank. "Yeah, I see your point," she said in a whisper. "Maybe we should move."

Matt nodded. "I was thinking that too." They were both silent for almost a minute. "It would make an easier transition. I just wish it didn't feel like I was running away."

"There is no running away," Maddie said, looking at the blanket and pulling her foot back, not wanting to be touched anymore. "Even if we move, people will know."

Matt took a deep breath and leaned back on the couch. "Yeah," he said with a shrug. "But it might be easier in a new place."

Another uncomfortable silence descended, and Maddie could feel herself getting angry, as she often did when she thought about the details they had waiting for them—and that it was Matt's fault they were facing this at all. She tried to change the subject. "When are you going to tell your parents?"

"After church," he said.

"And my parents?" she asked. "They need to hear it from you too."

Matt grunted and stood up. "There is only so much I can do all at once."

"You have to talk to them," Maddie repeated, realizing she was sounding like a school marm. She wasn't sure why she was pushing so hard. Maybe she needed to feel powerful somehow.

Matt turned and looked at her. "Thanks for the news break," he said bitterly, tightening his tie back up. "I need to get back to church; I'm conducting in priesthood today."

Maddie went back to her book but found it hard to focus until Matt left. She wished again that she could choose to let go of the anger the way she had chosen to come home and give their marriage a chance. She knew it would take time, but wished she could fast-forward things somehow. Being angry with Matt, in addition to everything else, was exhausting.

★   ★   ★

Matt didn't come home after church, and Maddie could only assume he had gone straight to his parents. When he came in the door, his tie had been loosened, and his hair looked like he'd pushed his hands through it a hundred times.

"How'd it go?" she asked, muting the television and feeling bad for adding to his stress that morning. It couldn't have been an easy day for him.

Matt snorted and shook his head as he placed his scriptures on the counter. "They were very proud of me," he said, his voice thick with sarcasm.

"It was bad?"

Matt turned and leaned his hips against the counter, dropping his chin and folding his arms across his chest. "It was humiliating," he said quietly, staring at the floor. "After I talked to the bishop back then and got Sonja's assurances, I went ahead and enrolled in school for the fall semester. I didn't turn nineteen until early November, so I told my folks I wanted to get some school in. I thought I was doing the responsible thing by not burdening them with something that wasn't their fault. Telling them the truth now was quite a shock. I didn't even get to the part about Walter maybe coming in the summer—they were hung up on how it was that I never knew before now, and how I could do this to you. My mom cried."

"Really?" Maddie said. She hadn't expected that, and though she felt bad about it, it made her feel a little better as well. Maybe people did understand how hard this was.

Matt sighed and lifted his head. "It was a shock—like it was for you, like it will be for everyone. I've worked so hard to never give people reason to doubt me. Now, when they learn the truth . . ."

Maddie stood up and came to stand in front of him. He didn't look at her at first, and when he did, he regarded her with suspicion. "I'm sorry, Matt," she said.

"Isn't this what you wanted?" he asked. "To have me punished this way?"

It *had* been what she wanted—a little. But he had a lot more of this ahead and he didn't need her to make it worse. "I'm sorry," she said, reaching up and smoothing back his hair. "I don't want people to hurt you." And she didn't. She knew his hurt wasn't going to make hers go away.

Matt didn't look like he believed her, so she reached her arms around his neck, and after a moment he reciprocated. They hadn't been very affectionate since her return, but it felt good to be close to him, to deaden the sting a little.

"I'll go with you to my parents," she said after a few moments.

"You don't have to," he said, but she could hear how much he did want her there.

"I want them to know we're together on this," Maddie said.

"Are we?" Matt asked. "It's hard to tell sometimes."

Ouch, she thought, pushing back the retort she had automatically come up with. She didn't want to make things worse, though, so she refused to give in to the temptation to punish him further. "I'm working on it, Matt. I'll go with you if you feel up to it tonight."

Matt groaned, and she pulled back. "I guess I might as well get it over with," he said. Then he smiled. "I don't want to give you time to reconsider your offer."

"No kidding," Maddie teased.

★ ★ ★

Having advance notice proved to be a good thing. Maddie's parents asked questions, but made no accusations or judgments. Maddie reminded herself that they had gotten used to their kids having interesting turns in their lives. Allen's marriage to his first wife, Janet, their divorce ten years later, and then the marriage to Kim right after all her turmoil hadn't been easy. Maddie had another brother who was in his late thirties, unmarried and inactive with a four-year-old son and a live-in girlfriend. Her parents had long ago given up on the perfect family. But until they embraced Matt and offered their support, Maddie had never considered how their challenges had made them so full of love and compassion. She cried, of course, but their kindness went a long way in helping her see how she wanted to be. It also helped Matt. For the first time he had disclosed his past to someone who wasn't completely shocked or angry with him.

Maddie's parents even offered to call her brothers and sisters and tell them the news themselves. These confessions were draining, and being spared them was a welcome and thoughtful gift. Matt decided to tell his own siblings via e-mail. Maddie felt the e-mail didn't give it the weight it deserved, but Matt looked exhausted, and she couldn't bring herself to add to his burdens by insisting he call each person individually.

"What about visitation?" Maddie asked as they drove home.

Matt let out a breath. "I don't know. It seems like the right thing to do."

"Yeah," Maddie said, looking out the window to avoid looking at him as the anger rose up again. She wasn't against Walter's coming. In fact, she thought it would be a good thing. But she also knew it would be hard. Matt reached across the car and placed his hand on her knee. It surprised her, making her jump, but then she placed her hand over his and gave it a squeeze, reminding herself she'd chosen to be here.

★　　★　　★

Maddie went back to work Monday morning, working only until noon. There was plenty to do, and after her half-day was finished, she was overwhelmed and wondering why she had come back early. But it felt good to be doing something, so she got up the next morning, and the next. During their lunch break on Friday, she met Matt at his new attorney's office. It took an hour to get all the paperwork signed, a Voluntary Establishment of Paternity officially submitted—thus avoiding a court trial so long as they could all agree to visitation and child-support issues without the interference of a judge. They listened as the attorney explained the many intricacies of not only the custody issues but the complexity of dealing with the Navajo tribe. It was overwhelming to hear so many details. Sonja had already prepared her requests—$350 a month for child support and she was happy to give Matt visitation, though she would retain full custody. Matt and Maddie agreed to her terms, but insisted that Walter be okay with the idea. The attorney assured them she would follow through on it. It was a relief to know they wouldn't have to go before a judge or even see Sonja face to face. Apparently cases like this had become so common they were relatively simple to do.

They both returned to work, and Maddie was grateful for the solitude of her car on the drive back. By the time she pulled into the parking lot at work, her eyes were dry again. She wanted to be strong and supportive, but each phase was like a knife twisting in her side. Through it all, however, at least since she had chosen to come back to her husband, she felt lifted up. When moments came that she was sure she couldn't tolerate, something kept her going, helped her bite her tongue—most of the time—and reminded her that she was here by choice. Somehow knowing she hadn't been forced into this strengthened her resolve to do it right.

But sometimes she still found herself dreaming of a studio apartment in Seattle and a job at K-Mart.

CHAPTER 24

*I*t's a simple question," Sonja said with frustration. "Do you want to go stay with him or not? Grandmother will fly there with you and pick you up when it's over. It will be fun." She tapped her cigarette, and the gray ash plopped into the dirty ashtray. The letter she'd received in the mail was open on the table, and she kept looking at it.

Part of Walter was excited to go somewhere new, but it was scary to think about leaving the Rez. He looked at Anna, who was doing her homework across the table from him. She nodded without looking up. That was what he needed. "Yeah, I guess," he said.

Sonja smiled, showing teeth that were yellow because of the cigarettes she was always smoking. "Good. I've got to go into Gallup to make the call. I'll be back later. Actually, I might stay with José tonight."

She left, and Walter waited until the truck pulled away before speaking again. "You think I should go?" he asked, using the butt of a cigarette to trace patterns in the ash of the ashtray.

Anna nodded and smiled at him. "I bet he's nice. The letter says he has a wife and a good job. It's only for *naaki* (two months)."

"I think I'll miss the stars." He rested his arms on the table top.

Anna laughed. "There are stars in the city."

"Sam says there aren't."

"Sam's wrong," she said. "You just can't see as many."

"I wish you could come with me," Walter said.

"Well, I can't wait for you to come home and tell me all about it. I've never lived in a city. Besides, I'll be working full-time at the Twin Lakes Trading Post this summer. Even if you stayed, we wouldn't see much of each other. I'll be really busy."

Walter thought about that. It would be cool to go somewhere none of his friends had ever been. Besides, he didn't want to be home all day without Anna in the summer. "You think they'll be nice?"

"I think they are real nice. I bet they're excited to have a boy there too. They don't have any kids yet, and don't forget they asked you to come—they didn't have to."

"They're Mormon. Mom hates Mormons," Walter said.

"They seem nice, and that's all that matters. Besides, I know a few Mormon kids at school, and they're okay."

Anna's liking Mormons was more convincing than his mom's not liking them. His mom didn't like lots of people—including Navajos. "Okay," Walter said, getting more excited the more they talked about it. "I hope they like me."

Anna leaned over and ruffled his hair. "Why wouldn't they like you? You're the best little boy in the world."

"I'm not little," he said with a scowl.

"Okay, you're the best big boy in the world."

"I'm not big."

Anna laughed again. "You're impossible."

"Can I have some chips?"

"We don't have any."

"Cereal?"

"We don't have that either. There's some fry bread, though."

"Can I have honey on it?"

"Sure," she said, standing up. "I'll help you."

CHAPTER 25

*M*addie took a deep breath and pushed the doorbell, holding the package in both hands. Kim opened the door, and for a few moments she and Maddie stared at one another. Then Maddie smiled shyly and held out a white package with a pink bow and said, "I'm sorry I waited so long."

Kim stepped out onto the porch, pulling Maddie into her arms for a hug. Maddie closed her eyes and willed away the emotion that sprang up at knowing that Kim wasn't angry with her. Little Sammy, short for Samantha, was almost six weeks old, and although Maddie had thought about Kim often, she hadn't been able to bring herself to see her or even call. Kim had left several messages Maddie hadn't returned, and Matt said she'd sent some e-mails too. Maddie avoided the computer like the plague, not wanting to be included in the lengthy discussions Matt had been having with several of their siblings as everyone tried to make sense of what was happening. Maddie had been back to full-time work for two weeks and had started feeling horrible for not talking to her best friend for so long.

It would have been easier if the paternity situation had been the only thing keeping her away. She could have gotten past that. But there was also Sammy. Sammy represented all Maddie had lost, and it was hard to get past that and rejoice in Kim and Allen's bounty. Today she had realized that if she allowed it to, the jealousy she was feeling would destroy the friendship she had with Kim. The thought had been terrifying enough to force her to the nearest JC Penney. Going to the baby department was a heart-wrenching experience. Little frilly dresses and tiny shoes seemed to taunt her. She rushed in and rushed out, but was grateful she had done it once she was back in her car.

Kim eventually let her go and wiped her eyes with embarrassment. "What women we are," Kim said with a laugh, and Maddie smiled. Kim invited her in, and Maddie entered, feeling oddly uncomfortable in the home she'd always felt very comfortable in.

Once inside, Maddie asked, "So where's this little niece of mine?"

Kim turned and led Maddie to the cocooned infant lying in the crook of the couch. Kim lifted her, showing Maddie the chubby peach face of her newborn daughter. Maddie smiled and put out her hands, unable to find words necessary to ask for permission. Kim transferred the bundle to Maddie's arms and then settled on the couch opposite the chair Maddie lowered into. Wishing the tears hadn't come so fast, Maddie looked up and with a watery smile whispered, "She's beautiful." She met Kim's eyes and looked away from the pity there. "I should have come a long time ago."

"It's okay. I've been really worried about you, though."

Maddie ignored the sympathy. "Is she a good baby?"

"She has her moments," Kim said, seeming to relax a little bit, but still tense. "She's not as content as Lexie was, but she slept three hours straight last night."

Maddie laughed. "Three whole hours, and that's a good thing?"

"For her it is," Kim said with a smile.

143

Maddie handed the baby back. "She's darling." She could feel the emotions piling up behind her carefully built wall, and she didn't want to lose it on Kim. She'd made progress, she knew that, but it was still so hard. If someone could say that after she'd held twenty-five babies it wouldn't hurt anymore, or after five hundred and eighty-nine days she'd be able to be happy for someone else's blessings, she would at least have something to shoot for.

"How is it going with . . . well, everything?" Kim asked, her voice sounding hesitant to bring it up. "We were pretty shocked when we found out."

"Yeah, so was I," Maddie said. "Matt asked to be released from his calling. I feel bad for him—you know how much he's loved the young men." Kim nodded. "But I think he was right to do it. The bishop knows, and I think he's told the other ward leaders, but no one has said anything to us. We listed the condo, got an attorney, and petitioned for visitation in the summer."

"Do you think his mom's okay with that?"

His mom, Maddie repeated in her mind, and took a deep breath. "Apparently she's in full cooperation, but it's up to Walter. If he doesn't want to come, we won't force it."

"How much is Matt going to have to pay in support?"

"Three hundred and fifty dollars a month, and they haven't had a phone, so he'll be paying for that, too. But they can't go after him for back support. That's a relief."

"And you?" Kim said. "How are you?"

Maddie shrugged. It was her best answer. "I'm here," she said with a fake smile she knew Kim saw right through. "And I'm making progress. I better get going, though. I'm meeting Matt at the gym."

"I meant to tell you how great you look," Kim said.

"Yeah, not having anything better to do has gotten me off my behind a little more. I'm back in jeans I haven't worn for years."

"Good for you," Kim said. She put Sammy back on the couch and gave Maddie another hug. "Keep it up."

"Yes, ma'am."

But then Maddie cried all the way home and canceled the trip to the gym.

★   ★   ★

The following Monday found them across the desk from the attorney again.

"Walter agreed to the visitation—at least for this year," she said as she looked at Matt. Matt let out a breath and forced a tenacious smile. "He said it would be 'cool,'" she added with a smile. Maddie smiled back, but her stomach dropped a little. The attorney continued: "I took you at your word concerning visitation, and we've worked out eight weeks for the summer. Walter will fly in from Albuquerque, the closest airport, in June and go home in August. If these terms are acceptable for you, then we can finish up the paperwork now, I'll submit the copies to the courts, and within the week all the legal issues will be put to rest. Your willingness to agree to Mrs. Hudson's terms made things go very smoothly." She pushed some papers toward Matt, who picked up a pen and signed. Maddie's head was spinning.

They finished up and went out to the car. Maddie had missed so much work that she had to be careful about time she took off these days, so she'd taken a late lunch break and Matt had picked her up. They got in the car and started toward her office.

"I don't think I can do this," Matt said after a few minutes. "Every time I think I've accepted it, I get some overwhelming realization that I haven't. This is crazy. He doesn't even know us. Why are we doing this?"

Maddie took a breath, remembering the reasons she had come

up with to make it bearable. "Because he's a little boy who needs, and obviously wants, a father. What a blessing this will be to him."

"I'm not a father," Matt said, staring at the steering wheel. "I'm no different than the other four guys who were tested—it's all about biology and nothing else. Why are we forcing something that will be so uncomfortable and unnatural for all of us?"

Maddie took a breath. "It's about a lot more than biology," she said, though she agreed that his intent had been no different from that of the other possible candidates. "And the difference between you and anyone else is that you *are* his father. You have a responsibility to him. We have the chance to make a difference in his life. We should be grateful for that."

Matt didn't say anything, and Maddie knew he was a long way away from feeling gratitude for any of this. They pulled up outside Maddie's office, and she leaned toward him and kissed him goodbye. "It's going to be okay, Matt."

"You keep saying that."

"Just try to accept it, all right?" She hoped he didn't pick up on the edge in her voice.

Matt looked at her. "I *am* trying," he said stubbornly.

She held his eyes for a few more moments, and in them she could see his continuing obstinacy. Sighing, she kissed him once more and got out of the car. There was little more she could do; the rest had to come from Matt. But it bothered her. Shouldn't she be the one with the hesitations and fear? She had more reason than he did. She pulled open the heavy glass door of her office building, smiling at a coworker she passed on her way to the stairs.

As she sat down at her desk, she realized that even though her arms were empty, her heart was full and ready to have children. She was a woman, a wife, and very much wanting to be a mother. Tears pricked her eyes as she pondered the idea that her longing might be what brought Matt to accepting his role in his son's life. A warmth filled her chest, and she knew that just as she'd chosen to come home to her husband, at some point she'd chosen to do right by this child. She wondered when it had happened, and then realized it was likely a gradual thing. Every time she looked at Walter's picture on the mantel, every time she prayed for strength, she was receiving it. Perhaps one drop at a time. But it was there, and she was overwhelmed with gratitude. She could only hope Matt would follow her example.

When she got home that night, Matt had left a note explaining he was with a client. He also apologized for having such a hard time with everything.

> . . . *I'm trying, Maddie, I really am, and I'll do better. I don't know what I'd do without your support in this. Thank you for being so strong, for pushing me forward and for being here at all. I picked something up for you on the way home from work—it's in the fridge. Love you,*

> *Matt*

Maddie smiled and then turned to the fridge. Inside was a piece of German chocolate cheesecake, by far her favorite dessert. Matt used to do little things like that when they were first married. She had worked full-time while he went to school. Between class and study groups, they had struggled to find time together. His little gifts had been a sweet reminder that she was missed—as was this one. Calories notwithstanding, she enjoyed the cheesecake, reflecting on the fact that just as she had chosen to be here, so had Matt. He didn't have to face the situation with this much conscience and maturity. It was powerful for her to realize that.

When she finished the delectable cheesecake, she changed out of her work clothes. She was hanging them up in the guest-room closet when she paused and looked around. Over the last six weeks she'd gradually moved her things into this room, and yet she hadn't quite realized it until this moment.

She looked at the jacket in her hands. "What am I doing?" she asked no one. Lifting her chin, she pulled all the clothes from the closet and took them back into the master bedroom. For the next hour she moved all her things back—her books, her jewelry, everything that didn't belong in a guest room.

Matt didn't notice when he came home. It had become normal for them to sleep in separate rooms. They hadn't even talked about it. She thanked him for the cheesecake, and he smiled, obviously pleased to have done something she appreciated. An hour later, Matt was deciding what he would wear the next day to work and gave her only a perfunctory glance when she came into the room and began changing into her pajamas. He stopped and watched her for a few moments, and then turned to study his shirts hanging in the closet. That was when he seemed to notice her clothes were back. He turned to look at her, but she spoke before he had the chance.

"I'm thinking of giving the bed in there to my folks," she said as she pulled her pajama bottoms on. "Mom's been talking about turning the den downstairs into a guest room. With so many kids and grandkids, she needs more room to put them up when they come in town."

"What about a bed for Walter?" Matt asked, hesitation thick in his tone.

"Maybe we could get a twin instead."

Matt was silent, and she sensed he was feeling her out. "Why not keep the double?"

She turned and faced him. "With a double bed in there, it's too comfortable for me to make it my room, and it isn't. It's Walter's room. I belong here."

Matt smiled and came to sit next to her. He pulled her down to lie beside him. "Can I take the lock off the door as well?" he asked. "Just in case a twin seems too accommodating some nights."

She scrunched up her face as if deep in thought. "I guess," she said with a shrug as she began running her fingers through his hair. She smiled and cocked her head to the side. "When was the last time we made love for fun?"

"Fun?" Matt repeated. "People make love for fun?"

Maddie chuckled. "That's what I hear."

"Well, I'll be a monkey's uncle. I had no idea." He put a hand behind her head and pulled her closer until their lips met. The spark she felt was something she barely remembered but wanted very much to become familiar with again. She'd missed it over the years and vowed not to let it slip away this time.

CHAPTER 26

*M*addie woke up remembering what day it was—as if she could forget. The second Sunday in May: the worst day of the year. Matt was still asleep. She crept out of the room and dressed in the jogging clothes she'd left in the bathroom for this very reason. As quietly as possible, she slipped them on, put on her running shoes, opened the front door, and escaped to the great outdoors. Thank goodness it was a nice day. In past years Matt would get her flowers, or make her a Mother's Day breakfast in bed. Even though she'd never really deserved it back then, she'd gone along with it and enjoyed the day based on the promise that the next year . . . But this time was different, and he seemed to understand when she told him she wanted to skip it altogether.

Last year's Mother's Day had been the hardest one up to that point. Before then she'd been so excited and hopeful. Last Mother's Day, however, the blissful hopefulness had begun to fade, and she'd decided not to stand to get her obligatory flower at church. Everyone knew by then that she and Matt were getting infertility treatments, and she didn't want the looks of pity as she stood above everyone and waited for her mum. Rather than stand and feel conspicuous, she shrank into the seat. Matt elbowed her, but she'd shut him down with a hard look he couldn't help but understand. Then Sister Christiansen, in the row behind them with her seven kids, had leaned down.

"Stand up, Sister Shep," she had whispered.

Maddie turned and looked into the woman's meaty, but kind, face. "It's okay," she whispered back, humiliated that someone had noticed and dared call her on it.

Sister Christiansen pushed at her shoulder. "It's not okay. You get on your feet and get your flower."

Maddie shook her head and prayed she would be left alone. But Sister Jensen, standing in front of them with her two kids and eight-month-pregnant belly stretching out in front, had turned and chimed in as well. Apparently they felt it their duty to make sure Maddie got the flower she didn't want and didn't deserve. Finally she had stood, beet red, looking at her shoes and willing herself not to cry or scream. Maddie was out the door within seconds once the meeting was over. She placed the flower back in the plastic tray in the foyer and hurried to the car. She felt certain Matt remembered, which was probably why he had agreed to let the day pass by this year.

They had taken their gifts to their moms yesterday, so they didn't have to face anyone today. This year she would have just as soon slept through it.

Maddie and Matt had been walking together for almost three months now and had just started running—but she didn't feel like running today. Besides, it was Sunday. They didn't usually exercise at all on Sunday, but she needed to get out of the house. Thanks to the months of exercise, Maddie was in better shape than she had ever been. In fact, she was beginning to enjoy it. When she finished circumventing the neighborhoods and side streets, she reached the park and followed the jogging trail. She'd forgotten her headphones, but even musicless walking was better than church. She looked at her watch after what she thought had been about an hour and smiled. Another hour and she would be too late to have time to get ready, thus staving off any argument from Matt, should he decide to try to talk her into going after all.

"You can't run from your problems—or walk, for that matter."

She whipped around and narrowed her eyes as Matt jogged to catch up. "You're supposed to be asleep," she told him. She wanted to be alone. To make that clear, she started jogging once he stopped to catch his breath. He caught up in a few steps.

"I wanted to wish you a happy—"

"Stuff it," she said, giving him a hard look.

"No—this is important. So happy—"

She turned and stopped, putting a hand over his mouth as he stopped too. "I wasn't kidding when I told you to not say anything about it, okay. This is the mother of all bad days for me, no pun intended. Please," she begged, wanting him to hear the sincerity in her voice. "Please let it go by this time. I don't want any flowers. I don't want to stand up and have people give me encouraging smiles. I don't want it—really."

Matt grabbed her wrist and removed her hand from his mouth. "I know all that, Maddie. I'm talking about No Socks and Have a Coke Day."

Maddie furrowed her brow. "What?"

"I looked it up, and May eighth is No Socks and Have a Coke Day. So . . . happy No Socks and Have a Coke Day."

Maddie tried to hold back the smile, but she couldn't resist. "You looked it up or you made it up?" she asked as they resumed walking.

"I looked it up," he said with a nod of his head. "It's official."

Matt found her hand with his own. They walked for several minutes in silence, enjoying the spring day.

"I'm not going to church," she said when she realized they were turned toward home.

"Me neither," Matt said with a nod. "I suggest we take a few

Cokes, drive up into the mountains, lay out a blanket, and take off our socks."

"We'd have to buy Coke on Sunday," Maddie said. "I might be a heathen for walking on Sunday and not going to church, but I don't know that I can justify that level of heathenism."

"Well, see, I actually thought about this before today," Matt said, casting her a sidelong glance and winking. "And I bought the Coke—and some cute fuzzy socks."

"But it's *No Sock* day."

"Well, after the No Socks, we could put on some socks. Our own little holiday."

He squeezed her hand, and she felt the emotion rise in her throat. It was hard to believe that a few months ago she'd been so disappointed in their marriage. That he had thought of something so sweet and so simple melted her. "You're delectable," Maddie said, leaning into him. "I think it sounds fabulous."

And it was. After drinking their Cokes in the mountains, they sprawled out on an unzipped sleeping bag with bologna sandwiches packed in a cooler at their feet. They took off their shoes and fell asleep. When they woke up from their alpine nap, Matt put the bright pink fuzzy socks on her feet and took a picture—several, in fact. They got home as the sun was setting.

"This was the best Mother's Day I've ever had," she said as they got ready for bed a couple of hours later.

Matt gave her an exaggerated look. "What are you talking about? It's No Socks and Have a Coke Day."

She laughed. "Thank you for making it the best No Socks and Have a Coke Day I've ever had."

"I'll do anything for a smile."

She grinned as widely as she could and wrapped her arms around his neck, grateful for the opportunity to focus on what she had instead of what she was missing.

CHAPTER 27

*D*uring the weeks that followed No Socks and Have a Coke Day, Maddie put together a care package for Walter, hoping it would make it easier for him to come. Even though she felt herself growing excited for the experience, it was nerve-wracking as well. The little she knew about Indian reservations wasn't positive, and though she promised herself not to put too much stock in rumors, it made her nervous. She worried that his beliefs would be very different from theirs, that their lifestyle here would be overwhelming to Walter. Allen had come over one night and answered many of their questions. It had helped immensely. He had suggested that they not push the Church, but include it as a normal part of their lives and let Walter ask questions as they came. Mostly he counseled them to be as patient and loving as possible, pointing out how hard it would be for Walter to leave the life and people he knew. Maddie found herself watching other boys his age and trying to prepare herself.

Another half-day Friday at the end of May gave Maddie the afternoon off, and she headed toward home deep in thought. The subject of adoption had occupied her thoughts a great deal, but she'd avoided taking any steps forward in the process. Then, over the last week or so, she had seemed to see adoption everywhere. It turned out that a woman she worked with had adopted two children from Korea almost fifteen years ago. Maddie had never noticed the multicultural family picture. The talk radio show she often listened to on the way home spent a whole day discussing adoption and, more specifically, how to integrate multiple races in one household. She had a dentist appointment, and the *People* magazine she picked up focused on celebrities who had adopted. She felt surrounded and couldn't seem to escape thinking about it. She kept telling herself she wasn't ready. But if God was giving her subtle hints, it was working. She couldn't shake the thoughts from her mind.

By the time she arrived home that Friday she had managed to transition from not feeling ready to finding herself excited. They had Walter coming, so why not get started on the rest of their family? Over the weeks since her surgery, her heart had softened to the point where she felt capable of loving any baby who might come her way. She hungered to be a mother—anyone's mother—and saw the hunger as a true gift from God.

She called LDS Family Services, and they said they would send her an information packet. Then she went online and ordered the books Dr. Lawrence had recommended to her months ago.

"What's this?" Matt asked when he returned from work that afternoon. Maddie was at the kitchen table, surrounded by things she had printed off the internet.

He picked up an article and scanned the page.

"I think I'm finally ready to get started on this," she said, underlining another tidbit she wanted to go back to later. Then she looked up at him. "I don't want to rush it, though, and if you're not ready we can wait."

Matt leaned forward and kissed her. "I'd been thinking the same thing. But I didn't want to push you."

"Yeah, right," she said and shook her head. They spent the rest of the evening getting started on their research. They figured out what they had in savings—less than they'd had several weeks ago, thanks to the medical bills for Maddie's surgery and six weeks of unpaid medical leave. LDS Family Services had said the costs were based on a sliding scale relative to household income. With that as a guide, they knew how much longer they needed to save up.

"It's almost hard to believe anyone ever has a baby for free," Maddie said as she compared some prices for private adoptions. They were so expensive—up to thirty thousand dollars.

"Yeah, with all we've spent, you'd think we'd get a discount some-where," he said. "The guys I work with are in these nice houses with nice cars. Their wives don't work, and here you and I work our tails off."

"Ugh, I don't want to think about that," she said, shaking her head. "LDS Social Services is looking better and better. We could have the money by July."

"Do we want to start all this with Walter here?"

Maddie shook her head. "No, so maybe we should shoot for September. By the way, Walter flies in on the twenty-first. We had to change the day."

Matt just nodded and started punching numbers into the calculator. He had made some strides in accepting the situation, but Maddie had been the one who had stepped up and taken over all the arrangements.

"Sonja isn't bringing him, is she?" Matt asked a minute later. Maddie had gone back to reading an article, and it took a moment to realize what he was talking about.

"No, his grandmother is going to fly with him to make sure he's settled."

"I thought his grandmother was dead."

Maddie gave him a look showing her disapproval of his blunt statement. "She is. This is a woman he *calls* Grandmother. She sounds cool. She taught Native American Studies at Penn State back in the sixties, then went back to the Reservation to teach at a high school there."

Matt made a face. "And I suppose we're paying for her ticket too?"

Maddie frowned back. "Would you rather he fly all by himself?"

"I guess not," Matt sighed.

"We've gone over this, Matt," she scolded. "You've got less than a month to change your attitude." She shook her head and continued reading.

"Did you talk to Kim?" he asked after another minute or so.

"Kim is definitely going to heaven," Maddie said. "She is more than happy to watch him while we're both at work."

"More like she's too nice to say no. She can't like watching my mist—"

"Matt!" Maddie interrupted. "He is your son. Ten years from now he will still be your son. When he has children of his own, you will be their grandfather, and someday you will have to give an account for your role in his life. I hope you'll have something to say that will work in your favor."

Matt looked over at her and said, "Can I ask you something?"

Maddie creased her brow and nodded.

"Why is it you can accept this so well?"

"*So well* might be too strong," Maddie said. She smiled, although there was sadness in her expression, and reached over, putting her hand over his. "He's your son, Matt. A part of you. I wanted so badly for us . . ." Her voice quieted and shook. She took a deep breath and went on, " . . . to have children, in part so that I could love even more of you." Matt's eyes filled, but he didn't move them from her face. "It

157

isn't the way I wanted it," she said, "but I got my wish, and I expect to make the most of this opportunity."

"And Sonja?" Matt managed to ask after another few moments.

"Is his mother," Maddie said. "That's all that matters now."

Matt nodded, "I'll try harder."

Maddie smiled and patted his hand. "Good. That's all I ask."

Maddie put the papers into the folder and stood up to stretch. Coming around the table, she kissed him on the cheek. "I also can't help but wonder why God would send us other children if we refuse to care for the one you already have." She kissed him again and went into their room.

CHAPTER 28

*A*nna poked her head through the front door. "Walter?" she said in a loud whisper. He was playing his Game Boy and craned his neck so he could see around the new entertainment center Sonja had bought with the first child-support payment. Anna had the front door open a few inches but was still standing outside.

"Yeah?" he asked.

"Is your mom here?"

"No—I don't know where she is."

Anna grinned. "Good," she said. She disappeared for a moment, then came inside carrying a big box under one arm.

"What's in it?" Walter said, pausing his game and standing up. Anna was excited, and when she got excited he had no choice but to become excited too.

"I don't know, but it's addressed to you and it came a few days ago. I hid it under the trailer 'cause your mom was home, and you know how funny she gets sometimes."

"I think she's back with José again," Walter said, kneeling down to inspect the box Anna had put on the floor. He'd never received a package before and didn't know what to expect.

"It's from your dad," Anna said as she put her backpack on a kitchen chair.

It took a minute for Walter to realize that she meant Matt and not Garrett. His dad must like him if he had sent him a present. Inside the box they found pictures, a denim jacket, and some bags of candy. There were also some plastic animals, markers, and paper.

"This is so cool," Walter said as he put on the jacket. It was too big, but he loved it. It was still cold enough at night that he could wear it sometimes. His cheeks were starting to ache from smiling so hard.

Anna was looking at the pictures. "They sure seem nice," she said with a smile. She handed him the picture, and he looked at the white man and woman. They looked really nice to him too. "Aren't you glad you decided to go?"

Walter was more excited than ever. "I still wish you could come," he said.

Anna laughed. "You'll love being rid of me."

But he still wished she was coming. Maybe he could ask his dad when he got there.

Walter gave Anna some Hershey's Kisses. "They really want me to come, don't they?"

"Sure looks that way," Anna said. She pulled Walter into a hug, which he quickly pulled out of. He'd told her quite often that he was too old for hugs and kisses. "Now, we better hide this stuff so your mom doesn't see it."

CHAPTER 29

Three Mondays later, the day before Walter was to arrive, Matt was surprised to come home and find Maddie waiting. Matt's stomach had been in knots all day. Finding his wife at home helped to lighten his mood. Though the progress in their relationship had been rocky at times, there *had* been progress, and he was grateful for it. They'd both worked hard, and worked together, to recapture what they'd once had. It hadn't been until things started getting better that either of them realized how bad it had been.

"You're home early," he said as she met him at the door for a hello kiss.

"I played sick," she said with a guilty grin that made his heart thump. "I figured we ought to make the most of our last night alone."

Matt liked the sound of that and said, raising his eyebrows, "How so?"

"Well, I thought first we could catch a movie," she suggested, putting her arms around his neck. "Then I thought we'd get something to eat, then we should come home, light a couple of candles, snuggle up together, and . . . see where the evening takes us."

Matt chuckled and bent down to nuzzle her neck. "Can we skip the movie and dinner part?" he whispered.

"No, it might be our last chance to go out for a while," she giggled in response, as his hand slid up the back of her shirt.

"Well, all right," Matt said with feigned disappointment—time with Maddie was all he wanted tonight. With a little luck he could forget all about the little boy coming in from New Mexico in the morning. "If you insist."

The evening was perfect, but later that night, staring at the ceiling, Matt couldn't sleep. Tomorrow was the day he would come face to face with what he'd done. He marveled at Maddie's acceptance, and envied it, though he didn't understand. At some point she had realized that this was their life, yet he still rebelled against it. Part of him hoped Walter would be horrible and miserable and ask to go home early. Yet he knew he was wrong to think that. But still . . . he couldn't talk himself out of his anxiety. It seemed redundant to say it, even to himself, but once again his life was about to change, and once again he didn't feel ready for it.

★   ★   ★

The next day Matt and Maddie stood beside the baggage carrier and waited for Walter and Grandmother to come down the escalator. Matt took his wife's hand and gave it a squeeze as they looked past the heads of the people for a glimpse. But it didn't do them any good. The airport was so packed they could barely discern one face from another. Matt felt sick and shook his head in disbelief. On the heels of this feeling came everything Maddie had been helping him to understand, and he resolved again to make the best of it. Thank goodness she was here and was so supportive. He knew he wouldn't be up to this challenge without her.

"There he is!" Maddie said, interrupting his thoughts, and he followed her gaze up the elevator. Matt's heart started thumping in his chest as he watched the little boy look around himself in amazement. In one hand he held a Spiderman backpack. The other hand was linked with the hand of a very old woman who was also looking around herself with a contented grin on her face. Matt and Maddie walked closer to the escalator and waited for the two arrivals to reach the bottom.

Walter was dressed in cutoff jeans and a faded T-shirt. His sneakers showed a great deal of wear, and he needed a haircut. His blue eyes were an interesting contrast to his dark skin and hair. The grandmother wore a multicolored skirt and a purple velvet blouse. She had several silver and turquoise necklaces as well as large earrings, multiple rings, and bracelets. Her steel-gray hair was pulled back into a thick bun, and her features were darker than Walter's, the lines in her face giving her skin the look of dark suede. The two of them stopped after stepping off the escalator, and Maddie pulled Matt along with her to greet them.

Walter saw them first and watched them suspiciously while Grandmother gave them a large smile that was missing several teeth. Maddie pushed Matt ahead when they reached the pair. For a few moments Matt looked down at the boy who was staring back at him. Then he cleared his throat. "Walter?" he asked.

Walter nodded and then lifted his hand with the palm facing Matt and said, "How." Matt didn't know what to say, and was relieved when Grandmother pushed Walter's hand down.

Shaking her head, she said, "He loves to do that, but I tell him it is not very nice." Walter broke into giggles, shaking his head at his joke, and Matt gave Maddie a look that said, "See what you've gotten us into?"

Maddie stepped up at that point and crouched down in front of the boy, giving him a smile that warmed Matt's heart. Again he questioned how she could be so kind and open. "Hi, Walter, I'm Maddie," she said, putting a hand on her chest and then motioning toward Matt, "and this is Matt, your dad." Matt's heart skipped at being called "dad," but he managed a smile. "Did you have a good flight?" she asked.

"Yes," Walter said with a sigh. "But we couldn't see the Reservation." Then his eyes lit up. "The mountains were cool."

"Well, I'm glad you enjoyed it. Why don't we get your luggage, and then you can tell us all about it on the way home."

Walter held up the backpack. "I already have my bag."

"Didn't you bring any other ones?" Maddie asked. He shook his head. Maddie smiled again. "Well, great then." She turned to Grandmother and said, "I'm afraid I don't remember what time you were flying back."

The old woman smiled. "I will return home around eight o'clock. My chickens need me." Matt and Maddie exchanged a brief look as Maddie stood. At five-foot-six, she looked very tall compared to Grandmother, who was almost a foot shorter.

"We can't get to any of the restaurants here in the airport because of security, but would you like to come with us to get some lunch?" Matt asked, hoping she would refuse.

Grandmother smiled and said, "That would be wonderful. I had hoped I might see where Walter will be living also."

"Um, sure," Matt said.

Once they got on the freeway, they asked Walter and Grandmother what they would like to eat. Grandmother said a sandwich would suit her just fine. Matt had thought she might prefer something closer to her native foods. At the sandwich shop, Walter and Grandmother ordered the same thing—a turkey sandwich with cheese on white bread, no mayo. They all sat at a small, round table. The silence was a bit uncomfortable until Grandmother turned to Maddie. "Walter is a good boy. He will like it here."

Walter smiled at Grandmother with a mouthful of food and then concentrated on his drink again. Matt watched Walter as if waiting for him to do something—though he didn't know what.

Grandmother continued, "He knows how to work."

Walter swallowed and looked at Matt. "Do you have chickens?" he asked.

"No, we don't have any chickens."

"Sheep?"

"No sheep either," Matt replied.

Walter looked back at his food in disappointment. "Mama said you wouldn't."

Grandmother looked at him for a moment and then pulled a dollar from her bag. Pointing to a rack of candy at the front of the restaurant, she said, "Go there and buy a treat."

Walter smiled and scurried away from the table. Before he left, he looked at Matt forcefully and said, "Don't eat my food."

Matt waved his arms a little and said, "Okay." Walter nodded, grabbed the dollar, and ran to the counter.

After another moment of silence, Grandmother spoke. "Anna has been getting him excited and not letting him worry."

"Anna?" Maddie asked. She looked at Matt, but he just shrugged.

"Anna is Walter's little mother, Sonja's sister. She cares very well for Walter. If not for Anna, I think Walter would have been too scared to come."

"Well, we'll have to thank her," Maddie said. Matt was thinking things would have been better if Anna had kept her mouth shut, but he knew better than to dwell on it.

"He should call her tonight," Grandmother said; then she turned to look at Matt. "It's good you pay for the phone."

He nodded and looked away, embarrassed by any praise. He'd expected some censure from this woman for the mess he'd helped make, but she was kind, and he didn't know how to react.

"What does he like to do?" Maddie asked with a smile. "I'm afraid we don't know much about little boys."

"He likes what all boys like—to run, to eat, and to play. His mother lets him watch too much on the television and play too many video games, but he is strong and smart." She tapped her head.

All three of them looked toward Walter as he stood before a candy rack. Looking back at Matt and Maddie, Grandmother asked, "You are Christian?"

Matt nodded but didn't know whether it would be good to tell her they were Mormon. Grandmother nodded, and with one hand took hold of a silver cross hanging from her neck that Matt hadn't noticed. "I am Christian too. I have taught Walter about God, the Holy One, but his mother has no belief in Him." She looked at Matt, making direct eye contact for the first time. "It is good for Walter to come here."

"We will do the best we can." Matt found himself wanting to please her, and it confused him.

"You know I was a professor," Grandmother said. She took a tiny bite of her sandwich and chewed slowly. "I sometimes miss the movement of big cities." She swept her arm, as if encompassing the city outside the restaurant. "But I returned to the Reservation with greater respect for the four sacred mountains and the mother earth that cares for us. I ask that you help Walter to see the greatness in all of God's earth, all his people. I don't want him to hate the white man, but I don't want him to hate his own people, as do many Navajo that leave the Reservation."

Maddie reached over and squeezed Matt's hand. "We want good things for him, I promise."

Matt could only nod, feeling weighed down by the burden he now carried. He had no idea what Walter had been taught and felt heavy with the responsibility of sorting it out.

Grandmother looked at him with firmness. "He needs to be a man one day."

So do I, Matt thought to himself, but he just nodded. One stupid moment didn't mean he deserved to be a father. He wondered when someone would point that out.

Walter scampered back and showed everyone the LifeSavers he was able to buy. He ripped open the package and gave everyone two LifeSavers, putting his aside for later. They finished their meals without saying much more and then walked out of the café.

They drove to the apartment, and Grandmother seemed pleased, though Matt wondered how she would have reacted if she had disagreed with the arrangements. They showed Walter his room and then walked around the complex. It was awkward, and Matt wanted to push fast-forward and get the day over with. Finally it was time to take Grandmother back to the airport. When they pulled up to the curb, she spoke to Walter in what Matt assumed was Navajo, and Walter nodded in agreement. He gave her a kiss on the weathered cheek before she got out of the car with Matt's assistance.

"Will you be able to find your terminal okay?" he asked.

She nodded and smiled up at him. "I will be fine, just as Walter will. Enjoy him."

Matt nodded and got back into the car as she walked toward the terminal.

Then it was just the three of them.

Maddie told Walter to put on his seat belt. Matt had thought he'd been wearing it before, but after a minute of trying, Walter admitted he didn't know how it worked. So Maddie helped him with it. Matt let out a breath. It was going to be a long couple of months.

CHAPTER 30

*W*alter was cautious around them both at first, not volunteering much information and watching a lot of TV. A few hours after arriving, he asked to use the phone. Maddie listened to him talk to Anna, the aunt that Grandmother had told them about. He took the receiver from his ear and asked Maddie what their phone number was. Maddie wrote it on a piece of paper, and he said it into the phone. Not long after that he hung up.

"That was Anna?" Maddie asked. Walter eyed her warily and nodded. Maddie considered asking more questions but didn't like the suspicious look, so she just smiled, and they all managed to make it through the awkward evening.

The next day, Maddie took Walter to Kim's around eight-thirty, where Matt would pick him up on his way home. As soon as Maddie came in from work that night, Matt was out the door, heading to a dinner with clients. Maddie took advantage of the opportunity by attempting to make some progress with Walter. Her fear was that the tension would never go away. That would make for a very long two months.

"Would you like to help me make some cookies?" Maddie asked. Walter looked away from the TV, but seemed hesitant. She wondered if the TV helped him feel like he wasn't here with them. It made her sad.

"I'll let you eat as much dough as you want," she tempted him.

"I don't like raisins," he said.

She scrunched up her nose. "Me neither. How about chocolate chips?"

"I don't like nuts," he added, still regarding her with suspicion.

"No nuts," she said. That decided, Walter stood up and came into the kitchen, acting as if he were doing her a great favor. Maddie had him measure the ingredients and drop them into the bowl one by one, then she mixed everything together.

"So tell me about your house," she said.

He shrugged and said nothing.

"What's your room like?" she asked.

Once again he said nothing.

"I'd love to hear about it," she tried once more, disheartened that her attempts weren't working.

"My mom said you would ask questions about her," Walter said.

Maddie paused for a split second before gathering her thoughts. She finished stirring and put the bowl on the counter. Walter stared at it but didn't try to sneak any dough. She got a spoon from the drawer and filled it for him. He didn't say thank you.

"I'm not asking about your mom," Maddie said, annoyed to even have to think about her. "I just want to know about you."

"Why?" he asked so quietly she could barely hear him.

"Because you're Matt's boy," she said, feeling stupid and wondering if she should send him back to the TV. "And that makes you my boy too. I want you to have a good time here, and I want to get to know you."

He finished his spoonful of dough as she dropped blobs from the bowl onto the cookie sheet.

"I wish you guys had chickens," he said.

Maddie couldn't help but laugh. "Where would we put them?" she asked, hoping he was opening up and it wasn't just her imagination that he seemed softer. "In the bathtub?"

"Where would you take a bath?" Walter asked with no hint of a smile on his face, making it hard to tell if he was teasing or not.

"Good point," she said. "Maybe we could put them in your closet. Would you like that?"

"They would stink," Walter said, and his face transformed. The humor Maddie had seen when meeting him for the first time was back, making her wonder at the stoic expression he'd worn the last two days. "We should put them in *your* closet."

"You mean they won't stink in my closet?" Maddie asked.

They kept trying to decide where to keep the chickens, and finally determined they would put them on the back patio and cover the whole thing with chicken wire. Walter then went on to ask where they would put the sheep, and they concluded that sheep were out of the question. But in the process Maddie learned a lot about this little boy, his shy laugh, and the life he had lived. By the time Matt returned home, Maddie felt they had made progress.

Every day after that became more and more comfortable. Maddie could get Walter to talk about anything and liked hearing about his life. It was so different from the childhood she'd had. He talked about hunting, ceremonies, Grandmother, and the things she taught him, like making fry bread and sewing. He even made fry bread for dinner one night, with minimal supervision. He seemed to know so much for such a young boy. By the weekend Maddie felt like she knew Anna as well as he did. Maddie couldn't help wondering if she was more of a mother to him than Sonja was. The fact that Walter never said a word about his mother helped drive that home. When a question seemed to be tied to her in any way, he clammed up, a suspicious look blanketing his expression.

Though he didn't say so, Maddie knew it was overwhelming for Walter to be in such a new place. Maddie tried to get him to talk about it, and he finally explained how different it was here. She tried to be sympathetic and make him comfortable, but he still had that stolid expression bordering on fearful for the first several days—she hoped it would go away in time. He was, however, exceptionally clean—showering every day—and very tidy. Matt and Maddie were familiar with the "dirty Indian" assumptions, but Walter, even at his young age, proved that not to be the case. It helped when he made friends with a boy at the complex and felt more comfortable playing outside.

The haircut was an issue. Walter's hair looked as if it hadn't been cut in several months, and as if he had done the last cutting himself. Maddie begged and pleaded with him to get it cut, but he refused. He said he was growing it long like his friend Jason Grey Bear. Finally he told her it was a Navajo tradition. She dropped it and bought him a baseball cap that he agreed to wear most of the time.

In accordance with Allen's advice to take the Church slowly, they explained only minimal things before taking Walter to church with them on Sunday. Before walking into the building, they exchanged a look—this was something they had dreaded. It was all they had thought it would be. Several people asked them straight out who Walter was. Each time, Matt or Maddie took a breath and said that Walter was Matt's son. Most people were polite enough not to ask any more questions, but curiosity burned in their eyes. Although it did get a little easier with each explanation, it was all they could do to ignore the looks and whispers they encountered. Maddie wished they had been able to sell the condo before now. It had been listed for over a month.

On the upside, several members went out of their way to say hello to Walter, to swallow their surprise and bite back the other questions they obviously wanted to ask. The Primary president was wonderful, letting them know that she had spoken to Walter's teacher and that she would make sure he was well cared for. The support of those people was tremendously helpful. All in all, it went as well as they could have hoped for—but they were relieved when the final prayer was said.

On the drive home they asked him how it was, and he said it was fine.

Fine wasn't too bad. They could live with fine.

CHAPTER 31

*O*n Monday night, six days after Walter's arrival, Matt and Maddie took him grocery shopping. It was the first time, other than church, that they had gone anywhere all together. When they passed the candy aisle, Walter grabbed Maddie's arm. "If I'm good, can I have a treat?" he asked.

"One," Maddie told him. "Pick it now, but I'll put it back if I have to." Matt knew she wouldn't have to—Walter was always well behaved. Soon the boy was on his knees weighing the benefits of one candy bar against the merits of another. After almost a minute Matt sighed, "Come on, Walter, hurry." Maddie gave her husband a look, but he ignored it.

Walter grabbed a Twix bar and ran back to the cart. Holding it up for them to see, he explained how this was his favorite because it had two. Maddie smiled as if she thought that was cute. Matt started toward the next aisle, trying to keep his frustration at bay. In some ways, watching Maddie be so good with Walter made it even harder—he felt left out somehow, as if he was the only one struggling.

"Can I get some pop?" Walter asked when they were almost finished shopping. Matt gave him an exasperated look.

"No," Maddie said. Even though Matt would have said yes, he liked that Walter was being denied something. But he felt guilty for it.

"Please?" Walter whined.

"No," Maddie said, continuing forward.

"Come on, pleeeeeeeaaaaaaase?"

"Walter," Matt said loudly. "Enough. She said no."

Maddie gave Matt a look, then she turned to Walter. "Okay, one six-pack, but we're about to check out, so come find us at the checkstand."

Walter turned and ran down the aisle.

Matt pulled some frozen vegetables from the freezer section and threw in a bag of Popsicles. "Thanks for being consistent," he said a few seconds later.

"Yeah," Maddie said with a snort. "I'm going to take parenting tips from you."

Matt swung his head around, eyes flashing, at the same moment someone called his name.

They both swiveled to find the voice, and Matt groaned inside when he recognized who it was: Dave Richardson, an old high-school friend. He lived in the neighborhood north of their apartment complex. Though they were in different wards, they saw each other now and then. Matt wondered why he hadn't tried to convince Maddie they should go to a grocery store on the opposite end of the valley.

"Dave, you remember Maddie, my wife?" Matt said when Dave reached them. Dave smiled. "Maddie, this is Dave Richardson, from high school. He's in the Sixth Ward."

Maddie smiled, "Oh, yeah. I thought you looked familiar."

Dave was all smiles. They talked about the rumor that the stake was going to split soon, a mutual friend's new call as Scoutmaster, and Dave's three kids. Just as the conversation ran down, Walter found them and handed Matt a six-pack of Coors Light. Matt was too shocked to know how to react.

The three adults just stood there, Matt holding the beer, and Maddie and Dave staring at it. Walter looked back and forth between them, his face falling.

"This is Walter," Matt finally said, not knowing what to do.

Maddie took the beer and knelt down to speak to Walter. "We don't drink beer," she said in a quiet voice.

"Walter?" Dave repeated, looking at the little boy like he was an alien life form.

"My son," Matt added. Maddie looked up and shot him an encouraging smile, but it didn't make him feel better.

Dave looked back at Walter and then back at Matt. He seemed on the verge of laughing, but after seeing Matt's face, he shut his mouth. "I didn't know you'd adopted."

Matt wanted to run out of the building and hide—preferably in the path of a bus. "No, he's mine," he said.

Maddie excused herself and Walter at that point. The two of them headed back down the adult beverage aisle.

Dave watched as Walter walked away from them. "Are you serious?" he asked. Matt nodded and tried to smile, hoping to hide his embarrassment. "How old is he?" asked Dave.

Matt cleared his throat, wishing Maddie would hurry back, create a distraction, and help him escape. But he had no choice but to answer. "He's nine."

Dave clamped his mouth shut and gave Matt a look that Matt didn't want to define. But Dave said nothing.

"It's kind of a complicated story," Matt said, wanting to disappear. "I didn't find out he was around until a few months ago."

Dave looked as if he wanted to ask more questions but apparently thought better of it. He'd been seminary president in high school and had always had a little Peter Priesthood in him. Of all the people Matt could have run into like this, Dave would have been at the bottom of the list. "Well, good to see you," Dave said, then turned and walked away.

Matt clenched his eyes closed and cursed the entire situation. Life was not supposed to turn out like this.

The drive home was uncomfortable and silent. Walter stared out the window and ran inside as soon as they pulled into the apartment complex. Matt and Maddie stayed in the car.

"I'm sorry that happened," Maddie said quietly.

Matt sighed. Then he tipped his head back on the seat and closed his eyes. "Is this what I get to deal with for the rest of my life?" he asked no one in particular. Maddie didn't answer—he took her silence to mean yes. "What did you tell Walter?"

"I told him beer isn't good for us, that God says not to drink it."

"What did he say to that?"

"He said we told him to get a six-pack. To him that means beer."

Matt shook his head. "How on earth are we supposed to mix these worlds for him, Maddie? No matter how much we try, he'll go home and live in the slums, and then he'll come back, and we'll deal with the awkwardness all over again. We're going to do this over and over? What's the point, Maddie?" His voice rose a degree. "We are fooling ourselves if we think we can change him. He was better off without all this confusion."

"We don't need to change him, Matt. We need to teach him. Any good we can give him will be for his benefit."

"Yeah, right. We're supposed to compete with a lifetime's worth of teaching—or nonteaching, in his case—with two months a year."

"That's not fair," Maddie protested. "He has far surpassed some of our expectations, and it's obvious someone is teaching him an awful lot. Find me one other nine-year-old boy who's as clean and polite as he is. You're overreacting."

"No, you're underreacting. Don't you see the differences between his life and ours? They'll never go away, and all the while we'll be exposing our own kids to those things."

Maddie took a deep breath. Matt could sense her anger rising, but he didn't mind. He was primed for a good argument. Anything to vent a little.

"Maybe you've forgotten we don't have *our own* kids, Matt. We have Walter. And we only get him for a little while." Matt looked away and clenched his jaw. "You're just embarrassed," she added with her hand on the door release.

Matt swung back to look at her. "You're right, but can you blame me? My son thinks beer is a soda."

"You chose the girl, Matt," she spat out. "Ten years ago the differences would have been something to consider—now it's way beyond that."

Matt narrowed his eyes and glared at her. "Very profound, Maddie." The reminder, however, cut to the quick, and he seethed in anger that this had ever happened in the first place. "You're the one who wanted him to come," he said, more than happy to share the blame any way he could.

Maddie narrowed her eyes. "You did this, Matt. Not him and not me. We both agree you were an idiot back then, but try to act like a grown-up now, okay? Let Walter be the child."

She got out and slammed the car door before heading up the steps. He didn't care what she thought, this wasn't the way he wanted to spend the rest of his life—tonight had just hit the fact home. For almost a minute he tried to calm himself down enough to go in and talk to her. It didn't work. He finally slammed the car into reverse and squealed out of the parking lot.

★　★　★

Once inside the house Maddie tried to keep herself from crying. Was that really what he thought—that having Walter come was all her idea? It made her boil inside, and yet she had to ask herself if it *had* been mainly her idea to push for this. A tear escaped her eye, and she wiped it away. She should go to Walter, try to explain, but she didn't know what to say.

For several minutes she waited for Matt to come in, but he never did. The groceries were still in the car, but when she ventured outside, she discovered the car was gone. Perfect. She went back in and knocked on Walter's door, coaxing him out with popcorn and root-beer floats. She got him to bed at ten, despite his pleading to watch one more movie, and then she went into her own room and tried to draw out her bedtime routine, allowing Matt as much opportunity as possible to come home and talk it over. At eleven she put down her scriptures and turned off the light. She didn't know what she would say to him anyway.

Maddie wasn't sure what time Matt came home. The only reason she knew he had been home at all was the fact that his shower in the morning woke her up. She snuck into the kitchen to see that the groceries had been put away—at least he'd done that much. But she decided to make him come to her this time. She got back in bed before he could realize she had been up. She lay quietly, listening, until the outside door shut behind him . . . without a conversation.

Matt called from work that afternoon to remind her he had a dinner appointment. He could pick Walter up from Kim's at three, but Maddie would have to hurry home from work as soon as she got off so he would make it to the restaurant. Their conversation was clipped and short, and Maddie hung up the phone in frustration.

The next day Matt was home in the evening, but they avoided each other—each waiting for the other to make the first move. By Friday Maddie gave in. This was all familiar territory—the avoidance, the unspoken thoughts between them—and she didn't need another lesson on keeping the lines of communication open. There was enough stress without it.

On her lunch hour she drove to his office, hoping he hadn't gone out. He was on the phone and looked surprised when she shut the door behind her. He ended the phone call after a minute. "Hi," he said in an even tone.

"Don't do this to me," she said.

"Do what?" he returned with irritation.

"Hide—run—avoid this. You did that before. I can't take it again."

He said nothing, but his face softened, and it gave her strength to continue. "This is hard, Matt. I've never said otherwise. But giving me the silent treatment, ignoring your son, and pulling inside yourself isn't going to help. I won't put up with it again. I won't."

Matt let out a breath and leaned forward, staring at the desktop. "I'm sorry, Maddie," he whispered, and she felt her anger drain away. She took a chair across the desk from him and leaned forward to take his hand.

"He's just a little boy, Matt. Yes, he's grown up different from us. Yes, there will always be things about him we don't understand or know how to deal with. But he's still a little boy. Don't shut me out. I mean it when I say I can't do it again."

He looked up at her and nodded. "I'm sorry," he said again. "I'll do better."

"Promise?"

He managed a humble smile and a nod. "I promise." They shared his sandwich and talked things over. By the time she left, she felt like they'd made an important step. He'd promised not to hide, and she'd promised not to let him. It was a good beginning.

★   ★   ★

Matt started by reading Walter a chapter from *Black Beauty* before bed that night. He didn't love it, but when it was over, he realized it wasn't so bad. The next afternoon, Saturday, they took Walter to the zoo, and Maddie seemed to make a conscious effort to make Matt step up. He couldn't help but notice, though, that Walter gravitated to Maddie. It was hard to blame him for that. Matt continued to marvel at how well she'd taken it on.

From that point on, despite the fact that it didn't come easily for him, he forced himself to spend time with the boy. Allen needed help putting in a sprinkler system, and Matt started taking Walter over there with him after work. It impressed him that Walter seemed more than willing to help out. Grandmother wasn't kidding when she said he knew how to work. Together they dug trenches and lined up the pipes. Walter was a great help, and his being there made Matt feel rather important and . . . well, paternal. Allen was a big help too, acting as a buffer zone and helping Matt see how easy it was to interact with a kid that age. The sprinkler system took the entire week and most of the next Saturday to finish. Walter was pleased with himself, and Matt was, too. "We make a good team," Matt said when it was finished. Walter just nodded. Though Matt was doing better, it was taking Walter a while to trust the new and improved dad. Allen told him that was normal. Normal but annoying.

When the sprinkler system was finished, Allen hosted a barbecue, inviting both sides of the family. It was the first time most family members had met Walter. There were looks and whispers, but a lot of good wishes as well, and with a few cousins close to Walter's age, he wasn't left out. Matt drove home that night feeling much more satisfied than he had to this point. They were a family, or trying to be, and they belonged to a bigger one that was helping to ease the transition. Walter fell asleep in the car, and Matt carried him to his room and helped him take off his shoes. For the first time since Walter had arrived, Matt felt like a father. As he shut the door to the room, he realized he liked it.

CHAPTER 32

*A*nna got up as soon as the early grayness filtered through the dirty trailer windows, though it was not yet *ha-yeli-kahn* (dawn). She showered, parted her hair in the middle, and wove it into two braids that hung over her shoulders. Though Navajo women traditionally wore their hair in a bun, she was young enough that braids were acceptable. The trading post was a tourist stop, and typically they hired only full-blood Navajos to work there. Her lighter skin worked against her—or at least it had. But Anna was one of the best weavers her age, thanks to Grandmother's teaching, which had started when Anna was five years old. It helped that she was willing to weave for hours at a time, five days a week. The tourists loved to watch a weaver at work, and Anna enjoyed few things more than sitting before the loom, even if she was making only small, relatively useless, decorative mats. Another loom was set up nearby with a full rug she also worked on, in between the souvenir rugs. When it was finished, the trading post would sell it for a good price, and she would get a percentage.

When Anna was ready to head out for work, she stood on the back porch facing *Tsishaajini* (Mount Blanca), the sacred mountain to the east, and recited her morning prayer.

> *May it be beautiful before me*
> *May it be beautiful behind me*
> *May it be beautiful above me*
> *May it be beautiful below me*
> *May I walk in beauty.*

Though some felt the Navajo and Christian traditions were too different to be lived in tandem, Anna saw similarities between the beliefs, appreciating the tradition of her people while respecting the detail of Christianity. The Holy One that the Navajo prayed to was the same God the Christians revered. She did not see the beliefs as going in separate directions, or overshadowing one another, but as two parts of a puzzle focused on care for oneself, for others, and for the land. Grandmother was a good teacher, and Anna credited her with the life Anna had lived thus far. She wished Sonja had taken the time to learn as she had, but she also knew Sonja had experienced darkness that Anna had been spared. Though Anna loved her mother, the men she'd brought home had not been good ones. The abuse Sonja had suffered on account of her mother's unwillingness to be alone had scarred her, and she had followed a path of heartache and anger ever since. Anna, however, tried to walk in beauty, as most traditional Navajos did. And she tried hard to pass those same beliefs on to Walter.

The sound of footsteps behind her caused her to jump. Sonja was never up this early. But as Anna turned, her face darkened to see not Sonja but José, her sister's on-again-off-again boyfriend. Anna hadn't realized he'd stayed here last night. She hurried back inside to get her things, ignoring the fact that he was wearing only boxer shorts with his beer belly hanging over the top.

"Good morning," José said as she passed him in the doorway. She gave him as wide a berth as possible and stared at the ratty carpet to avoid looking at him. She did not like or trust José and made a point to be around him as little as possible.

In her room she grabbed her bag and took a deep breath. With slower steps, not wanting to look scared, she left her bedroom. José said good morning again, and she ignored him again.

She was within a few steps of the front door when a large hand wrapped around her arm. She froze, and then tried to yank it free, to no avail.

"You should not be so rude," he said in a gravelly voice that attested to a smoking habit spanning at least twenty years.

Anna took a breath. "My apologies," she said, yanking once more on her arm and praying in her heart he would let her go.

He didn't. His thumb began to move in tiny circles on her inner arm. She swallowed. This wasn't the first time one of Sonja's boyfriends had made advances toward her.

"Let go," Anna said in a low voice. José pulled her backward, closer to him. In one fluid movement she spun around, knocking him in the head with her bag and aiming her knee at a much lower target. As soon as she felt his grip loosen, she twisted from his grasp and ran for the door. He caught her ankle just as she leapt out the front door, causing her to crash against the cinderblock steps. Pain shot through her face and down her back, and her nose began to bleed. She pulled her ankle from his grasp and, without pausing a moment, scrambled down the remaining stairs, jumped to her feet, and ran without daring to look back.

She ran down the dirt road for almost half a mile, sure that José was right behind her and that her feet would go out from under her at any moment. When she finally dared to look back, she was relieved to see that the road behind her was empty. As she came to a stop, her chest heaved for breath and the tears overtook her.

Placing her hands on her knees, she took long, deep breaths, try-ing to calm herself and think what to do while the tears dropped into the dust, disappearing into the starved earth at her feet. Her white blouse was streaked with dirt and blood. She couldn't go to work looking like this. The blood on her face was dried, but she worried that her nose might be broken. Looking around, she scanned the sagebrush peppered with litter blown across the mesa by the summer wind. Though the sun was just rising above Mt. Blanca, the baked earth still radiated yesterday's heat and made her dizzy. Seeing smoke from Grandmother's hogan another quarter mile off the road, she turned in that direction and began to walk through the dry grasses and rabbit brush as fast as she dared, careful not to step in any lizard or snake holes as she hurried across the desolate landscape. Grandmother's hogan lay at the southernmost edge of the land used by her clan, and Anna was glad she didn't have to pass any other hogans or modular homes belonging to Grandmother's family.

After cleaning Anna up, Grandmother made one of her horrid but healing teas and walked to a neighboring hogan belonging to her niece to use the phone and inform the trading post that Anna would be late. While Anna sat on a willow chair, Grandmother washed her shirt and hung it outside to dry. Then she came and sat across from Anna.

"It's not safe for you to be there."

Anna nodded. "I can't leave."

Grandmother didn't argue the point. They both knew it was true. Anna was glad Walter was gone for the summer, but he would be coming back—he needed to come back.

"Perhaps it is time to involve the elders," Grandmother said. "Perhaps they are the only ones who can fix things."

"*Dooda* (no), I can't risk Walter going to live with his father for-ever," Anna said, shaking her head. "He needs to be with his people." Though Grandmother had always helped them, she was of the

Tachii'nii (Red Running Into Water People), whereas Anna and Sonja were born into the *Ashiihi* (Salt Clan). Clans ran through the mother's line, and with so many generations of fractured women, Anna had grown not knowing her kinfolk. Grandmother had, in a sense, fostered them, and without her care, Anna feared she would have followed the same course as her sister and mother had. Walter needed her to help him avoid the same ruin and learn the traditions that had been lost.

They sat in silence for several moments, both contemplating their options and finding no solution. Anna finally stood, feeling much better, though her face was still throbbing. The small mirror above Grandmother's sink showed that her nose was dark and grossly swollen. But it couldn't be helped any more than Grandmother's tea could do. The dry desert heat had already dried her blouse, and she put it back on. Grandmother replaited Anna's hair before going to find someone in her clan willing to drive Anna the two miles to the trading post.

Another girl in another situation would have taken the day off, but Anna's reality was different. She needed this job, and she needed the distraction.

Grandmother exited through the hogan door again. The door faced east, as was tradition, and as the old woman exited the hogan the morning sun shone through the doorway. Had it been only an hour ago that Anna had said her morning prayer? She lifted her face to the sun and thanked the Holy One that she'd been able to make it to Grandmother's hogan in safety.

At the trading post, no one said a word about her swollen face. The Navajo were always respectful of one another's privacy. When her best friend, Skye, stopped in at the end of the day to offer Anna a ride home, even she didn't ask any questions in front of the others. When they were alone in the truck, Anna told her what had happened.

"Come stay with me," Skye offered as they bounced along the

rutted dirt roads. When they came to the turn that would take them to the trailer, Skye pulled to the side and stopped the truck. "You know my family would welcome you."

"I have to talk to Sonja first," Anna said, already having prepared herself for the offer she knew her best friend would make. "And I'll have to come back when Walter returns."

Skye pursed her lips and nodded her head, agreeing and disagreeing at once, as she made the turn and headed for the trailer.

They arrived to find the trailer empty, and Skye said she would wait in the truck while Anna gathered up her things. For almost a minute Anna stood inside the trailer, not sure what to do. Should she wait for Sonja? It could be days before her sister returned. Finally, she went to the phone and called Walter.

"Sheps," a woman said into the phone. Anna had called Walter once a week since he left and recognized the voice as Maddie, Walter's stepmom. She was always nice.

"May I speak with Walter, please," Anna said.

"Just a moment," Maddie said. A few minutes later, Walter was on the line.

"Anna?" he asked, and for a moment Anna thought how sad it was that he didn't even consider it might be his own mother calling him.

"How are you?" Anna asked. Walter went on to tell her all about what he was doing. She envied him and was once again thankful he had gone. Though she had wrestled with herself over encouraging him to leave the Reservation, worried that he would prefer it there over here, she knew it was best. From the sound of his voice and the report of all he was doing, that knowledge was reaffirmed.

"I'm staying with Skye until you get back," Anna said when he'd finished.

"Why?" Walter asked without any suspicion, as if it were perfectly normal.

"Well, the house feels too empty without you here, and I'll be closer to the trading post. I'll call when I can, but I won't be here if you need me, so let me give you Skye's number. Do you have a pen?"

She heard him moving things around, and after a few seconds he said he had one. "Are you okay?" Walter asked, after she told him the number and double-checked it.

Anna choked down a cry. No, she was not okay. Things were a mess, and yet it was her own selfishness that kept her from telling him so. If his father had any idea how bad it was down here, he might find a way to keep Walter forever. Anna couldn't imagine that, even though she knew Walter was safer there. "I'm fine," she lied.

"You'll be home when I get back?" he asked.

"I promise."

She hung up a minute or so later and wrote a note for Sonja to find when she returned. She packed a bag and ran out to the truck, anxious to get away now that her bases were covered. "I need to stop in and tell Grandmother," she said as she slid into the cab of the truck next to Skye.

"You okay?" Skye asked.

For the second time in ten minutes, Anna lied, "I'm fine."

CHAPTER 33

A month after Walter's arrival—two weeks since Matt had started acting like a dad—Matt greeted Maddie after work with a smile.

"My, don't you look happy," Maddie said as she put her purse down and kissed him hello. "Where's Walter? Not taped up in a closet, I hope."

"Funny," Matt commented. "He's at the playground." Noting her look of concern—she never let Walter go out alone—he said, "Don't worry, I can see him from the balcony, and I check every couple of minutes."

She seemed to relax—a little.

Matt leaned against the counter. "Remember the walk-through last week?"

"The ones who hated the carpeting?"

"Yeah," Matt said, having a hard time keeping his enthusiasm at bay. "They put in an offer this afternoon. I guess they got over the carpeting problem. It's five grand less than our new asking price, but it's an offer nonetheless."

Two weeks ago they had lowered the listing price on their condo. It was discouraging to consider taking even less than that, but it was still an offer. "Did you accept it?"

"I wanted to talk to you first," Matt said. "What do you think?"

"Yeah, it's a no-brainer," Maddie said.

Matt smiled. "That's what I thought too."

The next night, Maddie came through the door and said hello to Walter, who was playing Matt's old Nintendo 64 in the living room. He waved briefly and was instantly reimmersed in the game.

"We close on the eighth," Matt said, once the greetings were over and Maddie was looking at him with an expectant expression on her face.

Maddie's face fell. "That's just over two weeks away," she said. "We can't possibly find another place before then."

"Actually, I think I already did."

Maddie's eyes went wide. "What?"

"Remember that house we looked at back in February?"

"We looked at a lot of houses in February," Maddie said, going to the fridge and pulling out some things to make dinner with. Her mood was instantly somber. They had looked for homes then because they'd had a baby on the way. Life had taken several sharp detours since then.

"It was the one in West Valley. The tri-level with the big trees and the fenced-in yard," Matt continued, hoping she would rediscover her enthusiasm.

"The one that needed a new kitchen? Weren't the countertops green?" she asked.

"Yeah, that's the one."

"What about it?" she asked. She pulled out a pan and put a pound of hamburger in it before turning on the stove. Then she washed her hands and looked at him.

"After getting the final okay on the sale of the condo, I went back to the file I'd made of homes we visited and called on a few. The house did sell, but the buyers ran into all kinds of problems. The closing was delayed for a while and they eventually pulled their offer. Not long after that, the listing expired. The sellers decided to try to keep it."

Maddie nodded and wiped her hands on a dishrag hanging from the oven door. The hamburger began to sizzle. "But they're willing to sell now?"

"They're two payments behind and like the idea of not having the realtor fees involved. The price is incredible, Maddie."

Maddie turned to look at him. "How much would the payment be? With child support and the adoption stuff, are you sure we can afford it?"

Matt grinned. "Twenty-five dollars less than we're paying here."

"What!"

"I know, I was shocked too. But we can do this, Maddie."

Maddie smiled. "Really? I don't want to work if we get a baby."

"It still gives us some wiggle room with monthly expenses, and in another year or so I should get a significant salary increase. We'll have a room to paint and fix up into a nursery, another room for Walter, and a backyard to boot. How can we say no?"

"I don't know what to say," Maddie said. "It's so fast."

"I made an appointment to go see it tonight," Matt added, loving the surprise. "At eight."

"Eight!" Maddie said, turning back to the meat. "I'd better hurry, then."

★　★　★

Two hours later, the owners of the house went across the street to visit some neighbors so Matt and Maddie could walk through alone. Walter followed them from room to room without saying much. This house hadn't been one they'd fallen in love with. In fact, it had been on the bottom of their list, partly because back then they had thought they could afford so much more. But reality had shifted, and now the house seemed perfect.

"What do you think?" Maddie asked as they walked up to the top level.

"It's big," Walter said.

It wasn't that big, but he lived in a trailer on the Reservation, and their condo wasn't much bigger than that. "Which room would you want?"

Walter looked up at her with a confused look on his face. "My room?"

"Yeah."

Walter looked at Matt. "You'd give me my own room when I'm only here once a year?"

Maddie decided to make Matt answer. He'd been doing much better the last few weeks, but there was still some tension. Walter seemed suspicious of Matt's attentions, and Matt ran lukewarm as often as not. The silence stretched for several seconds before Matt figured out it was his turn to talk.

"Well, yeah," Matt said with a shrug of his shoulders as he opened the closet doors in the master bedroom. Maddie looked in and grinned. It was twice the size of the closet in their apartment, and the bedroom had its own bathroom. She was nearly giddy.

"Which room do you want?" he asked. "Other than this one. It's ours."

"Well, duh," Walter mumbled, looking toward the doorway. Matt opened his mouth to reprimand, but Maddie grabbed his arm and shook her head.

"Don't be rude," she said to Walter, but her correcting was much gentler than she was sure Matt's would have been. "There are the two other rooms up here, or the one in the basement."

Walter walked into the hall to check out the other rooms.

"What color does he want his room?" Maddie whispered.

"I don't know," Matt whispered back. They were in the master bathroom now. It wasn't huge, and it had only a shower, but it made a big impression. They'd only ever had just one bathroom. This house had three—well, two full ones and then a half-bath on the main level.

"That's why you go ask him."

Matt shook his head and walked out into the hall. Maddie followed at a discreet distance.

"What color do you want your room?" Matt asked.

Maddie stood in the doorway and smiled at the surprise on Walter's face. "I get to choose it?"

"Well, we get to agree on it. I think it should be pink."

Walter just stared, looking unsure what to do. Maddie smiled inwardly and busied herself with looking at the door frame when Walter looked to her for help.

"Well," Matt continued, leaning against the wall with a smirk on his face. "Do you want it pink?"

"Uh, no?" Walter said. It sounded like a question.

"Well then, we don't agree," Matt continued. "What color do *you* think?"

"Black," Walter said.

"Nope, we still don't agree. How about plain old white."

"Green," Walter said, catching on to the negotiations.

"What shade? Sea foam?"

"Dark, like a pine tree."

"Can we paint kittens along the top?"

Walter laughed a deep, giggly laugh that Maddie hadn't heard enough of. Her plan was working. She could kiss Matt for doing so well. "No kittens," Walter said, turning and heading down the stairs with Matt right behind him. Maddie continued to follow at a distance.

"Blue jays, then," she heard Matt say as they continued down to the basement to check out that bedroom again.

"Guns," she heard Walter say back.

"Okay, maybe no border. Pine green, you say?"

Their voices faded away as she stopped in the living room and looked out the front window. It was a nice neighborhood with well-kept yards, but it wasn't fancy. She knew they could afford much more if they waited, but with all the medical bills they still had and the years of saving they had made a habit, it felt good to be conservative. Outside, kids were enjoying the summer evening, and Maddie smiled, aching to see her own children among them. A family pulled up across the street. They looked Polynesian. Smiling at the realization that they would be right at home here, that Walter wouldn't stick out, she knew the fit was good. This would be their home.

Matt and Walter returned a few minutes later. She had already mentally painted and curtained every room in the house—except Walter's.

"I want the one in the basement," Walter said. "And Matt said we could paint it forest green."

"And I can make some nice curtains."

"Curtains are for girls," Walter said.

Matt and Maddie both laughed. Where did he come up with these things?

They got the ball officially rolling the next day. Whereas Maddie had been worried they wouldn't find a place before their buyers closed on the condo, it turned out they had a few extra days instead. The sellers were moving in with the wife's parents and were in as much of a hurry to get this over with as Matt and Maddie were.

They spent the next five days packing boxes, taking trips to Deseret Industries, and choosing paint while the sellers moved out. Matt worked on the loan and was able to get a little extra to help with improvements. The previous owners were out within a week, and they closed the loan a couple of days after that. Within two weeks of having their offer accepted, the new kitchen was installed and most rooms were freshly painted. It had taken every evening and all weekend to get it finished in time, but they were all grinning as they looked around at their new home. She was glad Walter had been part of such a monumental change in their lives—it seemed to bond all three of them a little stronger than before.

Maddie ran her hand across the new granite countertops and looked at the alder wood cabinets that had replaced the old Formica-covered ones. Life was coming together, but she still ached for what was missing. *Soon,* she told herself. *Just hold on a little longer.*

CHAPTER 34

$\mathcal{A}$ few days after they moved in, Matt's dad called him at work to say that while cleaning out closets he'd found the wooden chess set Matt had made back in junior high. He asked Matt if he wanted it.

"Well, yeah," Matt said. It had been almost three months since Matt's announcement about Walter, and they had seen each other a few times for family dinners and the move, but Matt's relationship with his parents had lost some closeness. Getting a call like this made him think that perhaps they could rediscover it.

"Good," his dad said, " 'cause I'm coming to take you to lunch and return it to you." Then he lowered his voice. "Your mom is on a cleaning rampage. I've got to get out of here."

It may well have been an excuse, but it went a long way to repairing those bridges that hadn't been fixed thus far. They went to a deli down the street from Matt's office, and once they were seated, his dad said he was sorry for how things had gone. Matt apologized for it happening in the first place, but his dad waved it off. Being men, that was all it took. Things were back to normal in a matter of minutes.

Then his dad gave Matt the box that held the chess set. "Remember when I taught you to play chess?" he asked.

"I sure do," Matt replied with a nod. "That's why I made this set."

"Now it's time for you to teach your boy to play. He's about the age you were when we first faced off."

Matt smiled and breathed a sigh of relief. He'd wondered if his parents would ever come to terms with what had happened, and felt the burden of his worry lift from his shoulders. "I think I might just do that, Dad."

★　★　★

"Hey," Walter said when he got into the passenger seat that afternoon. Matt said hello and waved at Kim as they pulled out of the driveway. Matt knew that coming home with him wasn't much fun for a little boy—at least, that was what he gathered from the way Walter watched Kim's house until it disappeared from sight. But Matt was excited to see Walter today, and he loved the feeling.

"You have fun today?" Matt asked.

Walter shrugged.

"I got a game for us to play."

"Not Go Fish, I hope," Walter said.

"Nope, not Go Fish."

"Uno? I hate card games."

"Not a card game," Matt said, shaking his head and putting on his blinker for a right-hand turn. "Chess."

"Chess is for nerds," Walter said.

Matt stuck his front teeth over his bottom lip and sucked his chin in. "Yah callin' me a nerd, Son?"

Walter gave him an adults-are-so-dumb look, but Matt caught the glimmer of a smile as Walter turned to look out the window.

It had been years since Matt had played chess. They set up the board, and he reacquainted himself with the rules while teaching Walter at the same time.

"So this guy can only go straight and this guy goes up one and over two? That's dumb."

Matt sighed in frustration. "Look," he said as nicely as he could, "I'm trying here, okay? Give it a shot." As a last thought, he added, "Besides, it will make Maddie happy."

That seemed to tip the scales. Walter shrugged, and they kept going over things.

Maddie came home at six-thirty with pizza.

"I hope it's cheese," Walter said as he jumped up to take the box from her hands.

"It is," Maddie said with a smile. Relieved of the pizza, she bent down to kiss the top of his head. He made a face, like he always did, but Matt suspected he didn't hate it as much as he liked to pretend.

"What are my boys up to?" Maddie asked as she flopped on the couch. She kicked off her shoes and placed her feet in Matt's lap, wiggling them as if to make him notice they were there. Matt looked from one corner of the ceiling to another, ignoring her, until she kicked him lightly in the stomach.

"They stink," Matt whined.

"So do you, but I've learned to live with it." She wiggled her feet more ferociously. Matt gave in and began massaging her feet. She sighed and closed her eyes.

"That's gross," Walter said, finishing off his first piece of pizza.

"I could kiss her instead," Matt suggested.

"Dude, you want me to throw up all over the place?"

Matt and Maddie laughed. After a few minutes, Maddie opened her eyes and looked at the game set up on the table. "Chess?" she asked.

"Yep," Walter said, suddenly enthusiastic about the game he'd been less than thrilled with all afternoon. "Matt's teaching me to play."

"Cool," Maddie said. "How's it going?"

Matt was about to say something about expecting it to be fun in a few more days, but Walter spoke up first. "It's pretty much awesome," he said with a confident nod. He moved onto pizza slice number three. "I love chess."

Maddie looked at Matt, and he smiled as if he'd expected nothing less. "It's kind of a man's game," he said, puffing out his chest.

"You can have it," she sighed. "I hate to run out the door again, but I've got Enrichment tonight. You guys going to be okay by yourselves?"

Walter nodded as if he had it all under control. Maddie smiled, sat up to kiss Matt, and headed upstairs to change.

By seven-thirty Walter was tired of chess again. They turned on the TV, but Walter didn't like sports. They ended up watching *The Crocodile Hunter*. Matt made popcorn and Walter ate it. When Maddie came home around nine, they had family prayer, and Walter went off to bed.

Matt and Maddie slumped on the couch and watched the news. "You know," Maddie started, "I always thought I would want a houseful of kids, five or six at least. But having Walter around . . . I think one or two more would be plenty . . . well, enough."

"That's good, 'cause adoption is expensive," Matt said. "I called a couple more private agencies, and I think LDS Family Services is our best bet. The wait is sometimes longer, but I'm feeling anxious to get it going. Are you ready to turn the paperwork in?"

"Yeah," Maddie said. "It makes me nervous, though."

"Why?"

"Why not?" she said. "New parents get months to prepare; we might get a call one night and a baby the next. It's hard to imagine."

"So was this," Matt said, waving his hand to indicate the house.

"And him," he said pointing over his head down the stairs toward Walter's room. "But it's been a good fit."

Maddie snuggled into him and looked at his face, her brown eyes drawing him into her. "Yes, it has," she said. He couldn't resist kissing those lips and touching that face, counting his blessings as he did so.

★　★　★

Friday night Walter and Matt were playing chess again when Maddie came in from work. They had played here and there all week, and Walter was getting the bug. As soon as Matt had picked up Walter that afternoon, the boy had demanded that Matt let him be black tonight. "Black is usually bad luck, but I think it's good luck in chess."

"Maybe the reason I keep winning is because I've played chess for years. Maybe it has nothing to do with the color of the pieces."

Walter shrugged, but Matt knew he wasn't buying it.

They both looked up when Maddie came in a few hours later. She looked tired and sad—not like he expected. She'd been feeling so good lately, he hated to see that change.

"What's wrong?" Matt asked.

"Two women on my team announced their pregnancies today," she said, stepping out of her shoes and heading for the pantry. "Two." She shuffled around the pantry and pulled out a package of Oreos, ripping it open. Matt hadn't even known they had Oreos around anymore.

"I'm sorry," he said. He moved to stand up, but she waved her hand for him to stay. He knew she didn't like too much sympathy when she was angry about something, so he sat back down.

"The one girl, Angie, can't spell my name right, and her husband's a drunk bum. The other girl, Cara—she's not even married." She looked at Walter, and her cheeks colored. She shoved a couple of Oreos in her mouth and chewed, her cheeks puffed out like a chipmunk. Then she chewed more slowly, and then her eyes filled with tears.

Matt stood now and pulled her into a hug. She cried for only a minute before pulling from the embrace and wiping her cheeks. "I hate Oreos," she said, as if trying to change the subject. "They're full of trans fat, you know." She picked up the package and dropped it in the garbage on her way to the stairs. "I'm going to take a shower."

Matt waited until the door to their bedroom shut. Then he turned to Walter. "You okay with Oreos that have been in the garbage?"

Walter nodded.

"Do you have a problem with trans fats?"

Walter paused, looked at the Oreos, and shook his head. Matt was glad. He pulled the package out, relieved to see the trash can empty except for a few paper towels. It was his move in the game, and while he considered his options, he tried to think what he could do for Maddie. When Walter groaned for the third time, six Oreos later, Matt moved his knight.

"Why is Maddie mad?" Walter asked as he contemplated his own move.

Matt wavered on how much to tell him, but realized that although only nine years old, Walter had a lot more education in some things than Matt had had at that age. He would probably understand.

"Maddie can't have babies. It makes her sad when someone else finds out they're pregnant, or when someone else has a baby."

Walter moved his pawn. "Why can't she have her own babies?"

Yikes. "Well . . . uh . . . boys have baby-making parts and girls have baby-making parts. But Maddie's parts don't work."

"Why not?"

"Well, she had some of them taken out during a surgery, because there were problems."

"Like when I had my wart removed?" Walter asked as if Matt had been there.

"Except you didn't want that wart, and Maddie really, really, really wanted to have a baby."

"So she's mad other ladies can have 'em?"

"She's not mad, she's sad. I mean—do you have friends who have something you want but can't have?"

Walter looked up and thought for a minute. "Sam has a super cool bike—but it doesn't make me sad as long as he lets me ride it when I'm over there."

"Maybe that was a bad example," Matt said.

"Or," Walter cut in before Matt could rephrase, "Harlan has a mom and a dad that live at the same house."

Matt paused in the middle of his move. He looked up. "And you wish you had that?"

Walter shrugged. "It's just cool, 'cause his mom doesn't go to work, and his dad teaches him stuff. He's the best bow hunter at my school. But my mom hates you, so you couldn't live with us anyway."

The statement shocked Matt, but he tried not to take it personally. Why would Sonja hate him? She made money through this whole venture and was quite happy to have the summer off. He chose not to dwell on it, calmed himself down, and ate another Oreo. "Well, that's what it's like for Maddie. She's glad other people can have babies, but when they do, it kind of reminds her that she can't."

Walter nodded, and Matt felt a little pride at having said the right thing for once. A few moves later, Walter spoke again. "I don't like it when Maddie's sad."

Matt felt a lump in his throat, picturing Maddie upstairs in the bath crying over the latest reminder. "Me neither," he said. Then he remembered something. "A few months ago, when Kim had her baby and it made Maddie sad, we decided that every time someone else had that kind of thing happen, we would reward ourselves—celebrate our infertility, we called it."

"Infantry?"

"No, infertility. I know, it's a big word. It means when someone can't have a baby. Anyway, we decided we should do something fun so that it wouldn't make us sad."

"Well, that's dumb," Walter said, looking back at the game.

"No," Matt laughed, realizing it did sound dumb, but knowing Walter didn't understand. "Maybe you and I can come up with something."

"And celebrate?" Walter said, looking skeptical.

"Yeah," Matt said, thinking hard about what he could do. "Something to cheer her up. I'm just not sure what it would be." She wouldn't want to go out now that she was taking a shower, and he didn't dare try to shop for clothes. She always took them back when he did. Maybe he could buy something for the new house—but what? She'd want to pick that out, too.

"When she took me to buy new shoes, she was looking at a fancy pair of earrings, but said she couldn't buy them that day," Walter said, moving his rook and killing off Matt's last bishop.

"That's perfect," Matt said, brightening. "Do you remember what store?"

"It's at the mall."

"Do you remember what store in the mall?"

Walter shrugged as if Matt had asked a stupid question.

"Well, we'll go look until we find it."

Walter smiled, obviously proud of himself for finding the solution. "Cool."

"Totally cool," Matt said back. He slid a note under the door of the bathroom, and they snuck away.

They started on the JC Penney end of the Valley Fair Mall a few blocks from the house.

"Is this the store?" Matt asked when they walked in.

"Um, I'm not sure." They found the jewelry counter, at which point Walter said it wasn't the right store.

"Was it a big store or a little store?" Matt asked as they walked into the main corridor of the mall, forty different stores shooting off to the sides.

"I dunno," Walter said, looking around. "Let's just look in all of them."

Yes, let's, Matt thought darkly. He wanted to hurry.

Every store had Matt asking the same question. "Is this it?"

And Walter always had the same answer. "Um, I dunno."

They walked to wherever the jewelry was, if the store had it, and then Walter would remember this wasn't the one. He even wanted to go into Foot Locker, but Matt convinced him it wasn't in there.

After almost forty minutes, they reached the last store, Mervyn's. Matt couldn't recall Mervyn's being known for its jewelry selection. "Is this it?" he asked with a sigh. Maybe this wasn't even the right mall. He started considering his other gift options. There were dresses displayed to the right. He cringed at the thought.

"I think so," Walter said.

It took a minute for Matt to realize what he'd said. "It is?"

"I think so," Walter said. "I remember that big black sign."

Matt looked at the big black sign that said Mervyn's and wondered why Walter couldn't have remembered it forty minutes ago. They found the jewelry case, and Matt was dismayed to see so many twirly towers of earrings. If it had been this hard to find the store, how long would it take to find the earrings?

"Here they are," Walter said excitedly as he poked his finger at the glass.

Matt smiled and bent down, resting his hands on his knees and staring into the case. "Which ones?"

"Those turquoise ones—shaped like long teardrops."

Matt scrunched his face up. "They don't look like something Maddie would wear."

"That's what she said," Walter said. "But she liked them—said they would look good with her black dress."

"I don't know," Matt said. Maddie was a simple, classic kind of girl. The earrings were over two inches long and bright turquoise. She'd never worn turquoise.

"She really did want them," Walter insisted, seeming to sense Matt's hesitation. "I told her turquoise helps with healing and bringing good friends," he said. "She said she'd come get them after her next paycheck, and they would remind her of me when I went back to the Reservation." He grinned, and Matt was reminded of how wonderful a woman his wife was to make this boy feel so important.

"Did she say anything about the necklace that goes with it?"

"Nah," Walter said, shaking his head. "It's not real turquoise, though."

"Why do you say that?"

"We're in the mall," Walter said, the look on his face showing that he expected Matt to know this. "Real turquoise is sold on the Reservation, and Navajo don't shape it like that."

"Is that so?" Matt said. "Did you tell her that?"

"Yeah, but she liked them anyway."

Good enough, Matt decided. It took a minute to find a salesperson. They completed the sale and had the earrings wrapped separate from the necklace. He knew why Maddie hadn't bought them before. They weren't cheap. But they were very pretty, and he was dying to see a smile on her face.

Maddie was stirring a mug of hot cocoa when they entered. "I'll make you guys some," she said without turning. She reached into the cupboard for more mugs. Matt smiled at Walter and nodded.

Walter stepped forward and put his small package on the counter. Maddie stopped and put the empty mug she'd just removed on the counter next to the box. "What's this?" she asked, picking up the box. Matt was still behind her, but he could see her smile when she turned to look at Walter.

"We're celebrating your fraternity," he said.

Maddie had the sense to laugh. "We are?" she said, turning around and resting her hips on the counter. She looked at Matt questioningly. "How did you know about that?"

"Matt told me that's why you were sad, so we needed to make you happy. Open it."

Maddie shook her head and removed the silver ribbon tied on the silver box. She opened it and inhaled sharply. She looked down at Walter. "You remembered these?" she whispered.

Walter was beaming. "Yup, I told Matt." He looked at Matt, and Matt gave him a quick thumbs-up sign before hiding his hand behind his back when Maddie looked at him.

"Thank you," she said. "That was very thoughtful of both of you."

"No, that was just thoughtful for me," Walter said, grinning. "Matt has his own thoughtful . . . thing."

Matt drew his hands from behind his back and handed her the other box. She opened it and stared at the necklace. Then she looked up at him and pulled Walter to her side. "A matching set," she whispered as a single tear ran down her cheek. "Just like the two of you."

She reached her hand out, and Matt walked to her, wrapping her and Walter in an embrace. "I love you guys," she whispered, kissing Matt's cheek. "You're both wonderful to me."

They watched some TV together and then went to bed. It was Friday, so Walter stayed up downstairs, but Maddie was tired, and Matt preferred going to bed with his wife over playing Nintendo with a nine-year-old.

"Thanks for doing that, Matt," she said after they'd lain down.

"I'm glad you liked them. I drew a blank until Walter suggested the earrings."

"I'll cherish them forever, but being thought of was what I really needed." She paused, and Matt reached for her hand under the sheet, giving it a squeeze. "I still feel so left out, so passed over. I don't exist when certain conversations come up. I hate it, and yet I'm realizing it's going to be a part of my life forever."

Matt pulled her close and kissed her temple. "It makes me bitter too, and I hate seeing you heartbroken over and over." He began stroking the side of her face. "I'd do anything to make it better for you."

Maddie smiled and lifted her hand to his face. "You're doing a great job of it," she said, her voice sounding lighter. "In fact, I'm hoping someone else announces a pregnancy real soon—there's these black cowboy boots I've had my eye on."

"Black cowboy boots?" Matt asked. "Since when?"

"Since I started liking turquoise," she said. "Walter pulled me into a leather shop and showed me the boots he wanted. I found some I liked."

Matt laughed. "Anything to make you happy."

"Oh, you've already done that."

Matt considered having her write that down so he could show her later and remind her she'd said it. But it would probably ruin the moment.

"I just love you, Maddie."

"I'm just glad."

CHAPTER 35

*A*nna tied off the rug she'd been weaving and began removing it from the loom. It was Sunday, and she had worked six hours at the trading post, but she was taking tomorrow off since Walter would be coming home. Skye had dropped her off at Grandmother's so she could finish the rug she'd been working on here and there for the last few weeks. Grandmother came inside and helped her. "It is very beautiful," Grandmother said. "Will you sell this one, too?"

Anna nodded. "I have to," she said, running her fingers over the patterns of burgundy and brown. People always thought there was some religious meaning in the patterns, but it was only the imagination of the weaver. Anna preferred the traditional patterns and the symbols of plants and earth included within them—this one was no exception. She'd been selling her rugs for three years now and was making quite a name for herself. Whereas the ones she worked on at the trading post earned her a percentage of the sale price, those she did on her own time were much more profitable. "The trading post wants another one in two weeks. Thank you for letting me use the loom."

"The loom is yours," Grandmother said.

Anna whipped her head around, staring at the old woman in surprise. "What?"

"My father made me the loom when I was your age, and I promised him that when I was too old to weave, it would go to my best student. I had hoped it would be my own daughter or granddaughter, but none are the weaver you are. It's in your soul. When you have a home, it will go with you."

Anna was in awe and looked back at the loom, running her hand across the top. The lodgepole structure was dark and smooth from so many years of use. "I don't know what to say," she whispered, overwhelmed by such a gift. It should be kept in Grandmother's family. However, it was not Anna's place to question her elders. Grandmother, of all people, understood tradition and appreciated the power of the gift she was giving. Anna was humbled by such a tribute. A warm hand on her shoulder caused her to look up at the woman who had been such a blessing in her life.

"Promise me you will weave and teach it to your daughters," she said.

Anna nodded, though children of her own seemed a far way off. "I promise I will," she said, placing her hand over the old woman's.

"You are going back?" Grandmother asked a moment later. She withdrew her hand and moved toward the back of the hogan where she kept her pantry items in narrow shelving fixed onto the walls.

For the last six weeks Anna had lived with Skye and her family, but Walter was coming home tomorrow, and she needed to be there. "I'm excited to see him again," Anna said, forcing a smile and an optimistic attitude. "He's had a wonderful time there."

"*Aoo'* (yes)," Grandmother said. "He deserves a home of safety."

Anna turned to look at the old woman, picking up something in her voice that piqued her curiosity. "A home of safety among his own people, right?"

"I left the Reservation for many years, Anna," Grandmother said with the sweet yet commanding voice. "But the way never left me. I worry for him with that woman."

Anna didn't question further, but she was surprised by Grandmother's words, pondering them as she walked to the trailer that evening. After so many attempts made by outsiders to take the Indian ways from their children, most Navajo, especially the older ones, were fiercely against their children leaving the Reservation. It had been only in the last forty years that the Navajo Nation had become strong again, teaching their traditions and running their society in accordance with their beliefs. There was no word for religion in the Navajo language. Religion was just who they were. Though many had been lost, such as Sonja and most of Anna's family, the fire of her origin burned within her. She had no greater desire than to go to college and bring the experience back to live out her life on the Reservation. She anticipated carrying on the traditions and weaving until, like Grandmother, she was old and wise—a blessing to the family she hoped to one day raise.

Anna saw herself as the preservation of a family line that was all but extinguished. She had always seen Walter as part of that preservation as well. Although she'd encouraged him to go to Salt Lake for the summers, she was committed to keeping his roots planted in Reservation soil. Yet Grandmother—a woman as devoted to preserving their people as Anna could ever be—felt his safety was the top priority. Was she insinuating she would choose Walter's father's home over the Reservation if it were the only way to keep him safe? It gave Anna a new, and not entirely welcome, perspective of the situation.

Anna also considered that in two years she would graduate from high school. She wanted to go to college, to get away from Sonja, and to learn the things she couldn't learn here—as Grandmother had done. But how could she leave Walter? It was something she'd thought many times, and a solution had not yet presented itself. But she had been prayerful and believed He would help her find the right solution somehow. When the trailer came into view, she took a deep breath and continued forward, praying in her heart that things would be better—that Walter would return to a home of safety, just as Grandmother wished for him.

CHAPTER 36

*M*att and Maddie made the most of Walter's last week. They took walks in the evenings and went to Lagoon, the local amusement park, with Kim and Allen on Saturday, trying to fit everything in. Monday morning they were standing at the airport security gate.

Whereas Walter had arrived in June with only one small backpack, he was leaving with two suitcases Matt had used on his mission. Inside were all the clothes Matt and Maddie had purchased for him over the short time he had been with them, as well as some toys and videos. Maddie had contemplated sending him home with the backpack and the exact clothes his mother had sent, but she realized it would be Walter who would lose. Walter didn't seem too excited to leave, and that helped Maddie in a weird, sadistic sort of way. But her pain was still very intense. She would miss him. They both would.

Walter was flying home alone. It made both Matt and Maddie very nervous, but Walter continued to assure them he was fine. At the security checkpoint, an attendant was assigned to help him get to his plane, and Walter hugged them both good-bye—something that had taken most of his visit for him to get comfortable with.

"We'll miss you," Maddie said, fighting back tears and forcing a smile.

"Me too," he said awkwardly. They all stood there for a few seconds.

"We love you, Walter," Maddie finally said. She'd been hoping Matt would say it, but she finally leaped in, not wanting it to go unsaid.

"Love you too," Walter muttered. He seemed embarrassed and gave Maddie one last hug before hurrying through the metal detector. He waved once more when he reached the top of the escalators—and they both waved back. Maddie watched until he was out of sight before she turned into Matt's shoulder and cried like a baby.

CHAPTER 37

*G*randmother and her son, Bearcloud, picked Walter up at the airport. Sonja wasn't home, but Anna met them at the road when they pulled up. She thanked Bearcloud and Grandmother, promised to visit tomorrow, and then helped Walter bring the bags in. "What's that?" Walter asked when Anna returned outside. She followed his eyes to the small tree in the front yard.

Anna let out a breath. "It's a beer tree," she said, recalling Sonja's explanation the night before when Anna had asked the same question. "Your mom read a book where someone hung beer cans on a tree. She thought it was cool."

Walter looked at the silver cans swaying in the breeze.

"My mom read a book?" Walter asked.

Anna laughed and shook her head. Oh, to be so young and so naïve. They headed for the steps. "Not the whole thing," she said, ruffling his hair. It felt softer than she remembered it. "I'm glad you're home," she said. "I've missed you."

"Where's Mom?" Walter asked when they got inside.

"With José," Anna said, annoyed that his own mother hadn't come back before Walter got home, but, as always, relieved not to have her around. "She'll be back soon."

As if on cue, Sonja's truck pulled up out front. With excited eyes, Walter turned and hurried back down the steps, reminding Anna that, for good or bad, Sonja was his mother, and he loved her. In her own way, Anna knew, Sonja loved him too. But as she often did, Anna wondered if Sonja loved him enough or if she loved him the right way.

"There's my boy," Sonja sang as she burst from the truck. Walter didn't seem to know what to do, but when Sonja hugged him, he hugged her back. "I missed you so much," she said. He turned to look at Anna, a huge grin on his face. *Maybe,* Anna thought to herself, *having Walter leave now and then will be a good reminder for Sonja.* Maybe the break would be good for everyone.

"I hope you're fixing something good for dinner," Sonja said to Anna before smiling at her son again. "This is something to celebrate!"

"I'll get right on it," Anna said, for once not upset to be treated like hired help. Sonja had accepted Anna's return as easily as she'd accepted her leaving. Not that Anna had been surprised. But she was glad Walter had received such a nice homecoming. She went inside to start a dinner of mutton stew with a smile on her face.

At almost nine o'clock the phone rang. Sonja picked it up, and Anna was just wondering who it was when Sonja's face lit up.

"Why, if it isn't Matthew Shep himself," she cooed into the phone, leaning back and smiling. Anna's stomach flipped, and she looked at Walter, glad he was absorbed in a TV show. She wished she'd gotten to the phone first.

"Of course he's home safe," Sonja said a few moments later. "No, I don't think you need to talk to him. You've had him to yourself for two months. You've got to let him spend some time with his mama—share and share alike, I always say."

Anna tried not to make it obvious she was watching, but she kept stealing glances as Sonja continued playing her game with Walter's dad.

"I'll have him give you a call, oh, next week or so. B-bye." Sonja laughed when she hung up, and Anna turned her attention back to the dishes, humiliated by her sister's rudeness, though that was nothing new. Her hope that things had changed seemed a little less likely, but she tried to be optimistic.

CHAPTER 38

$\mathcal{M}$att hung up and swallowed the lump in his throat. His head buzzed at hearing her voice, and his jaw was still clenched from his trying to hold back his temper as she made a fool of him. It was the first time he'd talked to Sonja since high school, and he hoped it would be his last. She made his skin crawl. He hated thinking of Walter returning to that. Walter had been careful not to say too much about Sonja, and Matt was pretty sure he'd been instructed not to— making Matt and Maddie wonder what it was she wanted to hide.

"Did you talk to him?" Maddie asked, coming downstairs in her pajamas.

Matt cleared his throat. "No, but he's home safe."

She looked at him for a few moments. "Did you talk to Sonja?"

He nodded. "She's awful," he said. "I hate having Walter there."

Maddie just nodded, and he was sure she was biting back the lecture on it being his fault for having conceived a child with the woman. He knew that—boy, did he know it. "I wish he could live with us full time," he finally said, voicing out loud what he'd been thinking for several days. "But that's probably ridiculous. I've only known he existed for five months."

Maddie ran a hand across his back as she passed him. "You never know," she said, coming around to face him. "Stranger things have happened. I would love it, and yet he has a family there—friends, culture. Trying to take all that away from him seems cruel."

That night they prayed for the Lord to watch out for Walter and keep him safe. It was little balm to the wounds of missing him as they did, but at least it felt like they were doing something. Perhaps the only thing they could do.

★　★　★

Time dragged by at a snail's pace once Walter was gone. Maddie likened it to the low she had felt after the surgery, and kept hoping something would happen to pull her out of it. She felt so heavy she could barely find the energy to get through a full day at work. Matt's younger brother's wife gave birth to a beautiful boy two weeks to the day after Walter left. They were now the only ones in both of their extended families without a child of their own. Now that Walter was gone, it didn't feel like he counted. They drove to the hospital in silence, and Maddie forced herself to be chipper and positive for a whole ten minutes. Once home she ran herself a shower and cried until the water ran cold, trying to believe that God had not forsaken them, that their doing well with Walter had perhaps proven them somehow. Their time would come soon, wouldn't it?

When she came out of the bathroom, there was a large box on the bed. A Post-It note stuck to the box had one word written on it.

YEEHAW!

She threw the towel she'd been drying her hair with over her shoulder and opened the box. Two shiny black cowboy boots winked back at her.

"Walter helped?" she asked a minute later when she walked into the kitchen with only her robe and her boots on. She modeled for Matt, who was sitting at the kitchen table working on his computer.

Matt smiled, looking up from his laptop appraisingly. "One of the last things I made sure to get his help with. I like 'em."

"Me too, but we're going to have to change our celebration of infertility."

"Why?" Matt said. "I like it."

"In the first place, it's getting more expensive every time, and we won't be able to afford it for long," she said. "And secondly, we need to save our celebrations for actually getting a baby."

"I say until we're delirious with sleep deprivation and up to our ears in diapers and bottles, we keep on celebrating the infertility thing. I like the excuse to get you stuff—it helps both of us."

It was hard to argue with a man who wanted to give her things, and with so many trials, she didn't want to create a new battle. So she valiantly gave in. Bending down to give him a thank-you kiss, she said, "Okay, but next time all I want is a Jamba Juice."

"Ahh," Matt said in disappointment. He started wiggling his foot, and she wondered if he had an itch. She looked down and smiled at the boots he wore—a match to her own.

"Now, I *know* we couldn't afford two pair," she said. Then she looked again and let her eyes travel up his body before meeting his eyes. "There is something very sexy about cowboy boots, however."

Matt shut the laptop with a snap and winked. "My thoughts exactly."

CHAPTER 39

*M*addie finished typing the document on her computer and then scrolled up to the top in order to proofread. In July she had been promoted to supervisor of special menus. This was one of those—a diet plan for a post-op cardio-bypass patient with diabetes. She sighed as she realized she had entered the wrong date. It was a small error, but even the smallest details irritated her these days. After deleting the wrong date, she typed in "October 8" and saved the document before hitting "print." Rolling her chair to the printer desk behind her, she took out both copies of the document and signed the bottom corners.

They finished their last interview with LDS Family Services in late August and were contacted a few days later with the final okay. They had received their preapproval for adoption, and Maddie's spirits lifted a considerable amount. Unfortunately, they realized, it could still be years before anything came of it. Their caseworker told them that their chances were good. In most cases the birth mothers chose the couples they would place their babies with, and Matt and Maddie were an attractive, young, relatively affluent family who would be happy with any ethnicity or blend thereof. But they also had Walter, and that presented a less attractive option to many young birth mothers. They prayed together morning and night for the process to be quick, as well as for the faith and patience they needed in the meantime. Maddie's heart ached in a whole new way after sending Walter to his real mother. Having tasted motherhood, she longed for it as she never had before.

They also petitioned through their attorney to have Walter come for Christmas. The house was empty without his presence, and they missed him. Since Sonja had been so easygoing about the summer visitation, they were hopeful she would agree to this one too. They needed all the hope and goodness they could get and clung to it with fervor.

Maddie put the document in her file as the phone rang.

"Madeline Shep," she said, hoping she didn't sound too frustrated.

"Maddie, it's Gayla." Gayla was their caseworker with LDS Family Services. Maddie stopped herself from sighing aloud. A few days after getting their final approval, Gayla had called to say the office had misplaced Matt's income verification, and could Maddie make another copy? Two days later Gayla said she needed Maddie's medical records; they had lost those too. Maddie had found and sent them to Gayla as well. How could it be a final approval if they didn't have any of this stuff?

"Hi, Gayla. What do you need?"

"How did I know you would say that?" Gayla said cheerfully. Maddie rolled her eyes and said nothing. "What are you doing tonight?" Gayla asked.

"Nothing that I'm aware of, but Matt has a dinner appointment. Did you lose the transcripts from our last interview or something?"

Gayla paused for a moment before saying quietly, "A birth mom wants to meet you."

Maddie dropped the paper she was holding and grabbed the phone with both hands as she leaned back in her chair. "What?" she breathed.

"I have a birth mom I've been working with. She's fifteen years old, seven months pregnant, and she and her mother have narrowed down the files to three couples. They want to meet you tonight. Can you be there?"

"Of course," Maddie said. As soon as she hung up, she called Matt.

CHAPTER 40

*M*att and Maddie met at the Olive Garden in Murray after Maddie got off work. They stood when a very young, very pregnant, brunette girl and her mother entered the restaurant.

"Matt and Maddie," Matt said, stepping forward with his hand outstretched. They'd been told not to give their last name at this point. The girl shook his hand limply, then the mother overcompensated, making Matt wince.

"So tell me about yourselves," the mother, Delores, said as soon as they had placed their orders.

Maddie took a breath and explained how they had met, what they did for a living, and what they liked to do in their spare time—though it was all in their file. The girl, Kirsten, didn't seem to be listening and played with her flatware, showing her age. But she seemed sweet, with large blue eyes and curly brown hair. Maddie couldn't help but think how perfectly this girl's baby would match them.

When they finished, Delores went on to explain the "delicate situation." The father of Kirsten's baby was sixteen. The two kids had met at a volleyball camp the previous spring. He lived in Wyoming, and his parents were in full agreement that adoption was the only choice. Maddie and Matt nodded, but Maddie's eyes kept wandering to the girl. She didn't seem the least bit fazed by all the discussion around her, not even when her mother talked about her sins or called the baby's father despicable—no emotion at all. But then, Maddie couldn't imagine being this girl. Perhaps she'd had to separate herself from the situation and was trying to block things out.

After three refills of her Diet Coke, Delores excused herself to use the rest room. "Why don't you come with me, Kirsten?" she asked.

Kirsten rolled her eyes and started eating instead of pushing the food around her plate. "I'm starving," she said. Her mother seemed to hesitate, but finally turned and left. As soon as she was gone, Kirsten looked up at them for the first time. "You guys are my first choice," she said. Matt and Maddie's eyes went wide. "But my mom's nervous about your son. She's not sure you're the best parents for this baby. When she comes back, you guys need to, like, try and make her feel better about it and all that."

"But isn't the choice yours to make?" Matt said. Maddie put her hand on his knee and squeezed. She liked them!

Kirsten shrugged just as her mom appeared. It was the fastest rest-room break Maddie had ever seen.

"Yes, so, where were we?" Delores asked as she settled back into her seat.

Matt cleared his throat. "I brought a picture of our son," he said, pulling his wallet from his back pocket. "He'll be ten years old in February, and he's a great kid."

"Don't you mean, *your* son?" she said, looking at Matt with disapproval.

Maddie cringed and felt her face heat up. She did not like this woman at all. Matt said nothing as he handed the photo across the table.

Delores took the picture, and her brow furrowed. "He's Mexican?"

"Native American," Matt clarified. "Half, anyway—Navajo. Great kid. He loves sports, is a really good artist . . ."

But a veil had dropped over Delores's face. He stopped, and she changed the subject back to Matt's job. Five minutes later she announced they were done. Kirsten hadn't eaten since her mother's return to the table. She smiled and said good-bye, leaving Matt and Maddie to stare after them. They said nothing. Almost a minute later, Kirsten waddled back to the table.

"I forgot my purse," she said, picking up the black vinyl handbag. The words "Too Cool for You" were written on it in hot pink letters. "I still like you guys best," she said, as if she were voting for her favorite soda. "And like you said, it is up to me, right?" She flashed them a bright grin. They both smiled back and watched her awkward body sway as she went back out the door.

"I don't think that went very well," Matt said.

Maddie picked up her own purse and nodded, but couldn't keep the tears from forming. She'd been so hopeful, and she tried to hold onto the fact that Kirsten liked them.

When they prayed together that night, Matt pleaded, "Please let us bring this baby into our home." It made Maddie hope even harder. It would be such a good fit—perfect for everyone. She couldn't imagine getting this close and failing again.

★　★　★

The next day Matt called Maddie at lunch.

"I hate that woman," he said.

Maddie pinched her eyebrows together. "Which woman?" she asked. She'd been thinking about Delores all day and found less and less to like about her.

"Sonja," Matt spat. "She won't let Walter come for Christmas."

Maddie's heart sank. Granted, she hadn't thought about the visit over the last twenty-four hours, but she'd been looking forward to it. In their minds it had been a done deal. Sonja had been so willing for him to come for the summer that they hadn't considered she would say no. "Why?" Maddie asked.

"No reason," Matt said, and Maddie could tell he was trying to calm himself down. "She just said no, and since I agreed to let her keep full custody, it's totally up to her. We can have him for six days over spring break instead."

"Well, that will be fun," Maddie said, trying to sound positive. "We can do an Easter egg hunt and color eggs."

Matt was silent. "I really wanted him to come for Christmas," he finally said quietly.

Maddie's eyes filled with tears, and she wondered, just for a moment, if perhaps it was good that Sonja had rejected the visitation request. Maybe getting mad would help Matt realize how much brighter life was when Walter was in it.

"I'm sorry," Maddie said.

After a few moments' pause, Matt asked, "I don't suppose Gayla's called you?"

"No. I'll call her if I don't hear from her by about four-thirty."

"Let me know what she says," Matt said, though she could tell he was as worried as she was.

"I will."

At 4:45 Maddie called Gayla.

"I was just about to call you," Gayla said with an even tone that told Maddie right away she didn't have good news. "I met with Kirsten this afternoon."

"And her mother?" Maddie asked, hoping Kirsten had met with her alone, but knowing the chances were slim. The more she thought about it, the more she felt that this adoption was more Delores's choice rather than Kirsten's.

"Yes, and her mother." Gayla paused and took a breath. Maddie steeled herself for what she would hear next. "They chose another couple."

Maddie stared at the keyboard of her computer, taking it in. A-S-D-F-G she said in her mind, reading the keys, trying to block the emotion. H-J-K-L.

"Maddie?"

"Did she say why?"

Gayla hesitated.

"Was it Walter?" Maddie asked. "Things changed when we talked about Walter."

"I didn't realize that we hadn't specified Walter's ethnicity in your file. We should have."

A chill ran down Maddie's back. "They didn't choose us because he's Navajo?"

"Uh . . . I didn't mean it to sound that way," Gayla stammered. "They had some concerns about a mixed-race household."

"I see," Maddie said, keeping the anger out of her voice as best she could. For the first time in many months, she resented Walter all over again. How unfair that they lose this baby because of him! But she chastised herself. She was not like Delores—and she wouldn't let that way of thinking enter her mind. *He's our son,* she said to herself, trying to internalize it. *There is still a family out there for us to make.* "Have you added the information to our file?" Maddie asked, never wanting to run into this again. "Would you like me to send a picture?"

"Um . . . that might be a good idea," Gayla said. "I'm very sorry, Maddie."

"Yeah," Maddie said. "Me too."

She left work after that, only a few minutes early, and drove up to her cul-de-sac again. Someday someone would finish what they'd started and put homes on the building lots. For now, with this heartbreak close on the heels of the heartbreak of not getting Walter for Christmas, she needed this place, this time-out from the world. She hoped the builders of the fine houses that would one day grace the mountainside would wait until she didn't need the solace anymore.

After almost an hour she turned around and headed home, dialing Matt's cell phone number. How many more times would she have to have this conversation?

CHAPTER 41

The doors of the school bus hissed to a close behind her as Anna adjusted the strap of her backpack. She tucked a lock of her long black hair behind her ear, hoping it would stay there. The sagebrush bent in the stiff December wind, and the stupid beer tree Sonja insisted on keeping tinkled as the cans hit one another. Anna scowled at the tree. Since reading the book that had inspired the idea, Anna found it even more humiliating. But Sonja thought it was a great joke. Anna wondered, not for the first time, if she was just harboring a vain and stupid fantasy that Sonja would ever straighten up. When Walter had come back from Utah, things had been better. José had been around less often and kept his distance when he was, for which she was grateful. But Sonja was spiraling down again. She was drinking more than ever and leaving for days at a time. A gust of wind sent the beer cans careening into one another again, and it seemed to be an answer to Anna's musings. How could things get better when Sonja was only getting worse?

Anna had one foot on the cinderblock step when the trailer's front door burst open. Something big and silver was suddenly coming at her face. It looked like a cartoon bullet, but felt completely solid as it smashed into Anna's head. The force sent her spinning around to land facedown in the dirt and rocks. For a few seconds she felt nothing, and then wondered if her head was still attached to her body. The world spun, her stomach turned, and she could barely breathe. Sonja's screaming brought her back to her senses, and she blinked a few times, her head feeling as if it had split in half. A beer can, unopened, rolled to a stop a few feet away. Anna tried to focus on it, but blood was dripping in her eyes, making it all that much harder to see anything at all. Spitting out the dirt from her mouth, she slowly lifted herself onto her hands and knees, watching the blood drip onto the dust and trying to understand what had just happened. Sand and dirt crunched between her teeth.

In the next moment Sonja was at her side. "Where's José?" she screamed.

Anna recoiled, backing away from her sister and looking at her as if she'd gone mad. Sonja's pupils were huge, and she smelled horrible—like nothing Anna had smelled before. It wasn't peyote or marijuana; she knew those smells. This was something different. "What?" Anna asked, confused at what was happening. She wiped at her face, and the whole left side of her head stung as if she'd been hit again. Looking at the blood on her hand almost made her throw up. She looked at the beer can on the ground.

"Where's José!" Sonja screamed again. Then she stood and started walking in circles, shaking her fists and yelling. Anna used the moment to escape into the house. She had to stop the bleeding.

After running a washcloth under cold water, she pressed it against her forehead, wincing at the fresh wave of pain. She stared at her face in the mirror. She looked like something out of a horror movie, and while holding the cold rag in place with one hand, she wet another one to try to clean up the mess. Sticks and dirt had stuck to the blood, making the washcloth gritty. *Did she really throw a full can of beer at me?* Anna asked herself. Sonja was far from gentle, but she'd never done anything like this before. Anna had to keep herself from crying, not from the pain, but from the fear.

And then she remembered.

"Walter," she whispered, her stomach sinking. He always got home before Anna. Where was he?

"Walter?" she called as loudly as she dared. Sonja's screams had turned to wailing sobs, sounding like a woman in mourning. Anna knew she needed to get out of the trailer before Sonja came inside. It smelled funny, and Anna wondered what new substance had been added to Sonja's lifestyle.

"Walter?" she called again, abandoning her cleanup efforts, but still holding the cold rag against her head to control the bleeding. She checked his room, but he wasn't there.

After searching the trailer, she went out the back door. "Walter?" she called in a loud whisper, praying Sonja wouldn't come around to the back. She heard a scraping sound and hurried toward a hole in the metal sheeting that hid the crawlspace below the metal house. Walter peeked out a few seconds later, and Anna breathed a sigh of relief. His face went pale when he saw her, and she remembered how scary she looked.

"I'm okay," she whispered. "It's just a little blood. We need to get out of here."

Walter hesitated; then Sonja started up with a war cry. Apparently Sonja was feeling a little more Apache than Navajo today. Sonja's piercing screams spurred Walter to scramble out from his hiding place. He took Anna's hand, and together the two of them hurried away. They headed for Grandmother's hogan half a mile away. She was their only refuge.

By the time they reached Grandmother's, Anna felt light-headed and sick to her stomach—very similar to how she'd felt months earlier after her encounter with José. Grandmother was standing in her doorway as if waiting for them.

"Walter, feed my chickens," she ordered in a mild voice that managed to be firm and comforting all at once. "Anna, come inside."

She said nothing as she tended to Anna's injury, which turned out to be an inch-and-a-half semicircular gash extending from the middle of her left eyebrow nearly to the corner of her eye. Grandmother treated it with an herb poultice and natural bandages before making Anna drink another vile-tasting tea.

"Do I need stitches?" Anna asked when Grandmother finished.

"No stitches," Grandmother said, "but lots of attention." She sat down opposite Anna and looked at her with soft, dark eyes. "It is getting worse," she said.

Anna swallowed the lump in her throat and nodded. It was definitely getting worse. Her commitment to keep Walter on the Reservation was feeling more like a betrayal than a blessing. Hot tears came to her eyes as she realized that unless things took a drastic turn for the better, he might one day be *taken* away. The thought tore her up inside, but Grandmother's words from several months before came back to her: "I worry for his safety with that woman."

Sonja hadn't been physically violent before. But Anna had all but given up on things getting better, and it was depressing to think that the best she could hope for was that things wouldn't get worse. It seemed like an idiotic thing to put her faith in.

★   ★   ★

Walter and Anna stayed at Grandmother's for two days, during which time Anna gathered her strength and prepared for a confrontation with her sister. She couldn't let this continue.

On Wednesday she skipped school and, after seeing Walter safely on the school bus, walked to the trailer, praying for strength with every step she took. As she had hoped, she found Sonja still asleep. When she got up, she would be sober.

It was nearly eleven before the door to Sonja's bedroom opened. Anna was finishing some dusting and turned to face her sister.

At first Sonja pretended not to think anything was wrong, and Anna allowed her to do so. But after a few minutes, Sonja asked where Walter was.

"At school," Anna answered. Sonja sat down at the table and lit a cigarette, her hands shaking. Anna knew she needed a beer, but was glad she hadn't had one yet. "Sonja," she began, relieved that her voice was sounding stronger than she felt. She pulled out the other chair and sat down across from her sister. "I'm scared for you."

Sonja looked up. To Anna's relief, she didn't appear angry or offended. But she didn't say anything either. Her eyes were focused on the cut on Anna's forehead, and for the first time Anna was glad it was there. It seemed to serve as a symbol of all that had gone wrong—at least, Anna hoped Sonja would feel that way.

Anna took a breath and prayed again that the Holy One would be with her. "You are my sister, and I love you. But I fear for you. I do not think you are well." Anna realized that she was speaking like Grandmother did, without contractions and in a paced tone of reverent counsel. She hoped Sonja wouldn't be angered by it.

Sonja was still staring at Anna's face. "I did that?" she whispered, her cigarette burning down without her taking a single drag.

Anna nodded.

"And Walter? Did I . . . hurt him?"

Anna was surprised. Did Sonja not remember any of that day? "No," she assured her sister. "He hid beneath the trailer. I found him, and we went to Grandmother's."

"I know," she said, taking a deep inhale from her cigarette. "I walked there yesterday and saw you there." She looked at the table.

"I'm so sorry. José left me, told me he hated me, that I was nothing. It hurt too much."

Again, Anna was taken off guard by her sister's candor and shame. She had expected a battle of wills, not an acceptance—and certainly not an apology. The explanation made sense of that day a little better, though it did nothing to alter Anna's intent for this meeting.

"We need you to be well," Anna said. "You need you to be well."

The tears began to fall from Sonja's eyes, something Anna had never seen. "I don't know how to be well anymore," her sister said. "I am so lost inside myself."

"I can help you," Anna said. "If you will let me."

They talked for several minutes, until Sonja could no longer concentrate and had to get a beer from the fridge. Even then they continued to talk, to discuss options. As the beer kicked in, Sonja became more prideful, explaining away the depth of the problems. But in the end she agreed to work on things—to do better. Anna agreed to help any way that she could, and finally ended the conversation when Sonja opened her fourth beer of the day. Anna knew her progress had been stymied, and yet she was more hopeful than she had ever been. The mere fact that Sonja knew she had a problem, that she'd apologized for what she'd done, seemed to be a good omen. *We can do this,* she thought as she walked back to Grandmother's to tell her how the confrontation had gone. *Together, we can make this work.* Now, if she could just bring together the other parts of her plan.

CHAPTER 42

*T*his is Matt," he said into the phone, using the greeting he used at the office. He'd been home for over an hour and was putting the finishing touches on the only meal he knew how to cook—meat loaf. After dinner, he and Maddie would work it off at the gym. They were both in better shape than ever, and exercising had become a bit of an addiction. And a distraction too.

"Matthew Shep?" a soft female voice asked.

Matt paid a little more attention. "Yes."

The woman or girl on the other end took a deep breath. "My name is Anna Begay. I'm Sonja Hudson's sister—Walter's aunt."

Matt felt the hairs on the back of his neck prickle. "Yes, hello, Anna. Is everything okay?" He couldn't imagine she would call him for any other reason but bad news.

"Everything is fine," she said, but something in her tone made him not believe her. She hurried on. "I was wondering if there was any way Walter could spend Christmas with you?"

Matt furrowed his brow and leaned against the counter, paying very close attention to the conversation. "Sonja rejected our request for Christmas visitation back in October," he said.

"I know," Anna said, her voice laced with apology, though they both knew it wasn't her fault. "But I think she would reconsider."

Matt was confused. What was going on? "I'm not sure I understand."

Anna was silent. "Sonja would kill me if she knew I was calling you," she finally said. "And I know everything has to go through your lawyer, but could you please ask again? I know Walter wants to go, and I think Sonja would allow it now."

"Anna," Matt said, his anxiety increasing by the second. "What's wrong?"

She was silent for a few seconds. "Never mind. Please don't tell anyone I called."

The line clicked, and after a few moments the dial tone returned. Matt hit the caller ID button and called the number back. A different woman answered, and for a moment his stomach clenched as he thought that it was Sonja.

"Is Anna there?" he asked. The woman said yes, and for him to hold on. She didn't sound like Sonja, and when he checked the number on his phone again, he realized it wasn't from her house. He let out a breath of relief.

"Hello?" the same cautious voice asked.

"I'm sorry," he said. "I won't ask any questions, and I'll make the petition again."

Anna was silent for a few moments. "You can't tell anyone I called," she said. "If you tell the lawyers I talked to you about this, I'll say I didn't."

"I won't tell anyone," he promised, though it killed him to say so. He wanted to tell his lawyer, call the police—but he wanted her trust even more.

"Not even Walter," she continued. "He has to think you want him to come."

"We do want him to come," Matt said, mildly offended that she would insinuate otherwise. "That's why we petitioned in the first place."

"I know," she said. "That's not what I meant. He can't know I called."

"Okay," Matt said. "I'll make the petition today."

"Thank you," Anna said with relief.

"Anna," he said, not wanting to push too far, but unable to leave things as they were. He battled with what words to use for a few moments. "Call me anytime."

"Thank you," she said. "I will."

Matt called his attorney and asked to make the petition again. The attorney was confused, and Matt wanted to explain but couldn't. Instead he simply said he had a feeling. When Maddie came home, he told her about Anna's phone call.

"What do you think is wrong?" she asked, concern heavy on her face.

"I don't know," Matt said, putting plastic wrap over the last of the meat loaf before putting it in the fridge. "But she wasn't about to tell me, and she hung up the first time when I asked too many questions. We gave Sonja ten days to get back to us."

"I hope Walter's okay," Maddie said.

"Me too."

★　★　★

One week after making the request, Matt received a call from his attorney telling him Sonja had agreed. Through the week of waiting, he'd gone over a hundred possibilities of what had prompted Anna's call, and none of them were good. He wondered if he should have gone to the police, or told his attorney, or done . . . something. But through each scenario the soft, scared voice of Walter's aunt—the person he felt was more a parent than Sonja was—came back to him. Matt trusted her, and wanted her to trust him, and when he prayed he felt pretty certain the Lord agreed.

Matt told Maddie the news when she got home, and she was thrilled. They made flight reservations for Walter that night. Then they went Christmas shopping. They'd already bought some things that were ready to be mailed, should their petition be denied again. But since he was coming, they would need stocking stuffers and a few more gifts. They loved every minute of it.

Hours later, as they made their way home through the snowy streets, Maddie told Matt about the call she'd had from Gayla that day. "That girl, Kirsten," Maddie said. "The one we met with?"

Matt nodded, feeling the burn in his stomach that always accompanied thoughts of the experience. In the two months since they had met Kirsten, no other birth mothers had requested to meet them. They didn't talk about it very much.

"She kept the baby," Maddie said.

Matt turned to look at his wife. "She did?"

Maddie nodded. "The adoptive parents were there for the delivery and everything. Kirsten even chose not to see the baby after it was born. She waited twenty hours."

Matt let out a breath, feeling such sorrow for the adoptive parents. In Utah, the birth mother had to wait twenty-four hours before she could sign the paperwork. The fear that she would change her mind at the last minute was every couple's worst nightmare. "That's horrible," Matt said.

Maddie nodded. "She's fifteen years old and she chose to raise that baby."

They didn't say anything for several minutes, both reviewing the situation in their mind. Matt didn't blame Kirsten for wanting to keep her baby. It was amazing to him that anyone that young could make such a mature choice as adoption, but it still stung. "It could have been us," he said as they pulled into their apartment complex. "We could have been that couple waiting at the hospital and going home alone."

"I don't think I could have survived it," she whispered.

"Me neither," Matt said. He reached over and put a hand on Maddie's knee. "I suppose it did work out for the best after all."

★　　★　　★

Walter arrived on December twenty-first. He was all smiles. They spent the next three nights shopping, going to Temple Square, and attending a couple of Christmas parties. Christmas morning, Walter's eyes were huge when he came upstairs to see the tree. After presents—more than they should have given—they went to Matt's parents' house for Christmas dinner. Walter played with his cousins, showing off his new shoes and bragging about his Game Boy while oohing and ahhing over their gifts. One cousin in particular, Jeff, was close to Walter's age, and they got along fabulously. It did Maddie's heart good to see him blend in so well. When he had come for the summer, they had taken the transition slowly, but now it seemed as if he'd always been a part of this group. Maddie was relieved that he'd adjusted so well. It had been her fear that he wouldn't fit in, that he would be on the outside of things. But her fears had been unfounded, and she considered it a blessing not to have one more thing to worry about.

Two days later was the annual Shep sleepover at Grandma's house. All grandkids over the age of five spent the night at Matt's parents' home. Maddie had the week off from work, so she drove Walter over and then hung around to make sure everything was okay.

"He's fine," Cindy, Matt's oldest sister, said after almost two hours. She and her family had come in from Ohio and were staying with Matt's parents—though Cindy and her husband were escaping to a bed and breakfast for the night. "Enjoy the break."

Maddie just smiled, not wanting to get into the fact that her breaks were when Walter was *with* them. As much as she wanted him to bond with his cousins and grandparents, she was selfish about her time with him too. "I'll go tell him good-bye," Maddie said. She went downstairs, interrupting the movie to kiss him good-bye. He waved her off like any nearly-ten-year-old would do, and she walked slowly upstairs, telling herself not to take it personally.

"You okay?" Cindy asked when Maddie got to the top of the stairs.

"I'm fine," she said. "I'll just miss him."

"You're a great mom."

Maddie was startled and froze midstep.

"What?" Cindy asked, looking concerned. "What did I say?"

Maddie tried to swallow the lump in her throat. "No one's ever called me that before," she whispered, feeling silly, but somehow relieved of a burden she'd forgotten was there.

Cindy smiled. "Well, get used to it. You're a natural."

★　　★　　★

Four days later, on New Year's Day, they waved good-bye to Walter as an airport worker led him to the plane. It was hard to see him go, but they were more used to it this time. On the way home, Matt pulled into a Jamba Juice. "Got a craving?" Maddie asked.

Matt turned to look at her. "James called me this morning, but I didn't want to bring it up before. Sheryl's pregnant."

"Again," Maddie said. Matt's best friend had three kids already. Her instant expectation was to feel bitter, but she noticed that the raw anger and envy weren't as strong as they used to be. She had no desire to get in deeper and dredge up the hurt. So she didn't, and was surprised how easy it was. *When did it change?* she wondered. She was happy for James and Sheryl—she really was.

"Yeah," Matt said in a flat tone.

Maddie smiled and opened her door. "I want a cookie, too."

★   ★   ★

Sonja was waiting for Walter when Bearcloud dropped him off that evening, and she pulled him into a huge hug. While Anna put the finishing touches on a mutton stew, Sonja asked Walter all about his trip. She didn't make any demeaning comments about Matt or his wife, and was very complimentary in regards to Walter's gifts. Anna couldn't have been happier.

After the trip to Salt Lake had been confirmed, Anna and Sonja had planned out their own undertaking. Sonja had dealt with the rehabs before and didn't want to go back, so Anna had agreed to oversee her detoxification. It had been horrible. For five days Sonja had been sick and delusional, and she cried most of the time. There were many times Anna didn't think they would make it through. But as a tribute to the commitment Sonja had made, she weathered the storms. On the fifth day, she finally held down some food. It had been uphill since then. The sisters had gone for walks, they had deep-cleaned the trailer, Sonja had even woven on Grandmother's loom for the first time in many years. Sonja had also agreed to start smoking outside. They had enjoyed a quiet holiday, and for the first time in Anna's life, she had felt she really had a sister.

Now Walter was home, and she saw Sonja being the mother he had never had. Anna smiled and filled the bowls with stew.

"Dinner's ready," she said with a smile. They all circled around the table and enjoyed what may have been the best family dinner they had ever had. Merry Christmas indeed.

CHAPTER 43

anuary came and went without much happening. Matt and Maddie took a country swing class, to break in their cowboy boots, and had a great time, but it was impossible not to notice the emptiness of life in general. Sonja was letting them have spring break too, and so, even though Easter was months away, it gave them something to look forward to. Matt requested, through his attorney, for joint custody of Walter, offering an additional one hundred dollars a month in child support if Sonja would agree. She did so without much hesitation, and they both felt better having some legal say in Walter's life. Thanks to several months of regular exercise, Maddie fit back into a size six by the end of the month—she was grateful to be making progress somewhere.

February second, Groundhog Day, Maddie was at her desk when the phone rang.

"Madeline Shep," she said as she placed the receiver to her ear.

"Maddie, it's Gayla. Are you up to meeting another birth mom?"

Maddie straightened and stopped working on the computer. She had always known this was coming, but she had feared the actual moment. Meeting another birth mom meant opening themselves up to failure again. But it was also a necessary step in the process.

"Really?" Maddie asked, wanting to make sure.

"Her name is Jenny. She's eighteen years old, and I've been working with her for almost three months. She is very studious about this decision and has looked through almost every file I have. At first she said she didn't want the baby to go to a family that already had kids, so you and Matt weren't included. But she's run out of couples, so I told her about you guys and the situation you have. Anyway, she wants to meet you, but I have to warn you not to get your hopes up. Her mother wants her to keep the baby, and she's still with the father, whose parents want them to get married and make it work."

"How determined is she?" Maddie asked, grateful for the honesty but disappointed that the chances didn't seem promising.

"Very," Gayla said. "Her parents married because her mother was pregnant with her. They divorced a few years later, and both have new families—that's her terminology, by the way. She wants to give this baby a real home."

"When does she want to meet us?"

"Tomorrow night," Gayla said.

Maddie took a breath. "We'll be there," she said. "What time and where?"

"The Olive Garden by the Fashion Place Mall. Do you know where that is?"

"Yes, yes . . . I do," Maddie said, her stomach sinking. That was where they had met Kirsten and her *lovely* mother. But she didn't want to overcomplicate things by reminding Gayla, so she kept her feelings to herself.

"She'll be waiting for you at six o'clock. She said you'd recognize her as the eight-month-pregnant teenager sitting alone."

"Alone?" Maddie asked.

"It's complicated. She'll explain it."

"Okay."

"Are you all right?" Gayla asked after a moment of silence.

"I don't know," Maddie said with all honesty. "After Kirsten, I'm nervous."

"Most couples are rejected at least once before an adoption goes through, but a hundred percent of couples who keep going—even though the risk of heartbreak is always there—get the family they're praying for."

★　　★　　★

The next evening Matt and Maddie tried to ignore the eerie similarities to their meeting with Kirsten as they entered the lobby of the restaurant. Despite how hard Maddie had tried not to get her hopes up, she couldn't help it and had been fantasizing all day long. Her insides were in turmoil, and she was sure she wouldn't be able to eat a thing. She reminded herself that the chances of this working out were slim. Still, the possibility . . .

Jenny was fifteen minutes late, a very long fifteen minutes. She was also extremely pregnant and looked uncomfortable as she walked in.

"I'm Jenny," she said and stuck out her hand when they approached her. Maddie shook it first. Jenny was about Maddie's height, with blue eyes, fair skin, and blonde, curly hair pulled back in a ponytail . . . and so young—though not as young as Kirsten. The hostess led them back to the table and handed out the menus.

For the first minute they were all silent, until Jenny folded up her menu and put it on the table. She started by quizzing them on almost everything—much as Delores had. Matt explained his job, his salary, the stability of his career. Maddie let her know she would quit as soon as they got a baby. Jenny liked that. They told her about Maddie's medical problems, their house, and their families. The fact that their parents on both sides were still married seemed to make a good impression. Maddie was aching to ask some questions of her own, but she let Jenny run the show. The young woman seemed to know what she was looking for and continued firing away her questions in an almost businesslike manner.

Jenny finally asked about Walter. It was the question they had both dreaded. Matt and Maddie had already decided to be very clear about Walter. They had kept information fuzzy before, and it had hurt them. This time Matt told her everything—how he had found out about Walter, the shock, and the eventual acceptance. Jenny listened, ignoring the salad placed before her.

"What's he like? I was hoping he could come with you."

"Walter lives in New Mexico with his mother," Matt said. "He's only here in the summers, but he's great. He knows we're working on adopting and thinks it's cool. He's Navajo."

"Yeah," Jenny said. "It's in your file. That's one of the reasons I picked you guys. Brandon is Latino. His parents are Colombian, so he's dark. Even though lots of couples put on their forms that they will take any ethnicity, I kinda didn't like the idea of the baby standing out."

"We get some looks when Walter's with us, but we're getting used to it."

"And you guys don't, like, hate other races and stuff?"

"Oh, no," Maddie said quickly. "Not at all."

" 'Cause I worry about that too. It would be horrible if he was raised in a home where they thought dark people weren't as good as white people. I met a couple last week, she's part Hispanic and he's white. I thought they would be perfect, that my baby would match, but the man pretty much said the only reason they were taking a biracial baby was 'cause no one would give them a white one since his wife was Hispanic. I hated that."

"That's horrible," Maddie said, more angry than she wanted to show at such callousness. She was also grateful that Jenny hadn't shown shock and dismay at the way Walter had come into their lives. Then again, she understood better than most how something like that could have happened.

"You're probably wondering why no one came with me," Jenny said, changing the subject. For the first time, they could hear the youth in her voice. She took a bite and swallowed before continuing. "My folks are divorced. Both are remarried now and have new families. I live with my mom. She isn't active in the Church anymore, not since the divorce, and she's got four other kids. She wants me to keep the baby or let her adopt it. It's her first grandchild and she's not very supportive about me giving it to strangers." Jenny took another bite.

"And what about your dad?" Maddie asked after a few moments, trying to get used to the abruptness of this young girl. She hadn't expected her to be quite so forthcoming.

"He doesn't even know, and he won't. He sends out his child support every month, and a hundred bucks for my birthday and fifty for Christmas, but that's about it. He lives up in Washington state, and I haven't even seen him for, like, four years, I think. He's got two kids with his new wife. I'm an expensive piece of his past he'd rather not worry about."

Matt coughed and took a sip of his water. Maddie put a hand on his back, remembering that he'd seen Walter that way at first.

"So he doesn't know," Jenny summarized as she took another bite and then pushed the plate away. "I get full so easy these days, but in another hour I'll be hungry again." Matt and Maddie had barely touched their meals. "Brandon and I didn't mean for this to happen," Jenny said, looking at them both. "It just . . . did. We'd been dating for a year. He's from a good family; a good kid. I've been to church more in the last six months than I ever went before." She smiled at the irony. "Anyway, it happened a few times, even though we knew better and all that. Then I found out I was pregnant."

The waiter came, and Jenny asked him to box the dinner up for her. She continued, "He's been good about it, offered to marry me and everything, but it didn't seem right. When his mom found out, she completely freaked, told him he *had* to marry me. I still said no." She smiled sadly. "My mom married my dad because she got pregnant, and it didn't do any of us any good—the last thing I want to do is replay their life."

Maddie reached under the table for Matt's hand and gave it a squeeze, hoping to communicate how impressed she was with this girl. This meeting was so different from the one with Kirsten—Jenny was so different. That had to be a good sign, right?

"Brandon's mom is still freaking out about it. She wants to adopt it, but there's no way I'm going to do that." She shook her head, showing her resolve. "That's why Brandon isn't here. His mom forbids him from coming around. My mom came with me the first two times I met with adoptive parents, but when I turned them both down, she said she'd had enough." Jenny shrugged as if it wasn't a big deal, but Maddie knew it had to be painful for her to be doing this alone. "The counselor offered to come with me, but I'd just as soon do it alone."

"Are you and Brandon together now?" Maddie asked, feeling such sadness for the struggles this girl was facing and yet grateful in a twisted kind of way. The only way Matt and Maddie would ever get a baby would be through someone else's tragedy.

"Sort of," Jenny said with a smile. "His parents won't let him see me, but he manages to come over now and then. We've gone to see his bishop, and he's helped us out a lot. Brandon calls me when his mom isn't around. But it's really hard. We're working things through. I think once the baby's born, it will be easier for us. We'd like to get married someday."

"But it must be hard, placing it up for adoption," Maddie said softly. Maybe it wasn't appropriate to say, but it seemed silly to ignore it, and she wanted to be sure Jenny was clear about the choice she was making.

Jenny nodded. "Sometimes it is, but I've learned a lot these last few months, about God, about the Church, and about myself. God doesn't want me to give up my life for this baby." Tears came to her eyes and she shook them away. "No one should give up their life like that. I've never had a job, I've never lived on my own, and I know this baby deserves someone who wants it, not someone who's obligated to take care of it."

"That's a very mature opinion," Maddie said after several seconds of silence.

Jenny let out a hollow chuckle. "If I were mature, I wouldn't be here. I'd be getting ready for college and picking out prom dresses. But God's will is not for me to raise this baby."

They were all silent, as if they had run out of things to talk about. Matt offered dessert, and at first Jenny said no, but then agreed to take some home. Matt and Maddie waited, wondering if they had passed the test. Would she say no to their face? Did she need to think about it? What happened now?

Jenny stood up awkwardly and then caught her breath and put a hand to her stomach. She smiled. "Want to feel it kick?" she asked, and Maddie nodded. She stood and leaned across the table. Jenny took her wrist and guided her hand to where she had felt movement. After only a moment, a distinct object bounced against Maddie's hand, and she sucked in her breath. It kicked again, and she could feel the tears come to her eyes as she shook off how close she'd been to living through the joy of that very thing. Her own baby would be five months old now. But she focused on the situation at hand. A living person was in there, a baby, maybe hers. The next thing she thought was that it was the dumbest thing in the world to feel it kick. It would make a "no" so much harder.

"I think she's mad 'cause I refused the dessert," Jenny chuckled when the baby kicked against Maddie's hand again.

"She?" Maddie asked, looking up into Jenny's face. Jenny had called the baby "it" or "the baby" throughout the entire dinner. Maddie had been waiting for a clue.

"It's a girl, but I try not to think about it." She smiled sadly. "Well, I better go. Someone will call you guys tomorrow."

They watched her leave and wanted to chase her down and force an answer from her. The waiting was agony. They sat back down in silence.

"Do you want dessert?" Matt finally asked.

Maddie shook her head. "I don't think I'll be able to eat anything until we hear from Gayla. This felt different, didn't it? I mean, not like Kirsten." Still, it was painful to hope after so many disappointments.

Matt nodded. "How about we start a fast right now. We'll order two desserts to go, and when we get the call it will be our celebration."

"What if she rejects us?" Maddie asked.

"If she rejects us, we'll throw them away and wait until next time."

Maddie smiled and nodded. They ordered two fudge caramel cheesecakes, paid the bill, and left. Matt unlocked Maddie's car door, and she was about to climb in when he grabbed her arm and pointed at an old, red Honda a few spaces down the parking lot. Jenny was in the driver's seat with her head bowed and her arms folded over her large stomach. They watched for a few seconds as she sat there alone, praying. Finally Maddie got in the car. Matt soon slipped in as well.

"I think she's got the right idea," Matt said, and they both bowed their heads as Matt began a prayer of his own, opening their fast and asking that if it were God's will, they might have the opportunity to raise Jenny's baby as their own, to build their family, to find what they wanted more than anything in the world.

CHAPTER 44

*T*he next day was agonizingly slow. Maddie had meetings all day long, which kept her away from her desk. At every opportunity, she raced to her phone and listened to her voice mail—nothing. She was also starving, since she had eaten very little of her dinner the night before. She was too nervous to eat anyway. She and Matt had prayed in the parking lot together, before bed, before Matt left for work, and she had continued to pray every time she had a free moment. It all felt different from the time with Kirsten, yet that earlier experience wasn't far from her mind. When she focused on how she felt, she admitted that she felt good. But was that God's way of telling her things were working out with Jenny? Or was it His reminder that He loved her even though this baby wasn't for them?

She tapped her pencil against her cheek as she looked up at the clock: 4:12. She wanted to scream. They had been in this meeting for over an hour—twice as long as they should have been. Someone was droning on about the latest hospital they were certifying. Maddie had zoned out a long time ago. She had decided she would call Gayla when she got back to her office. If, that is, she ever got out of this blasted boardroom! Finally they dismissed, and Maddie gathered her things and made a beeline for her office. Her heart was thumping as she pulled Gayla's card from her desk and picked up the phone. She was three numbers into it when someone knocked on the door. It was Joyce, her director.

Maddie tried to decide whether to put Joyce off and finish dialing or hang up and do it when she could be alone. Choosing the latter, she returned the phone to the cradle and tried not to let her frustration show.

"I'm sorry, Maddie. Could you sign this?"

"Sure," Maddie said with distraction, grateful that all she had to do was sign a form. As a supervisor, she signed a lot of things. Joyce put the paper in front of her, and Maddie picked up a pen and scanned the page for the signature line that should be in the bottom corner, as it was on every form the company produced. But the line wasn't there. Her eyes caught the first sentence, and she looked up at Joyce, confused.

"What is this?"

Joyce smiled just as Matt poked his head into the office. "It's your letter of resignation," he said. Maddie gasped as her eyes widened and the pen dropped from her hand.

"You're going to have a baby," Joyce added with a smile. Maddie screamed and exploded from her chair as Matt came around and scooped her into his arms. Maddie hugged Matt tightly, babbling questions without giving him time to answer. Joyce slipped out of the room and shut the door.

Matt put her down and wiped her wet cheeks with his thumbs. "Gayla called you a few times but didn't want to leave it on your voice mail."

"I can't believe it," Maddie choked. She pulled Matt back to her again, laughing. "I can't believe it," she repeated and clenched her eyes shut. "I was so sure . . ." She was smiling too wide to speak. She knew they weren't home free, or at least she told herself so, but it didn't diminish the thrill of the moment.

Matt wiggled out of her arms and reached down to pick up the bag with two small, white Styrofoam containers. Maddie laughed and wiped at her eyes again. "I hope you brought forks, because I'm fresh out."

CHAPTER 45

*M*att rushed to the elevator in a panic and pushed the buttons as he looked on the directory for the floor housing Labor and Delivery. Fourth floor.

"Come on," he muttered under his breath. The elevator was taking forever. Maddie had called just as he'd returned from lunch. Jenny had gone into labor the night before and was close to delivery. She'd asked Gayla to call them so they could be there as soon as the baby was born.

Their baby.

Maddie was on her way to the hospital, where she would get to see the baby as soon as it was brought to the nursery. It had taken Matt almost an hour to finish up some pressing phone calls and push some appointments to next week before he could leave the office. His stomach quivered with anticipation. February twenty-third, one week past their fifth anniversary, eight days past Walter's tenth birthday. The day their daughter was to be born. In just one year, February had become a busy month on their calendar.

Maddie had put in her last day at the office on Friday. They had spent the weekend painting one of the upstairs rooms for a nursery and shopping for the final bits and pieces. Family and friends had hosted three baby showers for Maddie, and despite how cheesy she said they were, the light in her eyes denied her opposition. They had received a crib from Maddie's co-workers, dresses, shoes, diapers, and some weird-looking underwear from Matt's family. Maddie's family had supplied more clothes, as well as a stroller and a bassinet. Just yesterday they'd received a package from Walter. Grandmother had helped him make a dream catcher for his new sister. They had hung it in the window, where the crystal tied to the center of the web-type design caught the light and sent little rainbows dancing around the nursery walls.

Several people had asked if they were worried about Jenny changing her mind. Of course they were. There was a mandatory twenty-four-hour waiting period. But after that, the birth mother and birth father could sign the forms relinquishing their parental rights. Once those papers were signed, it would be hard to undo the adoption process. There was still a very real risk that Jenny would change her mind, but without taking the risk they would never have a baby at all. After six months, the adoption would be finalized, at which time they could be sealed in the temple. Matt got chills just thinking about it.

The elevator arrived, and he hopped in, punching the illuminated 4 button. The doors opened, and Gayla was at the nurse's station. She was all smiles. Matt walked out of the elevator looking hopeful, and she held something out to him. He took it and looked down. It looked like a pink cigar, with "It's a girl" printed on the cellophane wrapper.

"Don't worry, it's bubble gum," she said as she took his arm and led him down the hall. Matt couldn't speak, even though he had a thousand things he wanted to say; he just stared at the object in his hand and went where Gayla led him. They stopped, and Matt looked up. They were standing in the hallway facing a large window. The sight on the other side of the glass made his heart skip a beat, and a lump filled his throat as he realized how long they had waited for this.

There, on the other side of the glass, was Maddie. Her face looked like a huge lightbulb, and her clothes were covered with a yellow paper coat. Two nurses were with her, instructing her on how to bathe the red, wailing infant she held in her arms.

The baby had been born—their daughter. Her tiny mouth was wide with what he could only assume was a loud protest, and her fists flailed through the air. She had a mop of black hair, and he noticed that the remaining umbilical cord on her belly button was still gray. He couldn't hear what was being said, but he watched Maddie laugh, and his heart fluttered at the sight. Then she saw him and smiled before lifting the tiny body out of the bathwater.

A nurse helped her swaddle the baby in a large towel, and Maddie held up the tiny, pinched face next to her own and looked at Matt. She whispered something to the baby, who looked like she was almost asleep now; the only word he made out was "Daddy."

★ ★ ★

The hospital was as dark as it got, and Matt sat down in the rocking chair. Maddie shifted the bundle and transferred the tiny infant into his arms. The baby didn't stir. Maddie had finished giving her a bottle, and now it was Matt's turn for some daddy-daughter time. Visiting hours were over, but the nurses let them stay a while longer. Throughout the afternoon, Matt had held the baby for brief periods of time, but they never lasted long. And there were always so many doctors and nurses around that he didn't feel he could concentrate. Now it was just the three of them.

"So what did you decide to name her?" Matt asked as the tiny hand curled around his thumb. They hadn't been able to agree, so they had decided that Maddie would choose the first name and Matt would choose the middle name. If they adopted again, which they hoped they would, they would reverse the order.

"Esther," Maddie said. "In the Bible, she was strong and beautiful, with a big heart and a powerful faith in God."

"Esther," Matt whispered back. Why hadn't he liked it before? It seemed perfect now.

"And did you choose the middle name yet?" Maddie asked.

Matt nodded and looked at his wife. "Madeline. Esther Madeline Shep."

Maddie's face filled with emotion, and she leaned over to seal it with a kiss. They sat there for several more minutes, inspecting their baby daughter and relishing the family-ness. Matt looked up toward the window when something caught his eye. A teenage boy stood watching them. His sadness and longing, coupled with his dark features, told them both who he was. For half a minute he stared at the infant in Matt's arms, then he looked at them both, first Maddie and then Matt. He held Matt's eyes, and Matt said softly, "Thank you," knowing the boy couldn't hear it, but hoping he would understand. The boy nodded and turned away. As they watched him disappear down the hallway, a whole new emotion gripped them. Brandon and Jenny had given up so much. Not just in the baby they gave away, but in the innocence lost along the way. They would never be the same, and as Matt and Maddie looked back down at this miracle in their lives, they both felt deep and sincere gratitude for the selfless gift Jenny and Brandon had given to them.

The next evening Esther was given the thumbs-up sign to go home. Jenny and Brandon had chosen to see but not hold her during the twenty-four-hour wait, and they signed the papers as soon as it was legal. Maddie wanted to do something to show her gratitude, but Gayla let her know that Jenny was in no state to appreciate the gesture. Despite her surety that adoption was the right path, and despite knowing Matt and Maddie were the true parents intended for Esther, her pain was still raw and devastating. So without seeing the young woman who had brought their daughter into this world, they left. Brandon watched from a faraway vantage point as Matt and Maddie signed the release papers and listened to the last-minute instructions. This time when they looked at Brandon he managed a small smile.

Then began the real shock of it all. Esther ate every two hours and cried for most of the time in between. It took only a matter of days to learn that Esther had colic. All day, it seemed, every day, Maddie rocked and bounced and cried with her, wondering when it would end. She wondered when she would get a full night's sleep again, when she would do the dishes or the ever-increasing piles of laundry. Matt pitched in a lot, but Maddie took the brunt of it. Although she tried to be a good sport, she was frustrated and didn't know what to do except keep bouncing, rocking, and crying. She worried that Esther somehow sensed that Maddie wasn't her real mother, and it broke her heart. Despite everyone telling her otherwise, she had a hard time believing that didn't have something to do with it. But a lot of prayer, and several blessings from her father and her husband, reminded her that Esther was hers, and she need not question it.

At six weeks the colic seemed to be getting better, just in time for the ear infections to start. There were moments—golden moments, Matt called them—when Esther would be content and calm, gazing at her parents with the innocence and peace they had longed for. At those times, Matt and Maddie were reminded why they had relinquished their savings, why Maddie was asleep before her head hit the pillow every night, and why their house smelled like dirty diapers. At those moments it all made sense. If only those golden moments could come around more often.

Walter came for spring break, and they all enjoyed the holiday. They had their first family photo taken, with Esther's mouth caught in a scream—at least it was true to life. When Walter went home, the separation still hurt, but this time there was someone to hug in his absence. He'd been thrilled with his new sister, at least as thrilled as any ten-year-old boy would be. Maddie got tears in her eyes every time she looked at the family photo now hanging over the fireplace. They were a family—for real.

★   ★   ★

The smell of bacon woke Maddie up, and she smiled and stretched her arms over her head. She was under strict instructions to stay in bed until told otherwise. It was hard to do. Since jumping into full-time motherhood, she'd found it hard to keep still. It drove Matt nuts that she couldn't watch a movie without getting up and organizing things. But she had promised to stay put today. A few minutes passed, at which point the door to the master bedroom squeaked open. Matt stood in the doorway with a plate of food in one hand and a bundle of baby tucked in the other arm. Maddie furrowed her brow. Matt was wonderful, but doing two things at once wasn't his forte.

He walked in and was handing her the plate when Essy slipped. It wasn't much, but Maddie overreacted and lunged for the baby at the same time Matt shifted. Maddie knocked his arm, and the plate flew through the air. Matt fumbled with it, making a gallant effort, but egg was already going everywhere. Moments later he was apologizing, Esther was wailing in his arms, and Maddie was pulling scrambled eggs from her hair.

The eggs were hot, the bacon had likely stained the comforter, and juice had splashed all over the place. Maddie ignored the mess, took Esther, and held her close, calming her down. Then she looked at Matt's dejected face. Reaching up, she grabbed the front of his shirt and pulled him down to her eye level.

257

"Thank you," she said as he picked another clump of egg from her hair.

"For bathing you in eggs and jam?—you're welcome." His tone showed how disappointed he was.

"It's the best Mother's Day ever."

Later they went to church, and, without being too proud about it, Maddie stood and received her complimentary petunias. It was a small thing, but very powerful. She'd always felt like she was cheating before, but this time it was for real.

When they arrived home, Matt gave her a can of Coke and a new pair of fuzzy socks, similar to the ones she had received last year.

"It isn't No Socks and Have a Coke Day today. It's the fourteenth."

"For us, Mother's Day will always include a Coke and a pair of socks. Deal?"

"Deal," she said with a laugh.

"And this came in the mail earlier this week. I saved it."

She took what looked like a card and opened it up. Inside was a picture of Walter, glued to a construction paper card. On the other side of the paper was a bouquet of crayon-drawn flowers. A little note said, "I would send flowers but I don't have enough stamps. Happy Step-Mom Day. Love, Walter." They'd never stopped praying for the opportunity to be a bigger part of Walter's life, and in some ways it had worked. Things like this card, pictures he sent them, and his excitement at their regular phone calls made them feel as if their prayers were making a difference.

Maddie wiped at the tears just as Esther started whimpering in the other room. "I'll get her," Matt said, standing.

"It's Mother's Day," Maddie said, pushing him back down and feeling as if she were on the top of the world. Being a mom was all she had ever wanted, and she had it—twice over. Better yet, no one could take it away from her now. The last thing she wanted was a day off. "Let me."

CHAPTER 46

*S*onja stumbled from her room. Anna only glanced at her before returning her attention to the book she was reading. Walter, absorbed in the TV, didn't even look up. It was ten o'clock in the morning, but Anna was surprised to see Sonja dressed. Her hair was done as well, making Anna think she was planning to go somewhere.

"Isn't there any milk?" Sonja asked after opening the fridge to find it nearly empty.

Anna looked up from where she was reading at the kitchen table. "You said you would buy some last night," she said.

"What did you guys eat?" Sonja asked, ignoring that it was her fault there was no milk.

"Eggs."

"I hate eggs."

"That's all we have," Anna said, returning to her book.

Sonja pulled a beer from the back of the fridge. Anna scowled when she heard the hiss of the top being opened. Sonja arched an eyebrow. "You want one?"

Anna didn't bother to answer. Things had gone so well after Christmas, she'd had very high hopes for the new year. But in February José had shown up on their doorstep. When he had come back into their lives, the fifty-three days of Sonja's sobriety had ended. They had gone to the bar that night, and the one time Anna had tried to remind Sonja of her commitments, she'd been told to keep her mouth shut or leave. José had seconded the idea, and Anna had watched her hopes vanish into cigarette-smoke-filled air. Now it seemed that the reprieve had never happened. Sonja was more arrogant and mean than she had ever been. She drank more than ever, and Anna suspected she was doing drugs—though she wasn't sure which ones. Anna was so disgusted she could hardly look at her sister anymore.

"You're such a prude," Sonja said, walking toward the table.

"At least I'm not a lush," Anna muttered under her breath—apparently too loudly. Sonja slapped her face so hard that Anna fell out of her chair. The room spun for a moment, and rather than jump to her feet right away, she stayed put, rubbing her jaw while Sonja delivered a long, obscene monologue that laid out in no uncertain terms how ungrateful Anna was. Anna told herself not to cry, but she couldn't help it. After telling Anna what a baby she was, Sonja stopped and went into her room to drink her *breakfast* in peace.

"Are you okay, Anna?" Walter asked when she finally got up from her spot on the floor.

"Yeah," she muttered as she got back to her feet. "But keep your distance—your mom had a late night." Walter nodded his understanding, and they didn't say another word about it. Walter went back to the TV. Anna sat back down, wiped away the tears, and tried unsuccessfully to ignore the residual throbbing and read some more. She had to finish reading the book for the test in her English class tomorrow, and since she never knew how her days would turn out, she felt a little frantic about getting it done. School would be out in two more weeks; this would be the final test counted toward her grade.

Sonja came back out of her room a few minutes later, and Anna tensed but made sure to remain absorbed in the pages.

"When did José leave?" Sonja asked, as if nothing had happened.

"Around eight," Anna said without looking up.

"We'll be taking off in a little bit. I won't be home till Wednesday."

"Where are you going?" Anna asked. Lately Sonja had been taking two- and three-day trips with José. She never said where they went.

"That's none of your business."

"Shouldn't it be?" Anna said. "Don't I at least get to know where you are in case we need you?"

Sonja glared at her. "Look, I'm trying to make some money to support us here, unless you want to start paying some bills—"

"I'm seventeen," Anna interjected, glad Sonja didn't know about the money she'd been saving. She did buy a fair amount of groceries and all her own clothes, but asking her to pay bills that Sonja received child support to pay herself wasn't fair, and her patience with her older sister seemed to wear thinner every day.

"When I was seventeen I was running a household, raising Walter, and holding down a job, so back off. Someone's got to pay the bills, Anna." A horn honked, and Sonja was gone. She didn't leave any money for food. She didn't even say good-bye to Walter. She just left.

★ ★ ★

Early the next morning, Anna opened the fridge and took out the six eggs Grandmother had given them. She noticed they didn't feel as cold as usual, but it wasn't until the stove didn't turn on that she realized the power was out. Could things get any worse? The Rez was known for frequent power outages, but Anna wished something could go her way.

They ate frosted flakes with water. They'd done it before, and she was grateful Walter didn't whine about it. She had to leave for school half an hour before Walter did, but as always she made sure he was ready to go by the time her bus came.

After school they walked to Grandmother's, since without electricity there wasn't much else to do. Grandmother gave them some squash and a watermelon. Her electricity was working. When they got back home at sunset, Anna flipped the light switch just inside the door. Nothing.

Anna called the power company, but the only information they would give her was that the service had been disconnected. She asked why, but they said they could only give information to the responsible party. She told them there *was* no responsible party and hung up. She put on a smile for Walter's benefit and fixed their dinner of squash, the last can of tomato soup, served cold, and watermelon.

They went to bed early since there was no power anyway. Anna lay in the darkness with a lump in her throat and hot tears in her eyes. When her mother had died two years ago and left everything to Sonja, Anna had begged Sonja to let her stay—knowing her sister would have no qualms about sending her to live with friends or some distant relation Anna didn't know. Anna had been grateful Sonja had agreed, if only for Walter's sake. *Poor Walter,* she thought. What could she do? She choked down a sob as she realized there was only one thing she could do if she were considering Walter's best interest. These trips of Sonja's had gotten longer and more frequent over the last few months, and there was no sign it was going to get better. There was something about their situation this time around that was different. She didn't know what it was, but she couldn't deny the feeling that something had changed.

Sonja had said she would be home on Wednesday. There were

some peaches and pork and beans in the cupboard—enough food that they could get by for a few more days. Anna would give Sonja one day past that, but if Sonja wasn't home by Thursday, she would call the Indian Child Welfare office in Gallup. Roots and heritage, tradition and training meant nothing if Walter's basic needs weren't met. She knew that. But she couldn't help feeling that she had failed somewhere.

★　★　★

Sonja squinted into the afternoon sun as they left the bar. "What time is it?" she asked.

José rattled off an obscene rhyme about time, and Sonja leaned into him and laughed, "No, really?"

"Two-fifteen, we got forty-five minutes—perfect."

They headed for the car, convincing each other they were walking just fine. José pulled out into the Santa Fe traffic without looking, and a car swerved to the right, honking. Sonja stuck her hand out the window and flipped them off.

"So tell me where we're headed," Sonja said once they got on the highway. José liked to keep the information to himself until right before a hit.

"This one is a gold mine," José said, clearly pleased with himself. "My brother used to make deliveries there. It's a little mom-and-pop gas station in the middle of nowhere, about forty miles from Santa Fe. Most people have an armored car come get their money, but this place is real old-fashioned and don't like nobody touching their money 'cept the bank. Every Thursday afternoon at three, the manager goes to the back safe and removes all the money they've brought in the last week. They close up early, and he drives twenty minutes to make his deposit at the closest bank. I'll sneak in the back and wait for him to go into the office. My brother drew me a map. You buy something right before they close, and after you pay for it, you pull out the gun and shout 'freeze.' That's my cue. I'll get the money and slip out the back, and you run out the front where I'll pick you up."

"Won't the lady remember my face? I can't hardly browse with a ski mask on."

"That's why I got you the wig," José snapped.

"Okay," Sonja said, then she leaned against the window. "Wake me up when we get there."

They had been running their little pranks—that was what José called them—since February. The first one had been a fast-food joint called Boggie's in Arizona. They had hit it right before closing and made almost two thousand dollars, which they split fifty-fifty. All she had to do was stand at the door and hold a gun on them, and the gun wasn't even loaded. It beat the pants off of welfare. Never having had much money, she was amazed at how quickly she could spend it when it was available—especially at the rate her vices were growing. It used to be that beer was enough, then vodka, but for the last few months, she and José had been experimenting with other stuff—and liking it.

Their second prank had been even easier, in Nevada this time. And then they pulled off one in Southern Utah. They had hit another one in Utah on Sunday. But the one they were doing today was different. This time they would be split up. She didn't like it, but knew it would do her no good to complain. José knew what he was doing; he told her that all the time.

They pulled up and parked around the side, out of view of the storefront. Sonja adjusted her bleached blonde wig, not commenting on how stupid and fake it looked next to her dark skin. José gave her a very wet good-luck kiss before they went their separate ways. After ten minutes, there was still a customer in the store looking at motor oil. Sonja was feeling uneasy. The man and woman José had told her about were both up front, and they kept looking at her as she browsed aisle after aisle. She ended up in front of the beer display, her mouth suddenly dry.

"Can I help you find something, dear?"

Sonja almost jumped out of her skin at the sound of the voice right behind her. "Uh . . . well . . . I'm just trying . . . to make up my mind," she stammered. The motor-oil man was paying for his purchase.

The woman smiled as the door swung closed. "Well, you see, we lock up early on Thursdays for inventory. I don't mean to rush you, but—"

Sonja grabbed a six-pack of beer. "I'll just get this, then," she said, holding the beer out to the woman.

The woman regarded her with a strange look, but took the six-pack and headed up front. Sonja's eyes darted around the store as she searched for the man, but he had disappeared. Where had he gone? Was she supposed to pull the gun out before or after she made her purchase?

"I'll need to see your ID for this," the woman said as she punched numbers on the register.

Sonja froze. ID! She couldn't show her ID.

"I'm twenty-six," Sonja stammered.

"Like the sign says," the woman said, pointing to a blue poster with white letters behind the counter, "if you're lucky enough to look younger than thirty, we'll need your ID."

Sonja didn't know what to do. Why had she grabbed beer, of all things? The woman behind the counter pinched her eyebrows together and opened her mouth to speak again when Sonja heard shouting from the back. The woman startled and began heading toward the doorway separating the store from the back area. Sonja pulled out the gun and shouted at her to freeze. The woman stopped and looked at her with wide eyes. The voices in the back got louder, and Sonja was trying to hear what José was yelling when the woman

265

moved toward the door. Without thinking, Sonja pulled the trigger. The woman screamed, clutching at her stomach with one hand and the counter with another. Sonja stared in shock as the woman fell to her knees, her face horror-struck and contorted with pain. Sonja's stomach turned when the blood started seeping between the woman's fingers. The gun was loaded! Sonja started to shake.

"Lori!" The man she'd seen earlier came running through the doorway.

"Don't touch her!" Sonja shouted, uncertain what to do and still searching for José. The man ignored her and bent over the woman. "I said don't touch her!" Sonja yelled again, trying to come up with some idea of what she should do. What would José tell her? Where *was* José? The man looked up, and his face contorted into an angry snarl as he stood and put one hand on the counter to help himself jump over it. He had just started putting weight on the arm when Sonja pulled the trigger again on impulse. The man took it in the shoulder and fell back, knocking the woman from her knees to the floor. The woman's screams turned to moans, and the man grabbed his shoulder and rolled onto his other side, rocking back and forth between grunts of pain. The gun fell from Sonja's hands as she stepped backwards into a candy display, sending it and herself sprawling to the floor. José emerged from the back room, hurried around the two bodies on the floor, and ran around the counter toward her.

Sonja, standing again, put her shaking arms out toward him and started sobbing. "José—didn't mean to—the gun—it was loaded— she—he—" With a cold look on his face, José walked right up to her and squeezed her jaw hard with one large hand. "Idiot," he said between his teeth. He swore and backhanded her across the face, spinning her around until she smashed into the counter.

The last thing she heard was the sound of tires squealing from the parking lot.

CHAPTER 47

*M*att got the call Thursday afternoon—the answer to his prayers and the mark of a new life for many people. He was home from work by then. Maddie was taking a nap with Esther. His stomach sank to his toes as he listened to Anna on the other end of the line explain what had been happening the last few days.

"After this call, I'm going to call the social worker, to make sure the tribe and state are involved and there's a record of what's happened. But I called you first so you could get working on the custody stuff." She sounded so grown-up and so tired. "I think you'll be able to come get him and take him home right away. This isn't the first time she's left us alone so long. I just want to make sure it's the last."

Matt absorbed the information as best he could, impressed with her choice while realizing what a hard one it was for her to make. "What will happen to you?" he asked. "Do you have somewhere to go?"

"I'll stay with friends, finish school. Then maybe I'll come to Salt Lake for college so I can be closer to Walter. I . . . don't want him to forget me, or think I've abandoned him. I really have done everything I can." Her voice broke a little, but she repaired it—as if he didn't know how difficult this was for her.

"I know you have," Matt said. It was hard to believe he'd never met this girl, with the role she played in Walter's life. "Walter talks about you all the time, and we're so grateful for all you've done." He paused. "My wife and I have been really worried about him, and the only comfort we've had has been knowing that you were taking care of him. We'll make sure you two see one another and stay close, I promise."

Anna said nothing, and he continued. "I'm so sorry this happened." And yet, he wasn't. Walter was coming to them—it was impossible not to be excited about that.

It was almost an hour before the social worker, Mr. Greenspan, called. Matt had his bags packed and a flight scheduled for that night. He wasn't sure whether to let the official know he'd talked to Anna, but was saved from making the decision.

"After speaking with Anna Begay, right after she spoke with you, we did a routine search for your son's mother and found her in Santa Fe."

Matt's heart sank to his toes. Getting custody would be easier if Sonja had stayed gone. "Oh," he said flatly, wishing he had discussed that possibility with his attorney when he'd spoken to him.

"She and a boyfriend were arrested for armed robbery and attempted murder yesterday morning. The system would have found the kids soon enough, but Anna beat them to it. Mrs. Hudson will be arraigned on Monday."

"What does that mean for Walter?" Matt asked.

"It means you need to come to New Mexico and appear before a tribal court. I understand you already have joint custody; that will help. I've already spoken to a tribal representative who will help you with your petition to the court," Mr. Greenspan said. "How soon can you be here?"

"Tonight," Matt said. "My flight leaves here at 6:17. I land in Albuquerque at 7:49."

"Walter is in Gallup, at the Indian Child Welfare office," Mr. Greenspan said. "That's a couple hours from Albuquerque. I recommend you stay there tonight and get Walter in the morning. We can place him in a shelter home for the night."

"No offense, sir, but my son has had quite a day, and I'd prefer he not spend the night with strangers when I've come so far to get him."

Mr. Greenspan paused, but he agreed. Matt hung up and kissed Maddie and Esther good-bye.

"I wish I could come with you," Maddie said, holding Esther against her shoulder.

Matt smiled, and the full impact descended upon him. Walter was coming to join their family, to make them whole. "Me too," he said, and yet he realized that as Walter's father, it was his job to protect him, to bring him home. The feeling of importance helped make up for the helplessness he'd felt for all these months when he didn't know what was happening, or if Walter was safe. "I'll call you when I've got Walter."

★   ★   ★

"Dad!" Walter yelled when Matt entered the ICW office in Gallup around ten o'clock. Walter ran toward him at breakneck speed, giving Matt just enough time to bend and catch him. "You came!"

"Of course I came," Matt said with a smile. He looked up to see a portly Navajo man, in his fifties, Matt guessed, whom he assumed was Mr. Greenspan. "I got here as fast as I could. Thank you for waiting."

Mr. Greenspan gave him a tired smile. That was when Matt noticed the girl he assumed was Anna, sitting in a chair on the far wall. She had the stoic blank expression Walter often used when he was trying to hide his feelings, but her eyes were sad. Matt smiled at her, and she looked at her hands in her lap, her long, dark hair falling forward and hiding her face.

"Well," Mr. Greenspan said, standing and shaking the wrinkles from his faded slacks. "I need to get Miss Begay to the group home. I told her she could wait until you arrived."

Matt swallowed. *Talk about a knife through the heart.* Walter seemed to be putting pieces together. "Am I going home with you?" Walter asked, a touch of sadness in his voice.

Matt smiled, "Yeah."

"Mr. Greenspan said Mom's not coming home," he said, looking at Matt for confirmation.

Matt sat down so that he was eye level with his son. "Your mom loves you, Walter," he said, though it was hard for him to believe it, based on what she had done. "But she did some bad things, and she has to make them right. You'll see her again, I promise. I'm sorry it happened this way, but Maddie and I are very excited to have you come live with us."

"What about Anna?" Walter asked, his voice almost a whisper. "Can't she come too?"

Matt glanced up at Mr. Greenspan, who shook his head and cleared his throat. It made so much sense to have her come with them, and Matt had been thinking about it, but he didn't know the answers.

"The tribe will decide," Mr. Greenspan said. "She'll live with a Navajo family. It's tradition."

"But I'm Navajo. How come I can go with you and Maddie, and Anna can't?" Walter asked with confusion and frustration.

"I'm your dad," Matt said. "But not Anna's." He looked at her, though she wasn't looking at him. "I very much wish she could come with us," he said. Anna looked up, startled by the offer. "And if there is a way we can make it work, I'll do it."

"You'd have to take it up with the tribe," Mr. Greenspan said. "But the chances are slim. I'll be turning her over to the tribal social worker when I get to the group home. Speaking of which . . ."

Anna nodded and stood with a look of resignation on her face. She came over to Walter, and Matt moved out of the way. She said something in Navajo, and Walter nodded.

"I love you, *shash*," she whispered. "You are *Diné*, of the Salt Clan, and we are family no matter where we are."

Tears began to fall from Walter's eyes, and he hugged Anna tightly. She hugged him back, and Matt tried to keep his own tears at bay.

A few minutes later, Matt and Walter stood next to the rental car as Anna got into Mr. Greenspan's Ford Escort wagon. "You'll need to stay over for the weekend," Mr. Greenspan was saying. "A tribal hearing will be set up sometime next week—will that be a problem?"

Matt shook his head. "My attorney expected as much."

Walter was quiet as they drove to the nearest motel. "What does *shash* mean?" Matt asked.

"It's the Navajo word for bear. Anna calls me that sometimes," he said.

"And *Diné?*"

"The name of the Navajo people," he said even more quietly.

He wasn't only leaving his home and his aunt and mother, he was leaving his people. "Walter," Matt said as they pulled into the parking lot, "Anna was right." Walter looked up at him. "The two of you are family. Maddie and I love you, and we'll do whatever we can to help Anna and to help you. We don't want to take anything away from you. Do you understand that?"

Walter nodded, but Matt knew he didn't understand. Not really.

"I love you, Walter," Matt said, realizing he'd never said it before and seeing the power of the words reflected in the eyes of his son. "Everything is going to be all right."

CHAPTER 48

*Y*ou're okay?" Maddie asked for the fifth time as she paced back and forth, bouncing a squirming Esther in the waiting area of the Salt Lake Temple. It was September first, the day Esther would be sealed to them, but Maddie hated leaving Walter out here. There were other family members waiting with him, but still. He belonged to them as much as Esther did, yet in this way he didn't.

Walter nodded and smiled, taking in the grandeur of the room with typical boredom. "I'm fine," he said, sounding very grown-up for ten and a half. His hair was long enough that he wore it in two braids, and the red leather bands stood out against his white shirt. Maddie hardly noticed the difference between him and most other boys his age—except when he asked her to help him braid his hair. She'd never imagined doing her son's hair in quite that way, but it was part of who he was—Walter.

"Matthew and Madeline Shep?" a temple worker asked. Maddie smiled, then turned to find Matt, who was talking with his parents on the other side of the room. He acknowledged the announcement, finished his conversation, and hurried to join his wife and daughter.

"You okay?" he asked Walter.

"Yes," Walter said, shaking his head. "I'm fine."

Maddie kissed him on the forehead, handed Esther to Matt, and walked toward the staircase leading to the sealing rooms. She took one final look at Walter and headed down the stairs, ignoring the tug at her heart. Walter's last name had been legally changed to Shep last month, making them a family in another way. Matt had also tried to terminate Sonja's parental rights so that Maddie could adopt Walter, but the Navajo issues made it nearly impossible. And unless Maddie could become his legal mother, he could never be sealed to them. But Walter had yet to be baptized anyway, making the sealing a moot point for the present. However, if she'd learned anything at all, it was that life was much more full of joy when she trusted in the Lord. She was making the conscious effort to trust that someday, whether in this life or the next, it would all be worked out the way it should.

Some time later, as she and Matt knelt across from one another, she looked deep into her husband's eyes as her mom placed Esther on the altar, her small hand placed on top of theirs. The sealer evoked the blessings of the covenant upon them, sealing them to their daughter and reminding them of their stewardship to her. Maddie's heart was full as she looked through the same mirrors she'd stared into on her wedding day. In a way this was a renewal of their vows, and she felt regret that not all couples got to experience this. It was a powerful thing to relive the blessings evoked upon them on their wedding day and to hear them including Esther by name.

After the ceremony, they had family pictures taken on the temple grounds before going to a luncheon at their ward house. It was a magnificent day in every sense of the word. So many desires remembered. So many dreams realized. Their son and daughter beside them.

The next day, Matt gave Esther a name and a blessing in front of their congregation. Maddie put an arm around Walter's shoulders and gave him a squeeze, hoping he felt the Spirit as she had these last two days.

After they got home from church and put Esther to bed, Matt and Maddie exchanged a look and waited for Walter in the kitchen. Walter was becoming comfortable with their lifestyle, enjoying Webelos and asking more questions about the Church. But one thing Walter had no respect for was a shirt and tie. They could count on the fact that Walter would be free from the confines of his church clothes as soon as possible every Sunday. Once he was changed into jeans and a T-shirt, he would come looking for food.

"Something was delivered on Friday," Matt said when Walter came upstairs. "We waited until things died down a little before showing it to you."

"What is it?" Walter asked with curiosity.

"Let's go see," Maddie suggested and led the way to the garage. Walter hadn't seemed to notice that they didn't use the garage all weekend, which was just as well, because there was nowhere else to hide the surprise. When Walter entered the garage, he stopped, staring at the loom with confusion for several seconds before turning to look at Maddie with questioning eyes.

"Grandmother's loom?" he asked.

"Grandmother told Anna that it would be hers once she had a home of her own," Maddie said.

"Yeah?" Walter said, still looking confused.

"Well," Maddie said with a smile. She exchanged a quick glance with Matt, who was looking mighty pleased with himself. "Anna turned eighteen years old last week, which means she can leave the Reservation if she chooses. She's considered an adult now."

A glimmer of hopefulness shone in Walter's eyes, but he was cautious. Maddie couldn't blame him. They had not included him in their discussions with Anna, not wanting to get his hopes up. Leaving the Reservation was a big decision for Anna to make. It was difficult enough for her to decide to finish her senior year of high school in a new city; they didn't want to force it by having Walter beg. Matt and Maddie had been ecstatic when she had called two weeks ago, after having a lengthy discussion with Grandmother, and accepted their offer. Matt had arranged for a shipping company to transport the loom with all the tender loving care he could afford.

"Anna flies in on Saturday," Matt said.

"And she'll live here?" Walter asked, his eyes wide.

Matt nodded. "She's your family, Walter, and that makes her our family too."

Walter erupted in hugs and laughter before he ran inside to call Anna. She'd been staying with Skye, and Walter knew the number by heart.

Maddie walked over to her husband and wrapped her arms around his waist. He drew her in close, and they stood there, swaying slightly. Maddie stared at the loom, considering all the aspects of life she had never imagined would become so familiar. Just like the rugs that Anna wove, their lives were toiled over, tightly knit, creating a pattern all their own.

"Who'd have thunk it," she whispered, pondering on all the twists and turns of their lives.

Matt kissed her, his lips lingering a breath from her own. "Who indeed."

★   ★   ★

Later that evening, Maddie left Matt and Walter to their chess game—Walter had beat Matt the previous week, and it had increased the level of competition to a fever pitch—and went to the grocery store with Esther in tow. The baby was getting a tooth and was a royal pain, initiating a last-minute run back inside for some children's

Motrin, which she administered before starting the car. As she headed toward home, she thought of something, and on an impulse she turned east. Several minutes later she was winding up the side of the mountain. It had been almost a year since she had come to her cul-de-sac; the last time had been when the first birth mother they'd met with had chosen another couple. As she pulled in, she smiled at a newly poured foundation at the far side of the circle—it looked as if someone was trying to get their house up before the winter snows began. It was only fitting that someone else should find comfort here, now that she didn't need it.

She got out of the car, wrapped her arms around herself, and stared across the Salt Lake Valley below her. For perhaps the first time ever, she hadn't come here to cry. Rather, she took inventory of her life and deemed that things had, in fact, turned out better than if she'd have planned them herself. There was a purpose far greater than her vantage point allowed her to see. She took a deep breath, a cleansing breath, and returned to the car. Esther was asleep in the backseat, and her men were waiting for her at home. She had no reason to linger here.

AUTHOR'S NOTES

• Infertility is a problem faced by increased numbers of people every year. Currently six million families, about 10 percent of married couples in the United States, struggle with infertility. With more and more women waiting until later in life to have children, that average will continue to rise.

In The Church of Jesus Christ of Latter-day Saints, where family is the nucleus of our religion, the emotional and spiritual struggle of infertility becomes even deeper. Adoption seems the easy answer, but with abortion on the rise, there are far more couples wanting babies than there are birth mothers looking for families for their children. Often, by the time couples exhaust the myriad of infertility treatments and determine that adoption is their only option, they don't meet the age, health, and financial requirements. For more information, please go to the web page for Resolve, the national infertility association:

http://www.resolve.org/site/PageServer
• LDS Family Services has become an important part of the

adoption process for many Latter-day Saints. The mission of Family Services is to counsel and support birth mothers, fathers, and their families in making the decision of whether or not to place the baby for adoption. They then assist in placing babies in LDS homes. Thirty percent of the women who meet with Family Services counselors choose adoption, and yet LDS Family Services places babies with 100 percent of the couples who meet the requirements and persevere through the process, which can take anywhere from a few months to a few years. To read more about LDS Family Services, visit their web site:

http://www.providentliving.org/familyservices/strength/0,12264, 2873-1,00.html

• The Navajo Nation is roughly the same size as the state of West Virginia. They are one of the few Native American tribes that have retained their sacred lands; at a time when many other tribes are decreasing in population, the Navajo tribe continues to increase. The Navajo people actively teach their language and traditions to their children as they try to overcome the loss of culture brought on by multiple government programs that removed Indian children from their homes. The result of these "assimilation" attempts was a "lost generation" of Navajos raised without an understanding of their own people. For more information please go online to *Wikipedia: The Free Encyclopedia:*

http://en.wikipedia.org/wiki/Navajo Nation

• The Indian Student Placement Program, often referred to as the Lamanite program, began in the 1940s as a way to offer religious and educational opportunities to Native American members of the LDS Church. It continued for nearly sixty years until the last graduate in the year 2000. Though critics suggest that the program's purpose was to take the Indian out of Native American children, for most participants and families who fostered the children, it was a positive experience.

• No Socks Day and Have a Coke Day are real holidays celebrated on May 8. I was unable to learn when these holidays were first declared, and for the sake of the story I combined them to be No Socks and Have a Coke Day. For more information on unusual holidays, go to:

http://www.thevirtualvine.com/days.html